CW00433382

Spies Without Borders

Spies Without Borders

T.M. Parris

A Clarke and Fairchild Thriller

Copyright © 2022 T.M. Parris

All rights reserved.

ISBN-13: 9798409089818

This is a work of fiction. Names, characters, businesses, events and incidents are either the products of the author's imagination or treated as fictitious with no factual basis. Any resemblance to actual persons, living or dead, or actual events is purely coincidental.

The Clarke and Fairchild series of novels

is written in British English

Hungarian pronunciations

Accents are important in Hungarian. Here are a few pointers as to how some of the names are pronounced. Names not listed here are pronounced more or less as they look.

Tas – An s is pronounced "sh" and an unaccented a is half way between "a" and "o". So Tas is pronounced somewhere between "Tash" and "Tosh"

Bálint – a long wide sound, like "baa": "Baalint"

Zsuzsanna – "zs" has a soft sound like the "j" in "bijou": "Jujanna"

János – like "Jaanosh"

Lajos – like "Lie-osh"

Gulyás – like "Gool-yaash"

Béla – an acute accented e is long, as in "knee": "Beela"

Pécs – cs is like the ch of "church": "Peech"

Tamás – "Thomaas"

Miksa – "Miksha"

út or útca (meaning street): "Oot", "Ootsa"

Ózd – o with an acute accent is long, like "Door": "Oozd"

Köszönöm – this o is a closed sound a bit like a u, as in "but": "Kussunum"

Nyíregyháza – a long "i": "Nyeeredge-haaza"

Spies Without Borders

Five Years Ago

Spies Without Borders

Chapter 1

Tas trudged along the side of the road. He moved slowly; it would be a long walk. From here to Nyíregyháza, from there to Debrecen, and then to Budapest, he had only a hazy idea of how long it would take. They had trains. When a train arrived, he'd get on it. That was his only plan.

The road here was proper tarmac, shimmering heat, almost burning through the holes in his shoes. He kept to the verges where he could. Occasionally a car would race by, hardly slowing, forcing him into the hedgerow. Sometimes a huge truck would roar past, or a tractor would toil by leaving a mist of diesel fumes. In the village where he started his journey the road was uneven, potholes filled with muddy water, pavements of pitted earth strewn with rubbish. He and his brothers and sisters would play in those streets, chasing each other through the stinking water, batting away the insects, their clothes becoming baked in mud. That was in the summer. In winter, it would freeze over and they would all huddle in the single room of their hut, plugging the gaps in the walls as best they could.

Approaching the town the roads got wider and busier. The flat farmland gave way to silos and huge stores with car parks, and neat rows of solid houses. Near a stadium a billboard rose up, a white background and a well-dressed man, solid and serious, looking down at him. Tas didn't know who he was and didn't care. He had a bag of bread and a pocketful of money. He'd taken the bread when everyone was in the field chasing a runaway horse. He'd stolen the money from the hiding place in the corner his father thought nobody knew about. He'd walked out of the village right then, straight away, without looking back. Then he just kept walking and walking, hour after hour, his legs aching, his clothes damp in the heat.

He wondered when they'd notice that he'd gone, whether they'd come for him, chase after him like they did for the horse. But no one did, and he was glad. Whatever was on the road ahead, he'd take it. He'd left the village now.

He'd never come back here again.

Five Years Later

Spies Without Borders

Chapter 2

Here we go again, John Fairchild was thinking as he stood outside the Széchenyi Baths waiting for Gregory Sutherland to turn up. True, this was a nicer spot than the last place Sutherland had stood him up. It was warmer, to start with, and the trees of Budapest's city park were starting to unfurl into bright green life, under a blue sky studded with fast-moving clouds.

Fairchild had offered his services to Sutherland, often known by his erstwhile street name Grom, back in December. Since then Grom had spent weeks giving him the run-around, finding original ways of telling him nothing about Fire Sappers, the hacking organisation he claimed to be involved with, this culminating in a summons to Stockholm mid-January which Fairchild crossed half the globe to meet, only to get a text from Grom cancelling the thing. And that was only after he'd waited half an hour. Truth was, Grom played games with people, and the games he was playing with Fairchild suggested that Grom had much more to offer their arrangement than Fairchild did. Fairchild needed the old man. If Grom needed Fairchild, he was yet to explain why. It was a worry. But he had to carry on; he could think of no other way.

He'd been waiting here forty-five minutes, checked Grom's text, texted and phoned Grom, got no response. The place was busy, a steady stream of visitors in and out of the legendary spa complex despite the chill in the air, or possibly because of it. He'd walked all the way round and this was the only obvious meet point, outside at least.

Outside. His eye followed a group of young people as they made their way up the steps and in through the imposing Baroque façade, each carrying a bag of personal items. Could Grom have meant that?

Fairchild followed them in. It was all tiles and echoes, a high ceiling, elaborate plasterwork and yellow mood lighting. He didn't have any swimwear with him so he joined a lengthy queue to hire a set, his impatience growing. Eventually, equipped and changed, he embarked on a search of the complex and its fifteen pools. He tried inside first, feeling foolish as he plodded practically naked the whole length of the complex, the plastic slippers they'd given him little help on the wet tiles. No sign of Grom amongst the bathers around the edges of the pools, or emerging from steam rooms, saunas or showers. Outside, a towel provided little protection against the March breeze. A systematic search finally revealed the man in the hottest of the pools, comfortably submerged with only his head visible in the steam, observing a bathers' chess game.

"Ah! Finally," said Grom, as Fairchild discarded his towel and came down the steps into the pool. "I thought you'd find me if I stayed in one place. Better than us both wandering around chasing each others' tails. Besides, this match is pretty close."

The match seemed to be proceeding slowly, every now and then a bare arm reaching up to move a piece on the board, set up on the pool ledge. Grom looked relaxed and pretty good for his age, Fairchild had to admit. His white hair was scraped back off his head and smoothed by the water, he had a little spare weight around the waist but otherwise he was pretty trim. A body that occasionally saw the light of day, and a gym, by the look of it.

"I assumed we were meeting outside," said Fairchild. "It would have made a lot more sense."

"Would it?" As if the thought hadn't occurred to him.

"I was trying to phone you but you didn't pick up."

"I look forward to listening to your messages later." Like everyone else, he would have left his phone and valuables in a locker.

"At least you're here at all," said Fairchild. "You're expecting gratitude for that, are you? I should be glad I haven't been sent half way across the world for nothing again?"

"Now, now." The old man talked as if addressing a schoolboy. "As I said, that was unavoidable, and besides, you spend your life trotting the globe. What difference did it really make? Come on, relax a little."

He sunk and disappeared for a moment under the surface, emerging a few seconds later clearing the water from his eyes. He turned back to the game, blinking. "What would you say? Four moves away from checkmate?"

Fairchild played, but had no interest in the game. "Why Hungary?" This was what was really bugging him. "Fire Sappers is global, so why come here? The FBI team will be right on the case here. Milo was their only physical lead and they have his real ID. They know he was Hungarian. This is the last place we should be."

"You're really afraid of them, John? You know you and I can outsmart them any day. Or are you worried your friend Rose will show up?"

Rose Clarke was a name that was never entirely absent from Fairchild's mind, and the old man knew it. Fairchild wasn't going to indulge him. "Afraid, no, but I think it's about time you explained yourself. All I've been doing for weeks is follow you around on some futile journey across continents. If you want me involved, it's time you let me in."

"Yes," Grom said thoughtfully. "Yes, you're right. It is time." His look was suddenly intense, as if he were eyeing

Fairchild up and down like a possession, something he could control.

"Well, go on, then! What's the plan? Why Hungary?" Fairchild's impatience seemed neutralised by the steam. A public spa wasn't a good place for an argument.

Grom wallowed back to rest his head against the edge of the pool. "You're aware of Béla Kornai's influence on the politics of Europe, I take it?"

"Of course I am." He may have sounded a little defensive. He knew about Hungary's self-styled anti-establishment prime minister, but Fairchild's network, his research and first-hand experience of Hungary were greatly lacking compared to many other parts of the world.

"Then you know that he's setting himself up as a leader of the nationalist right wing in Europe, determined to defy the so-called liberal international influence of the EU, amongst others. Protecting the values of the Christian majority, supposedly. Anti-immigration, anti-Islam, anti-gay, anti-multiculturalism."

"Yes, I know about that. So what?"

Grom smiled at Fairchild's impatience. "Hungary is becoming known as a hub of what they used to call the alt-right, a kind of pan-national grouping of right-wing ideologies that's very much on the up. They're starting to share more and more in terms of knowhow, resources, ideas. A more joined-up and networked far right. Not just your racist thugs any more."

"Really?" Fairchild's scepticism showed.

"Well, I say, not just. That thuggery is in there, of course. You need your foot soldiers. But the people pulling it together are much more savvy now. Technology, comms, propaganda, they know what they're doing. And Hungary's at the heart of it. Right around us, what do you have? Croatia.

Serbia. Slovakia. Poland. Then you have Austria, Germany, Denmark, Italy. The scene is changing, and what they're capable of is changing as well."

Grom's enthusiasm was evident. He had no empathy with far right values, or indeed any values at all as far as Fairchild could make out. But he loved manipulation, and the field was ripe for it. Fairchild dipped underwater to hide his distaste. The water, bath-warm and slightly sulphuric, enveloped him and dulled all sound. He stood, full height, and shook the water off his face. Droplets sparkled in the sun. Up above them in white marble, Leda stood with a swan draped over her. That look was there again on Grom's face as the man cast his eye over Fairchild's body almost possessively.

"You're not in bad shape, are you?" Grom said. "A few war wounds, but on the whole…"

Fairchild sank back into the water. "Flattered."

Grom was amused. "It bothers you, doesn't it, associating with me. All the terrible things I've done. Mummy and Daddy, yada yada."

He was right, but Fairchild didn't allow himself to react. "You said it wasn't as simple as that. You said you'd tell me the truth. Tell me everything I can't get out of Walter, or Penny Galloway."

"Galloway? Haven't heard that name in a long time. Thought she'd be dead by now."

That was foolish. Fairchild was giving away information for nothing. He changed direction. "This alt-right stuff sounds like nonsense. A waste of time."

Grom pursed his lips. "I'm surprised you can't see the potential."

"Why would this be of interest to Fire Sappers? They just want to get rich. They've never been political. They're just hackers, amassing millions in crypto from their raids and their ransom demands. Why would they back a bunch of far right extremists?"

"That's what I intend to explain to them. You see, unlike the rather amorphous nature of most hacking enterprises, Fire Sappers has what they call a high command. A group of people who make the key decisions and have resources to enforce them. They have direction, John."

This was interesting. Possibly the first real piece of new information Fairchild had gained after weeks of this wild goose chase. "You have access to them, do you?"

"Oh, yes. I do." After decades of watching his words, lying for a living in two of the world's most sophisticated secret intelligence agencies, Grom wasn't one to elaborate without reason.

"Where are they based, then?"

"All over." Grom bobbed in the water, annoyingly concise.

"So how do you get in touch? How are you intending to influence this high command?"

"There are protocols. It's quite easy, with the right technical support. If you want to know how, I'll show you. Come to my hotel room." He was dangling bait, hoping Fairchild would give himself away by snatching at it.

"What I want to know is why you've dragged me to Budapest. These hackers can surely be accessed from anywhere. I have no interest in your hooligans. Why am I here? What do you want from me? We had an agreement. Time you started to honour it."

Grom seemed no more than mildly surprised at this display of irritability. "But that's what I'm doing, John. You're not comfortable here in Hungary, are you? Never spent much time here, if my intelligence is right. Your in-depth knowledge banks, your deep network of contacts and watchers and friends, they all seem a bit thin on the ground here. Ever asked yourself why?"

Fairchild shrugged. "I don't speak Hungarian. It's a difficult language."

"But you speak a number of Slavic languages."

"Hungarian isn't Slavic. It's completely different. From the Finno-Ugric family of languages. It's more like Japanese than Slovakian or Croatian or Polish."

"You speak Japanese."

"The resemblance is very distant. Little more than the order of words in a sentence."

"And Finnish, I believe?"

That was one of Fairchild's first languages, inspired by a Finnish girl at school with striking pale features and ash blond hair. She'd been flattered he'd learned the language just to impress her enough to get into bed with her. Less flattered when she eventually realised it was the other way round, that to him she was merely a means of learning a new language. She wasn't the last.

But Hungarian? He'd never asked himself before. Why did he not speak Hungarian? Everything else flowed from that; not being confident in the language, he'd simply avoided the country. In his decades-long search to solve the mystery of his parents' disappearance, there'd been plenty of other places to look.

Grom was observing him. "If you want to meet some people, you can meet some people," he said. "But if you want answers, you need to ask the right questions. I suggest you start with that one. There's more to it than you think."

Chapter 3

"Come on," said Danny. "Let's get outside. We've been cooped up in here all winter."

Rose followed Danny Bartholomew, MI6 Budapest Station Head, through the gates of the super-modern low-rise complex that was the British Embassy, past the security point and the police box, up and along to a tiny park perched on the side of the hill. The residential architecture of suburban Buda, browns and oranges and angled roofs set in trees, contrasted sharply with the gleaming white Embassy building harboured in its midst.

The park consisted of little more than a grassy bank and a dog exercising enclosure, and would have been unremarkable if not for the view. Rose and Danny sat on a bench by a flagpole flying the Hungarian flag and looked out over the Castle district. It was quiet except for occasional late afternoon traffic passing on the road below them. A sunburned man in brown stained clothing sat on a distant bench. A whiff of urine floated their way occasionally.

"I'll never get bored of looking at this," said Danny, sitting back and crossing his legs.

"You've been in Budapest a while, haven't you?"

"Too long, probably. Officially. But it kind of had my name on it. My mother's Hungarian so I speak the language. Was recruited from the civil service. Never thought to apply, but they found me."

"You have a family?"

"Two boys, pre school." Danny was in his forties, only a few years older than Rose and young for his level. "They love it. We all do. But at some point we'll go back. We fell into this, really, and it suits us for now."

Danny seemed refreshingly normal compared to those of the gentlemen's club era. He represented the way MI6 ought to go, and probably was going, but slowly. He had a sturdy build, brown eyes and thick dark facial hair, but it was his perfect grasp of the language that allowed him to pass so easily as Hungarian.

He turned the conversation to the present issue. "So, you're back."

"Hopefully for longer this time. The online leads have dried up again, and Hungary is the last place we had a physical lead."

Rose's role in the global task force set up to neutralise Fire Sappers had got off to a frustratingly slow start, mainly due to an insistence at senior level that the entire operation could be done online and there was no need for the expense of an on-the-ground operation. Her last visit to Hungary a couple of months earlier had done little more than establish that the real-life identity of the group's former leader Milo pointed them nowhere else. But the FBI operation, led out of Washington by the famously hard-ass Agent Alice Rapp, was getting nowhere either, so Rose had persuaded the Chief to authorise her return to Budapest. Or rather, she'd persuaded her boss Walter, who'd then engineered a change of heart in the MI6 top dog, Marcus Salisbury.

"What's your plan, though?" asked Danny. "I mean, the one identity we had didn't seem to yield anything, and the guy's dead, anyway."

"Follow up on the political angle. Fire Sappers seems to have developed an interest in right wing nationalist ideology. It's the reason why the task force was set up and prioritised."

"I thought that had gone cold."

"It did, in terms of the rhetoric the group is using. They're continuing with their ransomware demands, and after some incendiary anti-government statements at the beginning of the year, things seem to have resorted to business as usual. But there must have been something in that. They could be planning something or reaching out to these groups. Or there could be some kind of power struggle going on. In any case, if the wrong kind of group can somehow access the financial reserves and technical knowhow of Fire Sappers, the threat could be huge. And we have history with at least one person who seems to be involved."

"You can't go after them?"

"He's a former FSB senior officer. Now on the run from the Russians as well as us. He knows how to hide."

Rose didn't mention that Grom was previously MI6 as well, back before his Soviet and Russian days. People of a certain age might know something about Gregory Sutherland. Danny wasn't that old, and he didn't need to know the full story. He certainly didn't need to know that information mercenary John Fairchild, familiar to many in the clandestine world, may also have been drawn into the Fire Sappers web. Rose was still struggling to believe that one herself.

"And am I to know who he is?" asked Danny.

"I can tell you the names he's used recently. He had a couple of different Russian IDs, possibly even more. I'll pass them to you. In Moscow he used the street name Grom."

"Grom? As in, Russian for thunder?"

"He styled himself a kind of gangster. It's a persona that suits him, believe me. He also passes as British some of the time. But the way to get to him and Fire Sappers may be through these extremists. We have some intelligence there, don't we?" Rose had first-hand experience of this; in the past she'd worked in Croatia handling agents informing on extreme right groups there.

"If you want nationalist politics you've come to the right place," said Danny. "Kornai has pretty much said that Europeans with so-called traditional Christian values are welcome to treat Hungary as a haven, where they can preserve their way of life apparently under threat from Muslim immigrants and the EU. He's distanced himself from some of the more extreme characters and the positions they've taken, but we're seeing evidence that some of the nastier types view Kornai as an ally."

"Potential terrorists?"

"For sure. So far they're generally involved in inciting riots at football matches and acts of vandalism against Muslim or Jewish targets. But the threat is growing, and if they become more joined-up as you said, things could move up to a different level. Kornai is fanning the flames, though he claims to be doing exactly the opposite by giving the Christian majority a voice, as he puts it. He's using old anger. Many Hungarians hold the view that they've been deserted by western nations and left to their fate over and over again, starting with the Ottoman invasion. They're not entirely wrong."

"Really?"

"The Turks destroyed the place, razed every village, practically. It was rebuilt under the Habsburgs. Then in 1848 Hungarians wanted a revolution like they had elsewhere. It was quashed by the Habsburgs while the rest of Europe looked on. In 1956 Hungarians rose up against Soviet control. That was crushed and the west did nothing. This is the problem. When a charismatic politician who came out of an ordinary village himself stands up and says that Hungary is being set up by the west, for example by being forced to absorb wave after wave of Muslim immigrants, people listen."

"Even here in Budapest?"

"More than you'd think. The opposition gained power recently and there's a good number of noisy detractors, but Kornai still polls respectably. Okay, the fact that his government has effectively seized control of the media, the judiciary and the education system may also go some way to explaining the man's popularity. But the idea that your way of life is under threat is a very powerful one."

"It's powerful ideas that push people into extremism. And it's the people who do the pushing that we should be interested in."

"Indeed. Are you expecting company, by the way?"

"No. Why?"

"Someone seems to be watching us." Danny's tone and expression didn't change at all.

Rose resisted the urge to turn. "What does he look like?"

"Old. Well-dressed." *Shit.* Rose's heart turned over. "Waistcoat, cravat. Looks like an extra in a Noel Coward play."

"Ah!" Rose relaxed. "Sounds like Walter. It's okay." She turned, and it was indeed Walter, lurking under a tree waiting to be noticed. She beckoned him over. "Walter Tomlinson. My boss. You don't know him?"

Danny shook his head. Rose wasn't surprised; she'd worked for the Service for some years before Walter had appeared on her doorstep with a special assignment. His precise role was somewhat opaque.

"Did you know he was in Budapest?" Danny asked.

"Nope." Rose greeted her boss with a pointed *This is a nice surprise!* and introduced them.

"Yes, apologies for that," Walter said. "A last-minute decision to come myself. Your people at the Embassy seemed to know you'd be here. I hate to interrupt, but there is something I'd like to borrow Rose for, if that's all right with you?"

"It's fine," said Danny, "as long as I get to hear what it's about." He smelled some secret, and so did Rose.

"Danny was filling me in on the political context," she said. "Which we need."

"Of course. This won't take long. An old friend is in town. A little aside the current business, but I don't have much time. I'll return her in one piece, don't worry." This last was directed at Danny, rather patronisingly, Rose thought.

Despite Walter's mild tone and fussy appearance, people didn't say no to him very often. Rose allowed the man to hustle her into the waiting taxi, leaving Danny sitting on the bench alone.

Chapter 4

"What's going on, Walter?" said Rose. The taxi crossed the Margaret Bridge, the Danube a rippling brown mass beneath them. Traffic was slow. A tram glided past along the centre of the road. "That was pretty abrupt. Whatever's happening here, we'll need Danny's help."

"You're probably right." Walter stared out downriver at the Parliament building, which looked from this angle not unlike their own Houses of Parliament. "But before you get too engrossed in all this, there are a few things you need to know." He looked unsettled, moody almost. Rose hadn't seen him like this.

"Such as?"

"Fairchild's in Hungary. That's the reason your placement here was cleared. There's something going on, Rose. If Fairchild's here then so is Sutherland."

"Hang on, hang on." Rose made an effort to absorb this, fast. "First, how do you know Fairchild's here? He has multiple identities. We've had alerts on him since December and seen no sign of him crossing a border."

"There is now. He flew in from Kiev, travelling under his own name."

"Kiev?"

"Who knows what he was doing there, but it's outside the EU so he needed a passport to get here."

"But he could be anywhere within the Schengen area now, and we wouldn't know."

"Indeed. But he didn't have to use his own passport to come here. He must know we'd be tracking it."

"You're saying it's a message of some kind?"

"Quite. But we don't know what. It could be a trap, one of Grom's games."

"Or he could have done it without Grom knowing. To tip us off. Or he might not even be working with Grom any more. They could have gone their separate ways. If they were ever working together in the first place, because that was never confirmed, was it?"

She could hardly believe herself, defending the guy. She was supposed to have no time for him. But after their last encounter she realised that she did, after all, perhaps have a little time for John Fairchild. Immediately after that, though, he decided to get together with Grom using information he got from MI6 – and from her. She should have learned her lesson, though it nagged her that he'd done it. He must have had a reason.

"We should assume the worst, Rose. It went quiet after the initial intelligence, I know."

"It did. And the political element subsided as well. I'm surprised Salisbury hasn't taken the opportunity to cancel the whole operation, or UK involvement in it anyway. How did you persuade him to send me? Did you tell him Fairchild was here?"

"Not exactly."

She glanced across at him. They were making their way through the grid of central Pest streets, winding up and down one-way systems to reach an address Walter had given the driver. "It's time you were in the picture, Rose. There's more to consider than previously discussed. More history."

That was for sure. She knew, as did Fairchild, that some buried secret involving Sutherland was influencing current events in ways yet to be explained. Sutherland, to put it bluntly, had more friends within MI6 than he deserved. He deserved none. He had at least one. But that was one too many.

"You need to be fully apprised of the situation," Walter was saying. "The danger. And this isn't something to discuss with Danny Bartholomew or anyone else. For your ears only."

In a long straight road leading back to the river, they were slowing down. Heavy Baroque facades rose above them on both sides. "Why?" she asked.

"Because it's highly sensitive, and compromising."

"Then why tell me? And why now, when you've kept it under wraps for so long?"

"We may have to change the ground rules." His voice was grainy.

"The ground rules?"

"The rules of engagement, my dear. What's right and what's wrong. What's justifiable. What may be deemed justifiable given the circumstances. But first things first. I'm going to leave you in some very capable hands for a while. Flat four, please."

They'd stopped outside a doorway. Rose could see a panel of buzzers next to the door. "You're not coming in?"

"No need. You'll see me again. Now, please, if you don't mind."

She got out and buzzed. In the taxi Walter was leaning forward giving an instruction to the driver. The cab moved off just as the door clicked open. She went in. A lift shaft inside a cage was empty, the lift suspended some way above. She took the stairs which encircled the lift shaft. At flat four she knocked. The door was opened by a slender white-haired woman with rosy cheeks and a measured smile.

"You're here already? Goodness."

"Walter told me to come up."

"I see. Well, you'd better come in." She stood aside.

Rose hesitated. "I don't even know who you are."

The woman frowned. "Didn't Walter tell you that? Dear! What was he thinking of? Well, never mind. Nice to meet you, Rose. My name's Penny Galloway."

Chapter 5

Grom was staying at the Gellért, in a top floor suite. When Fairchild showed up as arranged, Grom appeared to be alone. Fairchild walked in to a vast octagonal space going big on wood panelling, with a thick red-gold carpet, heavy brown curtains and, of course, a chandelier. The room was overheated and smelled of furniture polish. Outside the windows, through copious lace, the city lights were starting to glow in the dusk.

"Life in exile is a modest affair, I see." He sat in a low armchair.

"You think I've forgotten how to stay under the radar?" Grom was in suit trousers and a shirt with a sleek black pullover over the top; he looked like a well-heeled businessman and certainly seemed to be living like one. "At my age I like a little comfort. I hear you do, too, or do I have that wrong?"

"On occasion." Fairchild enjoyed a good income from his business ventures, as Grom well knew. He had no permanent home but kept a few bases around the world. When he didn't mind being found, he'd stay in the best hotel in town – the most famous one, the iconic one. In Budapest that would be the Gellért, with its riverside location and grandiose spa complex. Otherwise, he'd turn to his network, take a back room somewhere. Here, with no network, he was in some unmemorable budget place.

"Drink?" asked Grom. "Oh! Let me guess. Gin and tonic? They do a nice pink gin at the bar."

He picked up the phone for room service. A man walked in from the adjoining room.

"Bogdan! What are you drinking?" asked Grom.

"Beer," said Bogdan, and plumped himself down on an armchair. He glanced at Fairchild and opened up the laptop he was carrying.

"Consider yourself introduced," said Grom. Someone answered the phone and he turned away to order the drinks.

Bogdan seemed absorbed by the computer. "You're Russian?" ventured Fairchild, in Russian. Bogdan glanced up at him. "Former FSB?"

"Maybe." He went back to the screen. Grom was reported to have had a Russian guy with him in Japan, who managed all the technical stuff. Bogdan was young, mid-thirties maybe, in jeans and a heavy metal band t-shirt, his hair curly and messy. He was either a hacker or posing as one. If he were an FSB-trained hacker, he was probably very good.

Grom joined them. "Here we all are, then. Fairchild said he needed to meet some people." He said this over-enthusiastically, apparently for Bogdan's benefit.

"Actually, I didn't," said Fairchild. "But if I had, I'd be disappointed. This is it?"

That earned a dirty look from Bogdan and a laugh from Grom. "Don't be old-fashioned, John. With Bogdan's skills and my access, the Fire Sappers high command is at our fingertips. Well, his, anyway." He watched Bogdan as the man typed.

"You're making contact with the high command now?" asked Fairchild.

"Well…no." Grom settled back in his chair. "Not yet."

A flash of impatience. The man was playing with him again. "So what's this about? Why am I here?" Bogdan looked sideways at him. "Come on, Sutherland. What do you want from me? Why summon me here? You've obviously got some kind of plan. What's my role in it?"

"All in good time," said the old man. There was a knock at the door. "Ah! The drinks."

When Grom went to the door, Fairchild leaned over to Bogdan. "Why are you with him? He's a wanted man. The Kremlin will hunt him down until they find him. What's worth so much you'll exile yourself for him?"

"Money," said Bogdan. "Money, of course." He didn't take his eyes off the screen.

"Money? That's all?"

"A lot of money. An unimaginable amount. I do this, I don't have to do anything else, ever."

"He's got that much? I thought he was cleaned out."

"Fire Sappers does." Now he looked up. "What about you? Why are you doing this, if not for money?"

Fairchild held him in a level gaze. "You don't trust me, do you?"

"No. Not at all."

Grom came back with drinks. Fairchild's was large and pink, in a bulbous glass. "Talking about me?" the old man enquired.

"No, actually," said Fairchild.

Grom sat. He had some kind of whisky, no ice. Bogdan necked his beer straight from the bottle and put it on the carpet to resume typing.

"So, what's the delay?" asked Fairchild. "There has been a delay, hasn't there? Hence all this messing me about. You're playing for time, trying to fob me off. You could have put your case to Fire Sappers weeks ago. Unless you've already tried. Have you fallen out of favour, Sutherland?"

"You can call me Gregory if you like," said Grom. Fairchild didn't like. He sipped and waited. "You could say there's been a little back-tracking. Basically, these people, John, they're just money-grabbers. Very good ones, well-organised ones, but prior to my involvement, they simply went where the money was and extracted it without giving a lot of thought to overall strategy. And that's still what they're doing now. But the net is closing. Oh, I know about the task force. It's not just FBI now. It's gone global. Fire Sappers has jumped up the priority queue."

Fairchild said nothing but some surprise might have been visible. He didn't know that himself. How did Grom know?

"It's also the case," Grom continued, "that they're getting nowhere. But they will, in time, if they cooperate internationally. A global response, that's the key to their success. Recognising common goals and finding the will to put their combined aims before their individual interests. That's what will do for Fire Sappers in the end. And that's why they need a strategy."

"You're mobilising right wing extremists against an international task force?"

"Goodness, no! Are you being deliberately dense?"

The corners of Bogdan's mouth curled up as he typed.

"Think long-term, John," said Grom. "What Fire Sappers needs is a political environment that suits their needs. Countries squabbling over borders and quotas. A general atmosphere of mistrust and secrecy. Politicians more concerned to score points with their home electorate than cooperate internationally to protect people's interests. There's far more potential in a broken-up, me-against-you regulatory environment than one where people are inclined to work together. It's worth a little investment. And given the resources these people have, it is a little, too. A tiny amount to sow the seeds that will undermine international accords and get leaders more focused on each other than on their common enemies."

"Well," said Fairchild, "I can see how they might need some persuading that all that will happen because a bunch of hooligans blows up a synagogue."

Grom swilled his whisky. "As it happens, you're right. I put that idea to them some time ago. They considered it, but backed off. It wasn't enough. You guessed right, my boy."

Boy? Fairchild made an effort not to gratify him with a reaction.

"But I've thought of something better now," Grom said. "More imaginative than your scenario there."

Bogdan's typing slowed and the Russian half-turned to the old man. But whatever he was going to say, he thought better of it. This was the most revealing thing Grom had said so far. Putting aside his view that the most objectionable thing about blowing up a synagogue was lack of imagination, Grom had just told him he had a target in mind. A specific plan, that he was intending to put to the high command. Why was he sharing this with Fairchild?

"Of all the words I could use of you," said Fairchild, "unimaginative definitely isn't one of them. Am I to be honoured to know more about this great plan of yours? And are you expecting me to play a role in it?"

Grom finished his whisky. "All in good time, John. All in good time."

More game-playing. It was almost dark outside the window. Bogdan, smiling now, resumed typing.

Chapter 6

"So you know who I am?" Penny asked. They were standing in a small high-ceilinged living and dining room with a polished wood floor, one single window at the end opening onto a tiny balcony.

"I've heard the name." Rose crossed and looked down. Street lights hung suspended from a wire running the length of the road. They gave off a pale glow. Walter's taxi was long gone.

"From Walter?"

"No. From John Fairchild, actually."

"I see. So he told you about me. He must confide in you."

"I thought he did."

"What did he tell you?" Penny had watchful blue eyes and a stillness about her, as though she had all the time in the world.

"He said you were hiding something. Whatever happened years ago that no one wants to talk about. You and Walter and maybe others."

"You believed him?"

"Yes."

"You still do?"

"Yes." More than that, it was Rose who'd asked Fairchild to dig around. Grom's over-familiarity with the activities of MI6 had endangered her own operation, and her life, and possibly those of her team. Maybe now she was going to find out what this was all about. "Walter was never straight with Fairchild. Maybe that's why he's gone over to Grom now, or seems to have."

"Only seems?" Penny was quick.

"There isn't exactly an abundance of evidence. I've got an open mind, that's all. Unlike Walter, who's moved from defending the guy on every occasion to jumping to the worst conclusions about him."

"He's always been sensitive about Fairchild."

"Yes, yes, he feels responsible." Rose had heard the sob story before. "But that doesn't excuse what he's kept from the man. Sutherland had a wife, or a significant other, anyway. Walter must have known that. I bet you did as well."

Penny sighed and perched on a dining chair next to a glass-topped table. The room was bare of any personal effects. A wheeled suitcase sat in a corner. "He had his reasons, though you might not accept it. But anyway, I'm not here to talk about that. I've come here to tell you what happened in Berlin."

"Berlin?" This meant nothing to Rose. She sat on an unyielding sofa.

"Yes, Berlin was where it all played out. But it started here, of course, in Hungary. You know I was posted here, don't you?"

"Why would I know that? All I know about you is your name."

"I see. Well, for most of the seventies and eighties I was in this part of the world. Prague, Warsaw, Bucharest, here. I specialised in the so-called satellite states, the more reluctant allies of the Soviet Union. Hungary was more fortunate than some of the others in many ways. They had, in the scheme of things, a more enlightened communist leadership. Some elements of capitalism were allowed. People could buy things, travel to a certain extent. You could see the difference on the faces of those who visited from elsewhere, Poland, East Germany. Some say it all stemmed from 1956. Of course many wouldn't have accepted they had it easy. It wasn't enough, I'm not saying it should have been. A few quality goods on the shelves don't justify such a loss of liberty. But it was a shock to some when it came, the change. Like having the carpet snatched away. Under communism, if you toed the line you were guaranteed a job. Those who did modestly well in professions or academia and thought they were set up for life, did everything they were supposed to do, the wall came down, the regime changed and their savings and pensions were worth nothing overnight. In the meantime people could make a fortune in obscure import-export businesses that provided ostentatious luxury to the super-rich. Not everything about capitalism is marvellous, is it? In those first years, the early nineties, I saw people counting out the *fillér* in their purses to buy a single vegetable. A *fillér* is a hundredth of a forint. If you dropped one, it would barely be worth stopping to pick it up, by our standards. Even then."

"But you've come here to tell me what happened in Berlin," said Rose. It was rude, but she'd been plucked away from Danny for a reason, and wanted to get to it sometime.

Penny seemed untroubled. "Indeed. But it started here, as I said. It was Hungary which ripped a hole in the Iron Curtain. Quite deliberately. They could see the whole thing wasn't working. It was the end of their own political careers as well, though. Quite a change from the current government. Critics of Kornai say that the man would take on any cause whatsoever to entrench his own position in power. Hence the shift from left to right. He'd go back again if he felt the need, or anywhere else. The reformist communists did the one thing that would end their own careers because they thought it was the best thing for Hungary. And I bet you've never heard of any of them."

"Look, this is all very interesting, but I don't need a history lesson."

"Your boss thinks you do."

They stared at each other for a few moments. Penny hadn't put any lights on and the gloom was growing. A radiator made a clunking noise; the place was cold.

"It gets more personal," said Galloway. "Marcus Salisbury features, for example."

This was more like it. "I'm listening," said Rose.

"I thought you might be. But it's the whole story or nothing. I'm too old to formulate some précis. You need patience for this job. That's what they used to say, anyway. Maybe it's different now. Walter said you were ambitious." Her face looked strained.

What was wrong with ambition? And of course you needed patience, but that was for agents and informants, not long-winded colleagues. Never mind, Rose. Just say what you have to say. "I'm sorry. I just don't know why Walter brought me here. I was in the middle of something and he dragged me out of it. I got the impression it was urgent."

Penny sighed and pulled herself to her feet, looking stiff. "Well." She glanced around as if only just noticing it had got dark. "It can wait till tomorrow. Come back tomorrow, why don't you? It's getting late. I'm rambling, I know. It's being back here. So strange after all this time. And I've only just arrived. I'll be more focused in the morning."

"Are you sure?" Had Rose blown it? With her impatience, it wouldn't be the first time.

Penny led the way downstairs and gave her directions to the Metro. She called the lift to go back up. "It's good to be back," she said, as it clattered down towards them. "The place is so different. But full of ghosts. If only they could see it now."

The dimness of the hallway made her cheeks sunken and her face pale. But she pulled the cage open and yanked it back without effort. She looked round at Rose as the lift slowed to a stop. "Take care," she said.

Chapter 7

Fairchild ran. He followed Rákóczi út up past Keleti Station then carried on, letting the busy highway take him out of the city centre. He'd had to pack in a hurry to get here in time for Grom's meeting, but he had running shoes at least. Kerepesi út took him into the outskirts, a zone that could have been anywhere: drive-through restaurants, shopping malls, offices, warehouses. It was what he wanted, to try and get the taste of Budapest, soured by its association with Grom, out of his mouth. When he eventually started to tire he turned back, pushing himself up almost to a sprint. Now wasn't the time to let himself go.

Back in his room he worked out vigorously then showered and lay on the bed, his muscles still burning. He stared at the ceiling. He wasn't used to this. Generally, wherever he went he had people to meet, to catch up with and exchange information. He wouldn't waste time lying in a hotel room. There would always be something he needed to do. He'd set things up that way.

His overall aim was the same everywhere – to get ingrained as deeply as possible into the culture and inner workings of a place. Originally, this was to search for any clue that might lead him to discover what had happened to his parents. Given their occupation, anything to do with political machinations, espionage and the trading of secrets was particularly relevant, especially pertaining to the Cold War, that period of time which put practically every nation into one of two tribes, their destinies shaped by a decades-long ideological rivalry. That system collapsed almost twenty years ago, but his parents, as he now knew, were already dead by then. Their demise was certainly influenced by the Cold

War but was actually the result of a personal grudge. And now, he, Fairchild, was working with the man who'd had them killed. That thought made him sick. Shameful, that he was making a mockery of his life's purpose.

He'd never invested in building his network in Hungary. Why not? Since Grom raised it, that question had filled his head. Hungarian was a difficult language to learn. Who had told him that? His mother, of course. She was the linguist of the family. But why pick it out? Grom was right about that; Fairchild had managed other languages that were just as challenging.

He didn't have reach in every country in the world. Of course not. He'd had to prioritise. He'd let fortune play some role, but why had he left such a gap here, in this small, eminently accessible country right in the heart of Europe? When he thought about it, it made no sense. What had his mother said, exactly? He couldn't remember that.

The air conditioning hummed. Footsteps and voices passed in the corridor. The room smelled very faintly of cigarette smoke. The décor was cookie-cutter familiar: the wallpaper, the cushions, the curtains. He could be lying right now in any city in the world. He was seeing the place as a stranger would. Stripped of his personal spies and lookouts and fixers, not understanding the language, he was just like a regular person in a foreign country where everything was different. He couldn't remember the last time he'd felt as lost as this.

Who could he turn to? Taking on this venture, he'd made the decision to step away from everyone. In the favour-trading milieu in which he operated, he'd made a promise in desperation without knowing what the consequences would be, the depths to which he'd have to sink to fulfil it. Darcy Tang looked like any other respectable Hong Kong grandmother, and it was only after a gruesome turf war had claimed the lives of several family members that she'd stepped up to lead the Wong Kai clan. Once there she'd proved herself ruthless and violent. Tang had a problem with Fire Sappers, and thought that Fairchild was the person to bring them down. The information she gave him in exchange was good – good enough to spring Rose Clarke and her brother from the group's clutches in Japan – but what a price he'd paid. Even at the time he didn't know. After the dust cleared from the rescue, the only way in to the elusive global group was through Grom, the last man on earth Fairchild wanted to do business with. But you didn't cross Darcy Tang. Fairchild had a job to do, and it was his job alone; bringing any of his contacts, least of all Rose, into something involving the sadistic, game-playing Grom, just wasn't an option. And then, as if the man were planning it all along, Grom led him to a place in the world where Fairchild was particularly isolated.

What game was Grom playing? That so-called meeting at the Gellért served no purpose. Fairchild had told Grom he was joining him in exchange for information about the past, to uncover the secrets Walter and Galloway were still holding from him. Grom had suggested at another secret. But what was his plan for Fairchild? He'd tried to kill Fairchild in the past, more than once. Now he seemed to have some use for him but wasn't saying what it was.

He got up and stared out of the window. Was Rose out there somewhere? Were they tracking his passport? Did they realise it was a deliberate pointer? He'd wrestled with it. Would a signal like that put her or others in harm's way? But he was getting nervous. Grom wasn't the kind to do nothing for two months. The more time he had, the bigger a risk he posed to anyone he bore a grudge against. And grudges he had aplenty. So in the end Fairchild had done it, left a clue, a little breadcrumb, and he didn't regret it. Grom was working on something, and it was likely to be unpleasant.

He shuddered. The quiet was getting to him. He switched on the TV. Here he was again, behaving like a stranger in a strange city. He never normally bothered with television, but needed some distraction. Duna, Duna World, M1, M2, TV2: he channel-surfed and let the sounds of the language wash over him. If you didn't know the words you heard the cadence of the language more clearly, he thought; it was deep and warm, vowel sounds varied and precise, an intelligent-sounding language. He caught a snippet of song, on screen an animal cartoon. Some children's thing. Why was it on so late? Must be a documentary or a history programme of some kind. He moved on, then stopped. He killed the sound. Then, heart beating, returned to it.

On screen, two animated cockerels were performing a jerky dance to music. But it was the words of the song that made him catch his breath:

Debrecenben csuda esett: Két kis kakas összeveszett.

The words danced along the bottom of the screen. The song, a simple children's rhyme, did something inside his head. The programme moved on to a guy in front of a piano talking. Fairchild silenced the TV and opened his laptop. *Debrecenben csuda esett*, he copied in, and the whole song came up in front of him. He read the lines on screen and realised he knew what they meant.

Debrecenbe kéne menni, Pulykakakast kéne venni.
We should go to Debrecen. We should buy a turkey there.

Something like that. He focused on the Hungarian words, playing the audio, and forming the words with his lips. He closed his eyes, hearing the words.

He was in a room, the curtains drawn, a bedsheet folded up to his chin, his mother looking down on him. She was singing to him.

Debrecenben csuda esett.

There was a miracle in Debrecen.

His mother, who told him Hungarian was too difficult to learn, did everything to discourage him from trying, spoke Hungarian herself.

Chapter 8

Tas got out of the shower and started to dry himself, opening the bathroom door so he could listen to Bálint complaining all the while.

"They're not even proposing a law in its own right," Bálint was saying. "They're in such a tearing hurry, with the election coming up and all that. So they're going to tack it onto some other laws about child abuse. Child abuse? How is it child abuse? Are you a child abuser, Tas?"

He was lying on the bed. Bálint got ready for Rebellion in about ten minutes. Tas took at least an hour. He liked to do things slowly, draw out the anticipation, know that he was clean and smelled good before thinking about what to wear. It was the event of the week. All the usual crowd would be there. Even after all these years Tas felt a thrill about it every Saturday night.

"You're a geography teacher," he said, coming into the bedroom. "You don't talk to the kids about that kind of stuff anyway."

"True."

"So what's the problem?" Bálint went on about politics too much. If you can get on with things, just get on with them. Let someone else worry. Tas picked a sleeveless top with a white trim, kind of sporty. Bálint said it showed off his arms. The lights in the club picked out the trim. The first time Tas stepped onto a dance floor he thought it was some kind of wonderland.

Bálint lifted his head. "The problem is that this government we have is treating us, you and me, its own citizens, as if we're criminals and perverts. For this!" He made a gesture that took in the whole room. "This is all wrong to them, Tas. Béla Kornai has a problem with how we live, and that means they all do."

"Béla Kornai has a problem with a lot of people."

"Not everyone, Tas. Not everyone." Bálint's head was back on the pillow, and he was talking to the ceiling. "If you have family values, Christian values they like to say, Hungarian values, Kornai loves you! Kornai protects you from the thieving hordes of terrorist immigrants, and the Jewish internationals who have no country and don't want us to have one either, and the liberal perverts who infect our children with immoral ideas."

"That's just talk, isn't it?" Tas checked himself in the mirror. Nice. Now for some gel to spike his hair.

"It's not just talk. How many times have you been stopped by the police and asked for your ID?"

"That's because I'm Roma. Settled Hungarians have always hated Roma."

"That doesn't make it okay."

"I take my ID card with me and I stay out of trouble." Tas didn't have any ID when he arrived in Budapest. He got by for a while, but it was Bálint who took it on as a project, assembled all the documents, went back to the office again and again. So Tas had to show it every now and then? It hadn't been a problem. He could do what he liked here in Budapest.

But Bálint wasn't finished. "And what is a family, anyway? They've told us what a family is. One woman, one man. *Only* one woman, *only* one man. Kids, of course. Raised traditionally, according to the Church. That's a family. Nothing else."

Ten people living in a hovel, that was a family to Tas. Here in their flat in Újpest, just the two of them, they had a kitchen-living room with enough space for a table and chairs and a sofa. A balcony. A separate bedroom. A shower room. Just for them, and it was clean. Always clean. Tas made sure of that. Bálint teased him about it, but he didn't care. Bálint was his family now, with his baggy clothes and his wide lips and his loud voice, his big hands and his hair that always needed a cut. Bálint, who could make a whole room peal with laughter, the most popular teacher in his school, who was watching Tas now as he opened his make-up box.

"Are you listening to a word I'm saying?" he asked.

"Of course I am." But Bálint had a lot to say. Tas took out a mascara wand. The ladies in the club had introduced him to this. They were the first number in the floor show, had been for years. They weren't all ladies, of course. Or all lady. Some of them went huge with wigs and dresses and the like. Some were only happy like that, with boobs and heels and stockings. Tas was all man. He liked his body how it was, small and neat but strong, because he worked at that. But he liked being pretty as well. The first time they'd done a makeover on him, they stood back and whistled. *Gorgeous boy! Those big dark eyes! Who'd have thought it?*

He applied a little mascara. In the mirror he could see Bálint watching him. "What?" he said. "You like it, don't you?"

That made him smile a little. "You know I do. But…"

"But what?" Tas checked his eyelashes, half-closing his eyes and raising his head. Nice long lashes. No one at the warehouse would see him looking like this. Unless they went to Rebellion, of course. He picked out a lipstick, a bright one that went with the colours in his top.

"Tas." Bálint sat up.

"Are you planning to get ready now?" said Tas. "Or are you going like that?" He opened his mouth and swept the stick over his lips, upper and lower, then pressed his lips together. So quick, but it made such a difference. He stepped back to admire the effect. Bálint was sitting on the edge of the bed. He reached and pulled Tas back to sit beside him. A hand on the chin to get him to look, make sure he was focusing. Like he used to do when he was teaching Tas to read. It took him months to realise that Tas couldn't read. Tas still felt a little proud he'd managed to hide it for so long. He could hide things from Bálint, if he wanted to.

"I'm being serious," said Bálint. But his droopy eyes and sad-face mouth made Tas giggle. He planted a kiss on Bálint's cheek, feeling the warmth of his skin, pale and soft as butter. He left a lipstick heart, perfectly formed.

"Look!" Tas pointed to it in the mirror. "It suits you. You should get a tattoo."

The heart creased as Bálint smiled. He pulled a tissue from the box next to the mirror and wiped it off, looking at Tas as he did so. The serious face returned. Then he reached and wiped the lipstick from Tas' own mouth.

"What are you doing?" Tas got a mouthful of tissue, but he let him do it.

Bálint scrunched the tissue. "Put it on when we get there. Take it with you."

"Why?"

"We're going on the Metro, aren't we? Or the bus. Best just to – not draw attention to ourselves, that's all."

"You've never said that before. We've done this loads of times."

"But things are changing. All this stuff, it's coming from the government. The politicians. People listen to them, though they pretend they don't. It changes how they think. People in the street, out there."

"In Budapest?" Tas loved the city, though it had taught him a lot, some of it the hard way. In the village Tas was a cuckoo's egg, as they liked to say. But not here. Plenty of cuckoos here.

"Yes, in Budapest. Some."

Tas searched Bálint's face. "But what about pride? Being proud of who we are?"

Frown lines appeared. "I know, I know. But – let's just get there, okay? Then slap on the face paint inside. It won't make any difference, will it?"

He leaned forward and gave Tas a kiss on the mouth, such a gentle one it hardly brushed his lips at all. Then the dimples appeared. "So, how much longer anyway? Half an hour? An hour?"

"Hey! I'm nearly ready! And you're really not going like that."

Tas pushed Bálint off the bed so he had to stand or fall on his rump. "Get moving, lazy! Less talking and more showering. Go on."

Bálint held his hands up as he lumbered off to the bathroom. "Okay, okay, I'm going!"

Tas turned to the mirror and with a fresh tissue finished off Bálint's poor job of removing his lipstick. At least he still had the mascara.

Chapter 9

Fairchild didn't sleep at all. He spent the entire night on the internet, doing what he should have been doing these past decades, digging and reading and digging some more to try and get his head round Hungary.

He knew the basic history of the place, of course, and its political story, particularly in the various European struggles of the modern age. But that was little more than general knowledge. Fairchild informed himself by reading books – lots of them. Immersed himself over time in the detail, got to know the key personae, the defining moments, the places and events that shaped perceptions and identity and formed a national culture and personality. A few hours with a search engine couldn't make up for that.

And generally, he learned the language. In the way it was constructed, its vocabulary, its sound, a language shaped a nation. His prowess with language enabled him to comprehend the differences between Polish, Czech and Slovak, for example, and see how their differing identities revealed themselves in the sounds and inflexions of speech.

The fact that he'd somehow glossed over Hungary, not seen it for all these years, scared him. What else had he missed? This he couldn't blame on Grom. The old man had been the one to point it out, though he surely had his reasons. This went straight back to his mother, and no doubt his father too. They'd sown the seeds back in his childhood. There was something to discover here in Hungary which his parents didn't want him to know. And Fairchild was monumentally unprepared to find out what it was. There were so many places to start and so much to catch up on. It almost seemed too late.

The sky began to lighten before dawn. He'd read everything he could find but felt just as lost as before. He abandoned the search, left the hotel and walked, with no plan in mind. At the river he crossed, climbing on the Buda side, finding himself raised above the city as it slowly woke. A castle fortress on one side, the river below, he kept on going, unseen, unconnected. He descended a zigzag route of lanes and steps into a vast square criss-crossed with tramlines, almost empty. At some point his lonely footsteps were joined by the clanking and whirring of the first trolley buses. Kiosks opened their shutters, emitting an eerie light. At a Metro station, commuters were already congregating and descending the fluorescently lit steps. He passed by.

Through squares and tiny parks and along the grey curves of awakening streets he moved while the sun rose behind him. A slight downward gradient led him to the riverside. A bridge opened up in front of him, busy now with city traffic. Half way across the road split, the bridge continuing to Pest in a dog-leg curve invisible from either bank. The other road led onto Margaret Island. *Margitsziget.* He walked that way. On the island he scrambled down to the water's edge and double-backed, coming up to the pointed tip of the island right under the bridge. Spars stretched away from him in both directions, to each shore, and back over his head to the island. He sat on the rough paved ground, feeling some slight warmth from the sun. Through the arches the vast expanse of water shimmered. A tram passed by above and left a rumbling echo. He could smell the river, freshwater and mud.

All the bridges in Budapest were destroyed at the end of the Second World War. Hungary's support of the Nazi regime was a disaster, and the incoming Soviet forces brought with them another one. Somehow the nation survived setback after setback, rebuilt its bridges, remembered its past, reinvented it perhaps at times, again and again over the centuries. His mother had been a part of that story somehow, there in the rubble and reconstruction of the later twentieth century. But it was all so long ago. Fairchild was ten when they disappeared. That was over thirty years ago, and the roots of all this went back further. Books and facts and names weren't enough. He got out his phone and scrolled through the contacts.

So many of these people he'd pushed away because of his unappetising alliance with Grom. He paused at Rose Clarke. He pictured her when he last saw her. She'd been asleep, or at least dropping off, on a sofa in a late night piano bar in Tokyo. He'd called a taxi for her and slipped away. She'd resent him for that at the very least, never mind what had come after. He kept scrolling on, right to the end, and stopped at the very last entry. Freja Ziegler.

Freja Ziegler was his accountant. She lived a life of orderly Swiss perfection, skiing in the winter, hiking in the summer. Freja Ziegler had secrets, though; in previous times she'd helped the British secret intelligence services move money around, creating mysterious accounts in order to pay people for their clandestine services to Queen and country. The speciality of the Swiss, though global demands for transparency were increasingly clipping their wings. In the early years Fairchild, angry and disillusioned, found her name in a batch of contact details he'd stolen from Walter, his supposed guardian at the time. He went about tracking them down, appealing to them for help. Some were sympathetic, others less so. He was still a teenager at the time. The experience taught him a lot – how to find people who didn't want to be found, how to protect himself from those who didn't welcome their secrets being discovered. But a few he'd stayed in touch with, those who had been moved by the story of a boy who'd lost his family and his childhood in one evening and just wanted to know why. Some helped him more than they should have, and for that he was grateful.

Freja Ziegler had moved roles several times since then but they'd stayed in touch. In life you had to trust people to get anything done. It was unavoidable. The trick was to choose who to trust. Freja knew his business inside out, not just his legitimate concerns but the less visible aspects, the structures needed to fund a global independent intelligence-gathering machine, and everything that might entail. Fairchild wasn't too fussy about who he did business with. The powers of law and democratic legitimacy had served him badly, and he made up his own mind about right and wrong. Freja didn't ask questions. She got on with doing what she was good at. She knew where he was coming from because she knew him. He'd taken the time to become her friend as well as her client. The arrangement suited them both; Fairchild was wealthy enough to be generous when he wanted to.

He checked the time. Freja was an early riser. By now she'd be in the office, an espresso in front of her, maybe a croissant as well to enjoy while checking her emails. Out of the wide sash windows of her office, the sounds of Geneva's commercial district would be drifting up to her, and if she looked up she'd see glimpses of the lake between neighbouring office buildings. He called her.

"Fairchild! Lovely to hear from you." Her voice was warm and low.

He returned her greeting. They always spoke German; it seemed the right language for banking. He asked after her family: all fine.

"I'm in Budapest," he said.

"Okay." He was listening for a pause, some guardedness. There was none.

"I think there's something here. Something important."

"What are you looking for, John? You know what happened now, don't you?" A slight motherly concern was creeping in. Freja was up to date. She knew Fairchild had already discovered how his parents died and who was responsible.

"But there's more," he said. "Things they didn't tell me."

"You were ten years old. A child. They thought they had more time with you, John."

She thought he was grieving. He could hear it in her voice. Still coming to terms with their loss by inventing things that weren't there. "No, Freja, more than that. The way they raised me, it was all planned. They anticipated that Grom would catch up with them and come after me. They tried to prepare me for it. It's the only thing that makes sense of it all."

"And you think they wanted you to go to Budapest?"

"No, I think they didn't. They steered me away from Hungary. They absolutely didn't want me digging around here. As a result I've neglected it. Freja, you know they did everything to get me learning languages."

"Of course."

"But not Hungarian. That was one language they discouraged me from taking on. Now it turns out that my mother spoke Hungarian!"

"She spoke a lot of languages. You told me that."

"Not Hungarian. It was too difficult. That's what she said. I think."

"Then why do you now say she spoke it?"

"I heard a song." He suddenly felt self-conscious. "A nursery rhyme. She used to sing it to me at night, to get me to sleep. Just a little folk song. I heard it, and I remembered it!"

"Oh." A pause. "That does seem odd, but there's probably an explanation. If they were here, they'd just be able to—"

"No, that's not it!" He was getting impatient, stupidly. Freja wasn't the only one who thought he read too much into things, saw connections that weren't really there. But this was real. "There was a reason why they didn't want me in Hungary, Freja. I can see that now. What was there? Can you think of anything?"

A long-drawn-out sigh. "As you know, I never met your parents, John." She was speaking slowly, treading carefully. "But I can't recall anything in particular. They were in Vienna a lot, of course. Not far from the Hungarian border."

"Yes, yes." Vienna was where he saw them last. It was where they were abducted from.

Freja moved on quickly. "Did Penny Galloway not mention it at all?"

"Penny Galloway? No. Why would she?"

Freja had been instrumental in helping Fairchild find Galloway. He'd known her name for years, knew she'd served as an officer back then, but had only managed to track her down a few months ago.

"Penny worked in Hungary. And elsewhere in Eastern Europe. She was in Hungary a lot. Budapest. She was there when the wall came down."

"She never mentioned that." But then, he'd never asked. It was only after Grom's cryptic suggestion that he'd got curious about Hungary.

His head was spinning. Penny knew his parents. She and his mother were friends. Penny was hiding something when he'd spoken with her, he knew that.

"Thanks, Freja." He spoke absent-mindedly, his thoughts in a different place.

"But are you sure you need to—"

"I'm sure, Freja," he said. "Don't worry. I appreciate it."

He ended the call and got to work.

Chapter 10

Rose pressed the buzzer at nine the next morning. She wasn't really expecting an answer. She'd blown it, she was sure now, after a sleepless night of worrying. How would she explain it to Walter? Would he tell her the story himself, or would he be too let down by her churlish behaviour with Galloway?

The door clicked open. Rose went up. Penny, looking tired, let her in. The flat was in exactly the same state as the previous day except that the wheely suitcase had gone. Penny brought two glasses of water and gave Rose one of them. They sat side by side on the sofa, the only soft furniture in the room.

Rose started to rehash an apology but Penny dismissed it with a wave. "Never mind, never mind. I'm all in a muddle so bear with me. I don't know where to start. Let's start with Gorbachev. He began it all, really. He was the lynchpin. But he didn't know it. He thought he was reforming the Soviet Union. He thought there was a middle way, that it could be changed for the better. But he was caught between the ultra-orthodox and the iconoclasts. One or other was going to triumph. In Hungary it was a different matter. Németh kept it quiet how much of a reformer he was. Or really, I should say, how much of an iconoclast. You know who I mean?"

"Miklós Németh? The prime minister of Hungary from 1988 to 1990." Rose had done some homework the previous night.

Galloway nodded. "Only two years, but he made them count. He wasted no time getting his friends into key positions. They were open about it, to us at least. Outspoken, in fact. Communism had to be destroyed from the inside.

The system wasn't working and they needed a new one. Democracy. Multi-party politics. More integration with Europe. In ways such as this are great changes brought about. Nothing to do with Ronald Reagan. That was years earlier. Excellent speech, though. *Tear down that wall!* They wanted him to take that line out but he refused. Good for him. Anyway…"

"Németh?" Rose prompted, softly this time.

"Indeed. Their tactic was to make changes that sounded bureaucratic and mundane but had huge consequences. So one day they announced that for fiscal economy – fiscal economy! – they were going to stop maintaining the electric fence that ran along the border with Austria." She giggled. "They were basically saying that you could step up to the border with a pair of wire clippers, cut a damn great hole in it and walk through, and no one would try and stop you. They even did it themselves. A few hours after that announcement the photos appeared – Hungarian soldiers going at it with wire cutters.

"It was the East Germans this was all aimed at. Hungary was a popular holiday destination for them, especially around Lake Balaton. Not far from the border. That year the region filled up with them, but they seemed reluctant to actually cross. Németh and his crowd had to give them quite a push, in the form of a picnic."

"A picnic?"

"I know. It sounds very unlikely. They gave out leaflets in all the tourist places, with maps and a so-called warning that the border would be open. 'Make sure you don't lose your way!'" She chuckled. "Honecker in East Germany was very displeased. He started complaining to Gorbachev, but you see, the Hungarians had laid the groundwork. They'd already been to Gorbachev and had his assurance that the USSR would no longer intervene in the affairs of its neighbours. Of course that could have gone wrong. He could have changed his mind, lost his nerve. He could have been ousted by the hardliners. But he didn't, and he wasn't. So Honecker fumed as thousands of his citizens marched out to the West. Of course, it took all of five minutes before West Germans started complaining about housing shortages and immigrants taking their jobs. But that's the way of the world."

Rose listened, fascinated by this first-hand account of one of the most significant political reversals of her lifetime. But what she really wanted was the juice on Salisbury. Who wouldn't? It was coming, though; she just had to be patient.

"It was around then that I was summoned post-haste to Berlin," said Galloway, as if on cue. "Things were happening all over the place – Prague, Warsaw, Bucharest. I remember the conference calls. I suppose you might think we'd have seen it coming, but we didn't. Not like that, anyway. Berlin was a focal point and Walter was sent there as things really started to hot up. He was one of the big guns back then. Still is, I suppose. And Berlin is where young Marcus Salisbury was posted."

She spoke as if Rose should already have known this. "Salisbury was in Berlin? What was he doing?" She suddenly felt breathless. Whatever this was, it was important. A lot of trouble had been taken, firstly to conceal it and now to reveal it.

"Low-level recruiter. He'd been in the Service five or six years. Wasn't anything remarkable. But he had German, which helped. Anyway, out of the blue Walter called me and said he needed a second opinion on something and could I join him as soon as poss. I jumped at the chance, obviously. I got there, would you believe, the day before what turned out to be that fateful press conference. But you know all about that, I'm sure." Penny reached for her water.

"I do," said Rose. "But not from someone who was actually there. Did you see it?"

"None of us did. There was no particular reason to be there. The spokesman just happened to mention in passing, that all citizens of East Germany would be eligible for an exit visa. As if it were some bureaucratic detail. Then when someone asked him when, he consulted his paperwork and said *ab sofort*. With immediate effect. That was it – with immediate effect. It was all planned for the following day. But he didn't seem to know that. So he made history. The audience – globally – took that to mean there were no further restrictions on travel. Our phones went mad, everyone from London calling to ask if it was for real. By late evening thousands of Berliners were standing by the checkpoints waiting to go through."

"You saw all this?"

"I certainly did. Checkpoint Charlie. We couldn't believe it, to be honest. Some feared a bloodbath. But the guards seemed to have no orders. The crowd was emboldened. They were gathering on the other side as well, the West, egging their fellow Germans on. Then the commander just shrugged. The gates opened and they piled through. No shots, no shouts. Crying, hugging, it was pretty emotional. I mean, there it mattered more. The Hungarian border was a fence separating one country from another. In Berlin it was a wall dividing a city, separating families and friends. When we saw it happening in Berlin, we knew. *Der Mauer ist weg.* The wall is gone. That was what people were chanting. You remember all this, do you?" Her blue eyes, almost tearful, turned to Rose.

"I do. But I was just a child. I didn't really know what the fuss was about."

"I suppose it is just a memory now, not even that to the younger generation. That wall cut the whole world in two. A lot of people died because of it. Then, just like that, it wasn't there any more." Her voice had become thick.

Rose gently brought her back to the present. "Was this what Walter wanted your opinion on?"

"Goodness, no! It was just fortuitous that I was there at that time. The full repercussions hadn't sunk in. It was the end of East Germany, I think everyone realised that, but not necessarily communism or the USSR. That came later. As I said, Gorbachev wasn't intending for that to happen at all. We didn't assume the Cold War was at an end. So when in the midst of all this, Salisbury says that he's been approached by someone on behalf of a senior KGB officer who's prepared to tell us whatever we want to know…"

"You take it seriously."

Penny looked at her quizzically. "We treat it like we'd treat any other approach."

"You assume it's a trap."

"Right. But we check it out in case it's legitimate. This guy said he was in Berlin temporarily and needed to meet up with someone while away from Moscow. His rank meant that he could cross into West Berlin. Salisbury was like a kid when the circus is coming to town. That was how Walter described him to me, anyway. Walter was less enthusiastic, naturally."

"He thought it was some kind of set-up? Strange time, though, for the KGB to be playing games like that."

"We thought they might be counting on our attention being elsewhere. Or that we'd overlook that within the USSR everything was operating as before. It might have been a very good time to feed the West false information about what was happening in Moscow. Or even part of some kind of internal Kremlin power-play. And we were screaming out for intelligence. Gorbachev could have reacted very badly to the wall coming down. Got cold feet, as I said before, or been ousted. So we were interested, to put it mildly. Perfectly feasible that someone at senior level would foresee events and want to abandon a sinking ship.

"But Walter disliked one or two things about it. Why had it come to someone so junior? It seemed too neat. Salisbury had an explanation, or had been provided with one by whoever approached him. And the guy was putting pressure on us to meet quickly, another thing Walter didn't like. But it was too big to pass up. They existed, the high-level informants, the Gordievskies and the Penkovskies. Their intelligence made a big difference, as you know. Even a small chance this could turn out to be like that..."

"So what did you do?" asked Rose.

Penny drank some more water. "We proceeded," she said, "with great caution."

Chapter 11

"A meeting was arranged between the KGB officer and Berlin's Head of Station. The Russian was adamant that this meeting had to happen while he was still in Berlin. The Service wanted him to come to London and meet with more senior staff there. He had the travel privileges. But via Salisbury he insisted that this wasn't an option. His superiors would get suspicious. Particularly given everything that was going on around then. So they went ahead and arranged it with as many safeguards as possible. The guy was told to come to a particular hotel and ask for a certain guest at the front desk. He'd be given a room number. That was the room where the Station Head was waiting with Salisbury. Watchers were posted around the entrance, and a security detail was present as well. It sounds over the top but it wasn't, not back then. Walter chose to haunt the lobby. It wasn't particularly desirable to show your face to a senior KGB figure, especially one you had doubts about. So he skulked in the shadows. But he wanted a look at the guy."

"Didn't you have his file? There would have been photos of him, wouldn't there, if he was known to you as KGB?"

"Not in this file. The intelligence was very slim. Very little about his role. He'd kept himself well hidden from our Moscow network. I took a position further inside, the inner lobby. I was feeling shy as well. Put on a bit of an act. I was wearing mink, I believe. And some kind of feather boa. Yes, I remember that." She smiled to herself. Rose struggled to picture this mild old lady glammed up like that.

"It was late afternoon," continued Penny. "Getting a bit gloomy outside. Bitterly cold." She shivered as if re-living the moment. "It was twenty-four hours since the wall had been breached and the streets outside were still buzzing. People were coming across with suitcases, yes, but also just milling about, curious. Coming to take a look. Tourists in their own city. It still seemed very fluid, like things could go pear-shaped any moment. We were all distracted, of course. And this happens right in the middle of it all."

"Why didn't he just walk away? If all he wanted was to get out of the USSR, he could have done it any time. And it had just got even easier!"

"It's true most of the privileged at the top had the wherewithal to defect, but they had family and friends back home. This chap – his file was silent on whether he had any family or not. Or, indeed, friends. So we weren't sure of his motivations. In any case he would have been much more useful to us in place, where he could continue to pass us information. Defection is what happens at the end of such a relationship, not the beginning. We'd have wanted him to go back to Moscow and carry on for as long as possible. Then at some point he'd come over. Salisbury did say the man voiced concerns about how quickly this could be arranged, if necessary. It seemed at the time that the whole system might be about to implode. Very unpleasant if a regime change led to retributions against those who had been running the Soviet security machine for all those years."

"Okay. So he showed up, I take it."

"Oh yes, he showed up. Didn't stay very long, though. He arrived at more or less the agreed time. From what I gathered later, by the time he got to the front desk it was all over."

"All over? How?"

"Walter was on an internal phone calling up to the room. Telling them to seize the guy."

"Seize him? Why?"

"Because he recognised him."

Penny waited, eyes resting on Rose, while she digested this. She thought she knew what Penny was saying, but it seemed incredible. "So, did you recognise him?"

Penny nodded. "I did. And it was me who caused everything to go wrong, because despite my attire, he also recognised me. I was further inside, as I said. From the front desk, he went to the lifts, called one, and waited. I was behind him and some way off, but the lift doors and panelling were all mirrored. He caught a glimpse of me in the reflection. Only for a moment, but our eyes met and it was enough. I couldn't believe it, that was the problem. I never set any store by the rumours, you see. So, to my mind, I was seeing a ghost."

"And it was really him? It was really Gregory Sutherland?"

"Oh, it was him. No one on our side had seen him for twenty years, but still."

Rose was still piecing it together. "But would he really do that? Approach the actual people he betrayed and ask for their help?"

"But the investigation was never concluded, was it? So he was never actually accused of anything. Fairchild's parents were investigating, but it came to a halt when the guy supposedly died in a car crash in some remote place in Scotland. That was officially the end of Gregory Sutherland. When Ed and Elizabeth came out with the idea that he was still alive and in Moscow, most people didn't believe them. Even Walter had his doubts. And a lot of people – anyone who'd joined in the past twenty years – would have no memory of him at all. Walter being in Berlin was a temporary situation. If he hadn't been there I wouldn't have been either. Back in London Sutherland would have been identified at some point, but he could have got quite a long way by then. Done a lot of damage."

"You think his approach was a subterfuge? Designed to trick MI6 and feed us false information?"

"I dare say we'll never find out, but I'm sure it would have been detrimental. That's the nature of the man, isn't it? As you said, if it was freedom he wanted, he could have walked out at any time. But what motivated him was turning the screw on other people. Imagining slights and offences and setting himself on long and involved paths to exact revenge. That was how he operated. Whether he was there with the knowledge of the KGB I don't know, but it could have been his own personal initiative. He spent a lot of time over there using his position to further his own ends."

"So what happened when he saw you?"

"He took off. And I went after him. The glamorous get-up was a bust anyway, so I abandoned the act. He belted into the stairwell and I made after him. He went up. I followed. Do they still train you how to run in heels? Anyway, by that time the security detail were already at the top of the stairwell. I shouted at them to get him. They tore down, I tore up – and we met face to face. No Sutherland. Disappearing act."

"I know the feeling." Vanishing into thin air was Grom's speciality.

"He must have exited the stairs on one of the floors in between. We took one each. I drew the short straw. I knew he was near when I heard muttering and shouting coming from a conference room. I stormed in, my boa streaming out all over the place. Some conference was in full flow and Sutherland was on the far side climbing out of a window. That led onto a flat roof which he ran across then disappeared. By the time I got to the edge he was away somewhere in the crowds below. Must have had it all planned as an emergency escape."

"He's good at those. I didn't realise he'd had so much practice. And then?"

"That was when things got really difficult."

Chapter 12

"We all sat down with Salisbury. He didn't believe us. Simple as that. He adamantly refused to accept that his man used to work in MI6. And we couldn't prove it, of course. No one got a chance to photograph him, but even if we had it wouldn't have been conclusive. A strong likeness to someone who hasn't been seen for twenty years and has officially been pronounced dead can be brushed away pretty easily. It didn't help that the Station Head rather took Salisbury's side, feeling a little over-ridden by the way the incident had gone. He said that Walter and I had blown it by being too conspicuous and the guy had simply lost his nerve. Suspected an ambush and made off.

"In terms of going after him, even if Walter could have persuaded anybody, we had little to go on. We assumed he'd hot-tail it back to Moscow. So we forgot all about it. The one that got away. We thought that was the end of the matter, a tantalising glimpse, an opportunity lost that would never come again. Walter was pretty cheesed off."

"It sounds like you and he were quite a team." Rose risked interrupting the narrative, and Penny did look a bit startled at the question. But Rose was curious, and there was no better time.

"We worked well together. Came from the same place. There was a mutual trust there. But nothing more, if that's what you're wondering."

Rose waited to see if she'd elaborate. She did.

"But my dear, you do know, don't you? I'm not his type at all. Far too *female*. Oh, you didn't know. That was why he never made it to the top echelon. He wasn't one to deny himself. Oh, he lived how he wanted to live. No sham marriage for Walter, like so many others felt the need for. Of course no one cares about that now. But they did then. They certainly did. Anyway. More water?"

She disappeared with the glasses, leaving Rose to digest. That was something she hadn't picked up about Walter at all, but it made sense. He'd said once he wasn't a family man. Back in the day that was a kind of code, less so now. She'd completely lost track of time but clearly there was more to tell. Penny returned with the water and settled again.

"So, yes. The consequences. Well, you don't brush with a man like that and expect there to be none. It didn't take long, though we had to figure out the connection ourselves. We were thrown back into things, the domino effect moving across the whole of central Europe. I came back here. Each country had its own issues, but change was unstoppable. Németh had got his wish. Communism was toppling, one country at a time but inevitably, and we were all up for it of course. Meddling as much as we could, though that wasn't even necessary. It wasn't the West that pulled the wall down. It was the East that pushed. It was destroyed from within, in the end.

"Anyway, it couldn't have been more than a week later that I was summoned back to Berlin. Briefed on the way, then there we were, all four of us again, sitting in a meeting room. Major setback in Moscow. We had some friends in a firm that helped us with logistics. When we needed cars for certain journeys, mainly at night. Coming to rendezvous points in the early hours, driving unidentified people up in the general direction of the Finnish border, that kind of thing. Sensitive. To put it mildly. They were good people, just keen to make a little extra for their families.

"They were raided. Only two or three days after our close shave with Sutherland. The whole place was closed down and the managers taken away for questioning. There was little Moscow Station could do. Any intervention on their part would have made the situation worse. They couldn't even check up on the families. By the time they got word, the police had come in and removed them to some undisclosed location. It was a swift and thorough job, they said. How did the KGB know about the courier company? That's what we asked Salisbury.

"He blustered at first. But he'd already said that Sutherland had asked about how he'd be extracted from Moscow. He was worried about it, Salisbury said. Needed some reassurance that a plan could be put in place quickly. So, Walter asked, what kind of reassurance did you give him? I can still picture his face. And still Salisbury flannelled. Just generalised, he said. Gave him a rough outline of how it might be done. Did he push for details, was Walter's next question. Salisbury couldn't keep denying it. He admitted that he may have made reference to a courier firm in a certain part of Moscow. Shouldn't really have known that himself. Picked it up informally somewhere. Anyway, it would have been enough for Sutherland to identify them, on his return. Salisbury was played, basically. Fell for it hook, line and sinker. Not his finest hour."

"Was that always part of Sutherland's plan, do you think?"

"Who knows? Me, I reckon he was on a fishing expedition. Just wanted to find out whatever he could and inflict some damage. He saw a weakness in Salisbury and exploited it. At the cost of a few lives, unfortunately. Those folk never saw their families again."

"What happened to Salisbury?"

Penny gave her another of her quizzical looks. "What do you think happened to him? Or, no. A different question. What do you think should have happened to him?"

"When I messed up in Croatia I got sacked. And I didn't do anything as bad as that. My agent gave herself away. Got discovered, on the eve of an attack. So we didn't find out where the attack was, and couldn't prevent it. People died." Rose's voice caught; she didn't talk about this very much.

"And you got the blame?" Penny's voice was honey-smooth.

"I certainly did. I'd have been out for good if it weren't for Walter. He made me an offer. That's how I ended up going after John Fairchild. But I expect you already know that."

Penny's face gave nothing away. "Salisbury wasn't sacked. The whole thing was swept under the carpet. An understandable slip, the Berlin Head apparently said. No need to curtail a promising career. He's learned his lesson. In fact, the enthusiasm of the young man should be duly noted. No need for the matter to go any further."

Rose sat back. Penny watched. "Your thoughts?"

Rose usually kept this to herself, but here there seemed no harm. "When a man messes up, it's a slip. When a woman messes up, it's evidence of her incompetence."

Penny sighed. "I was hoping things might have changed since my day. It seems not."

"Hardly. This guy is the Chief of MI6. He almost welcomed a traitor back into the country with open arms, and in the process destroyed some of our most sensitive operational capacity and got a number of our friends killed. Now that's someone to look up to. Couldn't Walter have rattled a few cages higher up?"

"Perhaps. But he decided not to."

"Why, for God's sake?"

Penny looked at her watch. "Do you know, I think we've sat here long enough." She stood up slowly, stretching. It was easy to forget her age. "It's a beautiful day out there. Let's go for a walk."

It felt good to be moving. The sun was high now, making sharp shadows in the narrow streets, one side warm, the other cold. It became clear very soon that this wasn't a random walk. Penny didn't hesitate once on the winding route she led them. They came out near the Metro on Bajcsy-Zsilinszky út. They crossed several lanes of traffic. A tram whipped past them, leaving a smell of oil in its wake.

"Want to see my favourite cafe?" Penny asked.

"Sure."

They went down the steps under a yellow archway and were immediately on the platform. "This is the oldest Metro line, the original," said Penny. "Look at the wood panelling, the tilework. This hasn't changed in decades."

"What about the rest of it? Budapest?"

"Oh, it's changed beyond all recognition. But at the same time it hasn't changed at all."

The train arrived. They took it to Opera, and crossed the street outside to get to the cafe with the brown awning. Inside was more of the same to Rose's eyes: brown padded wicker-backed chairs with ornate feet, a gilded ceiling and chandelier, framed oils hanging on tan walls, a sizeable fireplace.

"Like someone's living room!" Penny said excitedly as they passed through to the back. Not like anyone's living room I know, thought Rose.

"Ah! Here we go." Rose followed Penny's gaze. A waiter was withdrawing, having just placed a cappuccino on the table, behind which sat Walter.

Chapter 13

He seemed to be expecting them at that precise moment, but Rose hadn't noticed Penny making a phone call or sending a message. Were the morning's revelations so precisely timed? Maybe so.

"Well, my dear," said Walter. "You now know what happened in Berlin."

"Not entirely," said Rose. "I do have one outstanding question. Americano, please." That was to the waiter. Penny asked for a peppermint tea. The waiter left and Rose resumed. "Why the heck is Marcus Salisbury our glorious Chief? Why wasn't he turfed out like I was? Or at least chained to a desk somewhere."

"Yes, I rather thought that might be your question." Walter seemed less stressed than the evening before, but there was still a wariness to him. "That was our first thought, wasn't it, Penny?"

"Indeed." Penny's face had taken on a dreamy quality. It was as if she'd done the hard work of the morning and seemed happy to sit back and let Walter take over.

"But we'd have had a hard time persuading anybody. Salisbury had friends, most notably the Berlin head. Makes a difference if your section chief is on your side. Things can be framed as political. Territorial. It would have caused a row."

Rose leaned in. "You let a man like that, who could make an error like that, off the hook and watched him rise to the highest position in the Service, to avoid a row?"

"A row we were unlikely to win. That's my point. I say we, but it was myself making these decisions, not Penny. It was my call, though we discussed things, did we not?"

Penny's look was blank, impossible to read. "Plenty of people at that time would have put a sighting of Gregory Sutherland on a par with having a run-in with a poltergeist."

"But it wasn't just about that. His indiscretion! The consequences for those people in Moscow! That was real enough."

"True. But we were in a particular situation. Moscow wasn't too pleased about what had happened and asked a lot of searching questions. Which Berlin refused to answer. An internal investigation was conducted, said Berlin. The necessary disciplinary action has been taken. A similar thing won't happen again. The details will remain station-confidential. London was told something similar. A lot was going on at the time. The matter was dropped – without having really been aired in the first place."

"But you could have done that! You weren't part of Berlin Station. You could have gone right over the man's head."

Walter picked up his cappuccino and took a delicate sip. Penny had a faint smile on her face and was looking out of the window, but Rose was sure she was taking in every word.

"In our game, Rose," Walter dabbed his lips with a napkin, "when we discover that someone hasn't behaved exactly as they should, do we shout about it? Necessarily?"

Rose stared. "If it's a potential agent, of course not. We look for ways of gaining from it. We have the dirt on someone, we use it. But that's for assets! Not our own people! Walter?"

He turned his cup in the saucer in an annoyingly unhurried way. "You see, Salisbury thought Berlin did him a favour by burying this incident. But actually, that put him in a bit of a situation. The head himself, he didn't last long. Couldn't adjust to the new world order, life after the Iron Curtain had gone up. He was out within the year. Salisbury did rather well. Managed to put it all behind him and progress up the ranks. But people didn't know, you see, what had gone on."

"And you did. You made use of this, did you? Threatened to spread the word if he didn't do what you wanted?"

Walter's face shaped into distaste. "You make it sound so terribly threatening. Really, I've barely referred to the incident over the years. Only enough to make sure he doesn't forget about it."

It was an unpleasant revelation, but she couldn't claim it was shocking. Walter always had the air of a person who knew how to manoeuvre. That was what Fairchild didn't like about him. "Well, hasn't it worked out nicely for you? Salisbury now being the Chief. That's how you get approval for your ops, even when he isn't that keen on them."

"You're over-simplifying. Of course I've lobbied the man to support the priorities I think are right for the Service. It's just that from time to time my arguments have had a little more weight behind them. You've benefitted from that, don't forget. And I haven't won them all by any means. He'll push back, will Salisbury. There's just a limit to how much he'll keep pushing if I make it clear a line is about to be crossed. Consider it a kind of trump card. You can't play it all the time. You have to choose your moments." Another elegant sip of coffee.

Rose's drink was untouched. "You do this to everyone, do you? What if I messed up? You'd hold it over me for the rest of my career? Come running to me for favours?"

"You wouldn't be dense enough to let the situation arise in the first place. Salisbury was greedy. He knew he'd made a mistake. He could have avoided it all by taking the consequences. He saw an opportunity and grabbed it. But he didn't have the foresight to anticipate how it would turn out later."

"You did." Rose couldn't keep the disgust out of her voice.

Walter ignored it. "I did. And so did someone else, I fear."

"What do you mean?"

"Who else knew what he'd done? One other person did."

Now she got it, and it all started to make a horrible kind of sense. "Sutherland."

"Precisely. Now, for years after this incident we heard nothing about him at all. He seemed to disappear back into the shadowland from whence he came. The next thing to happen was the break-up of the Soviet Union. The KGB was a Soviet tool. It was officially disbanded. But in reality it continued under a different name."

"The FSB."

"Eventually, yes, and many of its staff stayed in place. Under Yeltsin it went into abeyance somewhat, but then we welcomed the arrival in the Kremlin of a former KGB officer himself."

"Putin."

"Exactly, and you know the rest. The FSB has developed into a security machine every bit as formidable as its predecessor."

"You're telling me." Rose had first hand experience from her time in Moscow of the ubiquitous power of the FSB.

"I heard nothing that even hinted Sutherland might have survived the regime change. In the absence of any concrete intelligence I was rather hoping he hadn't, and had either slipped off somewhere or fallen foul of some retribution along the line. However, as we know now…"

"He came back."

"He never went, my dear. But he seemed too caught up in his own affairs to worry too much about ours. However, all that changed when our mutual friend appeared on his radar."

"John Fairchild."

"That's right."

"But Fairchild didn't go looking for Grom. He didn't even know the man existed."

"He wanted answers about his parents. And Grom was the answer. Every road he took to get to the truth would have led, eventually, to Sutherland. You wonder why I didn't share more with him. Why I was so discouraging about his efforts to find answers. This is why. Sutherland didn't even know the Fairchilds had a son. When he worked out who Fairchild was, things changed gear. We were in his sights again, Fairchild himself and the rest of us by association, including you. I understand why he did it, but the truth is that he awoke a monster. Only a few of us really understood the implications."

Rose was still fuming. "You should have shared everything with him right from the start. It would only be a matter of time before he found out himself."

Walter sighed, his jowls drooping, eyes sad like a clown's. "You're probably right. I just—"

"Didn't trust him to keep his mouth shut?" Rose didn't mean for it to sound so sharp, but was struggling to control herself. "You were onto such a good thing with Salisbury it would have been a shame to jeopardise it by letting someone else in on the secret. Do you have any idea how much he's suffered over this? He was ten, for Christ's sake! That man took his whole life away, his home, his family, turned him into some kind of cynical itinerant. And you sat there and let it happen!"

Walter and Penny exchanged glances. Neither of them seemed exactly pleased with themselves, which was some comfort at least. "Perhaps," said Walter. "Although he didn't have to choose that life. He wasn't short of alternatives. But that's in the past. The point is, the threat posed by Sutherland now is greater than it's ever been. And we're starting to think, are we not, that he may indeed be in contact with Salisbury in some fashion."

"Of course he is, Walter. Grom knows things about our operations that he really shouldn't know."

Every muscle in Walter's face froze. Penny's eyes were fixed on Rose, too.

"Such as?" This was Walter's grainy voice, cold as steel.

"In Nice, we were being tailed as soon as we arrived. Someone knew we were coming and where to find us."

"And you didn't tell me this?"

"I didn't know who to trust." Walter actually seemed slightly hurt at this. "Come on, Walter, you haven't exactly been on the level."

He took a sharp breath but waited for her to carry on.

"I noticed a shadow. At least I thought I did, but changed my mind, thought I'd made a mistake. Then one of the others did exactly the same thing. Typical Grom game-playing. He was trying to unsettle us, make us doubt ourselves. When Grom caught up with me in Arles, I recognised one of his crew. It was definitely his lot right from the start. Salisbury must have told him there was a team down there. Marcus Salisbury, Walter. MI6 Chief. Did that."

Walter and Penny looked at each other, a long, slow look. Walter broke it off and shook his head. "Salisbury was never happy about that operation. He made every excuse to quash it. I thought he was just being short-sighted. Well – hoped."

"Grom was leaning on him. Salisbury's been trying to please two masters, you and Grom. That time he couldn't. So he approved the op but tipped Grom off. He's an absolute liability. He put all our lives at risk. Everyone in the Service, everyone, is his ultimate responsibility. But he'd throw me and my team under the bus just like that to protect his own position. Walter, he's got to go."

Walter picked up his spoon and stirred the remains of his coffee. "I do see where you're coming from. But I think we're diagnosing the problem wrongly here. Everything was fine until Sutherland resurfaced. He's the real issue here. Grom needs to be neutralised, Rose. You almost got him in France, but somehow he slipped through the net." He replaced the spoon and looked up at her. "Finish the job. Do it this time. Then this goes away."

Rose looked at the old man, his wispy hair, lines of tiredness on his face. Since the end of the Cold War, getting on for thirty years, he'd enjoyed a hold over the career-oriented Salisbury, watching him rise through the ranks taking roles that Walter himself missed out on. He wouldn't give that up in a hurry. The end of Salisbury meant the end of Walter as well. Someone new would come in, a new broom, a clean sweep. She didn't like it, but knew the limits of her own powers of persuasion.

"That wasn't the job," she said. "We were after his assets, not the man himself. You said something yesterday about changing the rules of the game. About right and wrong."

Walter's voice was quiet now, but every word carried weight. "For obvious reasons, we need to be prepared to sidestep the order of command here. Events happen. Don't they? We've all been trained. You have capabilities."

Four eyes were looking at her. The background noise of the cafe seemed louder – customers talking, crockery clattering at the counter, the coffee machine whirring. "Capabilities?" She needed more than a general hint. But she wasn't going to get it.

"It would be better in many ways if he didn't survive," said Walter. "Though such a step wouldn't be authorised."

She tried again. "What exactly are you asking me to do?"

It was as if she'd uttered some faux pas. Walter picked up his cup and drained it, looking away. Penny sipped her tea, consigned to silence now, as if she'd run out of words. A straight answer wasn't to be had.

"I see." She gave it some thought. She'd have no problem killing Grom, truth be told. But what about the consequences for her, aside from the risk of the act itself? Walter's requests always seemed to put others in harm's way. And this one, more than ever before, was transparently in order to shore up his own power base. That left a nasty taste in her mouth.

"What about Fairchild?" she said.

Walter rested his chin on his hand. "He appears to have joined the man."

He seemed regretful, she gave him that. "We don't know that for sure. No one has had any contact with him. We don't know what he's up to."

"Granted," said Walter. "But if he has joined Sutherland…we can't let this legacy continue. It has to end now, this time, one way or another."

She thought about all the things Walter had told her about John Fairchild. His role as a family friend, how he bought the boy presents. How aged ten, young John called Walter when he returned to the family home to find his parents missing. Those troubled years, Fairchild asking and Walter pushing back at every turn, until Fairchild lost faith entirely and went his own way. Even after that, it was Walter who backed the guy in the face of his Service critics and tried to effect some kind of reconciliation. That was the purpose of her very first assignment for Walter. He'd defended Fairchild countless times against Rose's own criticisms and doubts. But all that had changed now, far more than she would ever have conceived.

"I understand."

She didn't trust herself to say anything further.

Chapter 14

Fairchild arrived late afternoon, only stopping once on the nine-hour journey. While he missed his network, he didn't need help to rent a car, and it was autoroutes and major roads all the way. In Ljubljana he thought about stopping, remembering the Alpine Mittel European serenity of the city; there were people here he could look up. But not this time, not now. He kept driving, skirting the city centre then pushing on to Trieste, past Venice, then north at Verona to the uppermost tip of Lake Garda.

He hadn't given her any warning last time and he wasn't going to now. He parked by the lakeside and walked again up the cobbled streets towards Penny Galloway's terraced cottage. Last time it was autumn; now it was spring but the geraniums nodded regardless from window boxes and terracotta pots. Past the church, the dog didn't bark this time. Had Fairchild become a friend already, a known person? Or maybe the dog was sleeping, or dead. He read too much into things. So he'd always been told. Always been told by people who didn't want him to find things out.

As before he tried the terrace, climbing the steps at the side and round the back. The geraniums were out here, too, those that enjoyed both sun and shelter. The wind was strong and steady. What did she say it was called? The Ora? The doors were all closed up, blinds drawn.

At the unmarked front door his knock drew no reply. He sat on the steps, exhausted suddenly. He hadn't eaten or drunk anything all day. Now he was empty and drained. He had no other contact details for Galloway, only this address. He pictured her as he found her last time, white-haired, blue-eyed, perky and charming, yet deliberate and thoughtful, holding something back. Should he wait? She said she did the *Passegiatta* every day. But it was too early, wasn't it? Walking through town he would have noticed its inhabitants dressed up and promenading the streets. He thought about the terrace. Not that difficult to get onto it from the path. Then he remembered what she said last time: *Nobody creeps up on me.*

He went up again anyway. The patio furniture was put away. The flowers were surviving, but they wouldn't for long; the earth in their pots was sandy coloured and coming away from the sides. A few petals had fallen onto the decking. The blinds in the windows were fully down. Even from the terrace you couldn't see inside. Penny wasn't out; she was gone.

Was it because of him? Following on somehow from his visit? He had the creeping feeling as he often did with Walter and his cloaked cohort, that wheels were turning, momentum was gaining, things were coming together and interacting – and that he was being left behind. The train had left the station and here he was gazing down the tracks.

Back in town, the bars were opening as darkness fell. He tried one – small, away from the waterfront. With impeccable Italian he fell into easy conversation with a couple of locals. The Englishwoman up the hill? Not around. Left recently. Who knows where? No, there's no regular place she goes, no relatives nearby. Abroad, maybe. There was something a little hesitant about all that. *There are people I can call on*, she'd said. He hadn't heard it as a warning at the time.

He moved on and asked the men about the tourist season, the weather, the roads, taxes. Talking felt good. They brought *aperitivo*: focaccia, bruschetta, prosciutto, pecorino. More drinks, gin to beer to wine. He didn't want to go back to Hungary. Here he could do what he was good at. What he enjoyed. That was when it struck him, sitting with these guys who were fast becoming friends. What he did had been for a purpose. It only took a small separation from it to realise that his way of life was a part of him now. He'd always be like this. There were worse things to be.

They were the last out of the place, slurring their goodbyes in the silent street. Fairchild promised to return in a couple of months and look them up. He tottered back to the car and slept on the back seat.

The sun woke him early. He got out and stretched. No Ora now, just a whisper of a breeze. Mountains rose high and green above a calm blue lake. It was too early for espresso and pastries.

He got in the car and drove back to Budapest.

Chapter 15

Rose was so intent on working through her inbox that it took her a few moments to notice Danny Bartholomew leaning on the door frame waiting for her to look up. She was hot-desking at the Embassy, and after the best part of a day away had some catching up to do. Having said that, Rapp's task force progress had been, to cut a long story short, non-existent. Everything they were trying came up with nothing. The revelations of Walter and Penny, while enlightening, only gave her more to think about. None of it helped at all with Fire Sappers or actually finding Grom or Fairchild.

Danny was holding something, a small white envelope. "Ever go by the name of Anna?" he asked.

Rose sat back, slowly. "Maybe." Anna was an alias she sometimes used with agents. "But not in these parts. Why?"

He held up the envelope. "Hand delivered, though somehow no one remembers by whom and it wasn't caught on CCTV."

He passed it to her. On the front was hand-written *Anna* – nothing else. It was sealed. "It's not any of your people?"

"No one uses that name. We don't even have any Embassy staff called Anna. There's an Anne-Marie, that's the closest. Besides, who would send it like that with no surname? It's one for us, for sure."

He meant the MI6 team, the shady people who did things no one asked about. She turned it over. "Open it?"

"Please."

She did. Inside was a single piece of plain notepaper, the handwriting the same as on the envelope: *Halászbástya 2100 Szerda*. She handed it to Danny.

"Fisherman's Bastion, nine pm Wednesday."

"Where's that?"

"Castle district. It overlooks the river from the Buda side. A tourist spot. Nice views."

"A public place?"

"Very much so."

"Even at night?"

"At that time, sure. The night views are good and there are restaurants and bars. Any idea who it's from?" Danny had been a little distant. She could tell him nothing about what Walter wanted with her and where she'd been. He didn't ask, but was cheesed off about it, she could tell.

"A couple of possibilities, I guess."

Was it Grom? That was her first thought. She'd have to tell Walter about it, she supposed. Salisbury could have tipped Grom off again, though to be honest the man could probably work out for himself that she'd be in Hungary. But if it were Grom, how did he know her alias? Salisbury wouldn't have access to such details. And if Grom knew that, what else did he know?

Could it be Fairchild? The thought lifted her a little. He knew she sometimes used that name. Was this his handwriting? She had no idea. He could have just sent her a text, but maybe he was locked down somehow. She could think of no one else; she'd only just arrived here.

Her apprehension must have shown. "You don't look very sure about it," Danny said.

"It could be good, it could be bad. Either way, I should go. The task force is getting nowhere. It may be a legitimate lead."

Her mind went back to a phone call she'd made to her boss when she was working in Moscow. A lead had been dangled in front of her, a possible informant. She'd persuaded him, against his better judgement, to let her travel to Georgia to follow it up. It turned out to be the first time Rose would fall victim to Grom's sinister and quirky style of manipulation. She'd been lucky to survive. This felt unsettlingly similar. But the meet point was a public place and she'd be prepared this time. And it may not be him.

"You definitely want to go?" asked Danny, studying her face.

She put the note back in the envelope. "Any chance you could come with me?"

Chapter 16

Bálint was going out. Tas didn't like it. Not the fact that he was going out. Bálint could do as he pleased. But this, whatever it was, this he didn't like.

Bálint had a hardness in his face, a set look around his jaw, as he got ready. Tas distracted himself by putting on a pair of yellow gloves and cleaning the kitchen. He ran a bucket of super-hot water, so much cleaner the foam was spilling out of the top. A smell of soapy pine filled his nose when he soaked the sponge and the scourer. Floor, work surfaces, cupboard doors, shiny like new. Then to the cooker. This was more of a job.

Bálint wandered in, looking at his phone. There was a strange kind of light in his eyes. Tas broke away from the cooker hood. "Why won't you tell me what you're up to?"

"Because we don't know yet." Bálint didn't look up. "That's why we're meeting."

"You're planning something."

"That's exactly what we're doing. I told you that."

"Well, what?"

Bálint looked up now, impatient. "Something that will get noticed. Something that says we're not okay with this. Because we're not, are we?"

Tas shrugged. "I don't care. They're not stopping us living, are they?"

"That will come next, if we let them do this. We're the enemy, Tas. They've decided that. They need people to hate and fear, and it's us."

"So? We ignore it."

"You can't ignore it forever. Not when it's being made into laws. The law of the land. Our land. Our country. The laws we have to live by, they're going to say that what we're doing is wrong. What we are is wrong. We ignore it, they'll think we don't mind, or don't care. They'll carry on and do some more. We can't let it go."

He was so serious, so worked up, his Bálint who did nothing but joke around and make everyone laugh. This was a new Bálint, angry and maybe a bit scared, putting his phone in one pocket then changing his mind and moving it to another one. Bálint going off into something new. Why did he have to do this? Couldn't someone else?

Tas knelt by the bucket and wrung out the scourer so hard it was barely wet at all. "So who will be there? People from the school?"

"One or two."

"People from Rebellion?"

"Maybe. I don't know."

"When will you be back?"

"I don't know. Don't worry, Tas. You just keep cleaning. Maybe you'll be finished when I get home."

Tas threw the scourer back in the bucket. "Hey, I'm just trying to keep the place nice. Look at all the grease on this hood! Have you ever cleaned it at all?"

"I'm sorry, I'm sorry!" Bálint swept forward with big hands and a big hug. "It was just a little joke. Joke, that's all." He squeezed. Tas, his chin squashed into Bálint's chest, felt his eyes go moist. He pulled back, leaving suds on Bálint's sleeves. The grin was back, just a little of it.

"Take me with you." He was being left out. Bálint would lose interest in him, find new friends to be with. Suddenly he didn't want Bálint out of his sight.

"You're not interested in politics. This isn't for you." Bálint planted a soggy kiss on Tas' forehead. "It's no big deal. Don't worry."

"I love you." Tas had to say it, it just welled up in him.

Bálint's face softened. "And I love you too, little boy. Even in these gloves." He lifted Tas' hand and sucked one of the ends of the rubber fingers. "Yak! Gross." Tas cuffed him with the other rubber hand.

"Take care," he said, as Bálint was putting on his coat. Bálint gave him a look, serious again. Then he was gone.

Chapter 17

Another day, another summons from Grom with no explanation. This was in some place in the north east, miles out of Budapest. Fairchild had two hours in his hotel room to catch up on sleep before setting off again. Lucky he already had a car – he'd left it too late for the train. Even so, the address didn't seem to exist on the GPS, which made him late.

It was dark by the time he reached the town of Ózd, right up against the Slovakian border. The satellite map showed thickly wooded hills on three sides, agricultural plains off to the north. Before petering out, the GPS directed him into the middle of a derelict industrial zone, not blessed with street lighting or indeed any signs of life or use. The beam of his headlights picked out piles of concrete rubble, warped metal shapes lying randomly, the side of a long brick building with wide arched window panes missing a lot of glass. The road led to a dead end. He reversed with difficulty, parked, and explored on foot using his phone as a torch. He wandered about amongst rusting trucks and overgrown railway lines until he saw a light through a grubby window. He circled almost the entire building before finding what was left of a giant pair of doors standing ajar. Inside was a vast expanse of space beyond his inadequate torchlight. In one corner he saw movement, figures seated in the glow of a portable halogen lamp.

He approached. His footsteps echoed on the gritty concrete floor. There was a smell of mould and damp plaster. He could see perhaps twenty people, all men, sat in groups. Some of them turned when they heard him but it was clear who held their attention.

"Ah! At last!" said Grom. "I wondered if you were going to make it. This is John, everyone." Fairchild felt suspicious eyes on him. "Don't worry, he's with me. He can be useful to us."

"This place isn't on the map," said Fairchild, taking an empty chair between Grom and the others. He wasn't sure he wanted to be useful to these people.

"That's one of the problems," said Grom. "It used to be. But not any more. When communism fell, the West was supposed to bring opportunities. More than enough to replace the heavy industry that fell apart, the supply lines to the east that so many depended on. It didn't. And what happened to local people? Same thing that always happens. The new politicians sold off whatever they could salvage and got rich in the process. New owners were supposed to come in and invest, bring the country up to the supposed standards of the west. Well, look around. You can see how that's going. This place was well-known, the biggest employer round here. A proud name, now removed from history. Not even on a map any more. How many jobs were lost here?"

Murmurs of assent echoed around. Grom was speaking English. Now Fairchild understood the huddles of people. Grom's words were being quietly interpreted into three different languages by someone in each group. Hungarian, Polish and Croatian, he thought, after listening carefully. He also realised he'd under-estimated the numbers. A quick count came to more than fifty.

"Is there any other employment around here to take its place?" said Grom. "No one cared about that. Move to where the jobs are, they'd say. They want to turn everyone into rootless internationalists like them. They destroyed this place."

Words of agreement rose and died away in the room. This was all planned, Fairchild realised. Grom had deliberately given him a defunct address so that he'd be late and Grom could make that very speech. Probably also to cement himself as the lynchpin and keep Fairchild at arm's length from this group, whatever it was. White males, manual workers judging from their physique, but all ages and a mix of nationalities, clearly. Fairchild was suddenly aware of the length of his hair. If he were required to fit in here he'd need a haircut.

An older guy started talking in Hungarian. His words were rendered into English. "I worked in this place my whole life. My wages here paid for my family, my kids. My friends were all here. I had my engagement party in the canteen. People moved here because of the work. Then the work goes and we're left stranded. Dropped, like garbage. I thought my pension would take care of everything but it's worthless. My son has to buy food for us. It's all wrong. I did everything right, everything they wanted me to do." A couple of people leaned in and patted him on the back or shook his hand.

"We made a mistake turning our backs on Russia." This was another guy, Slovak, maybe. The Polish interpreter took it up; the languages were similar enough. "Communism was far from perfect but we did okay when Russia was looking after us. They believe in strength of character, being proud of who they are. Russia's big enough to stand up to America and Europe. When we went our own way, it went wrong and now we're tied in with the EU." Frustrated headshakes all round. "Run by a cabal of liberal elites in Brussels and their Jewish friends! They think they can throw their money around and tell us what to do! They don't want what's best for us. They want to line their own pockets."

The rumbling translation followed on after he'd finished like a long echo. Nods of assent came from around.

"Look at this place!" a younger Hungarian piped up. "It's ruined! They've taken everything and left us with nothing. It was always the same in Hungary. We were abandoned time and time again by the rest of Europe. Same with these immigrants. They want us on the frontier, absorbing all the Muslims, giving them whatever they want, so they don't go anywhere else."

Grom stepped in himself. "It's nonsense when they argue it won't make any difference. Of course it will make a difference when wave after wave of them come in with different values and beliefs. Neighbours don't know each other any more, don't speak the same language. It's like that in the big cities, isn't it? No sense of community, everyone isolated and alone, surrounded by strangers. And then they become terrorists, or their children do. Let them settle here and their kids will be planting bombs and blowing you up because you don't want Sharia law. Believe me, I know. I used to work in national security. I know how these things work."

His words continued on in three different strains, reverberating in the huge room like distant thunder. There was a respect in the way the room looked at Grom. He'd managed to steer the discussion away from a Hungary-only narrative to one that everyone could get behind.

"This stuff they talk about, integration, it's nonsense." This was a young man, another Slovakian. "Where I'm from, just over the border here, the place is full of Roma. You can't integrate them! They breed like vermin. They'd over-run everything if you let them. They're not interested in civilisation or Christian values. Hundreds of years and they're still living in hovels and shitting in the middle of the floor." This earned a few sniggers. "The only way is to give them their own space and let them stay there. That's all *we* want, isn't it? Our own space, where we can live the way we want to live?" There was plenty of agreement with that.

"But you're not supposed to talk about it," said another Hungarian. "Roma people can talk about how they're Roma. Muslims, blacks, Asians, whatever, but what about if you're white? White Christians, we're at the bottom of the pile now. No one cares about us. But I'm proud of who I am! Everyone in my village is white and Catholic, and that's how I like it. It's peaceful. It's beautiful. It's home. That's all I want, to keep my home. Is that so bad? I grew up there, I worked hard, I got married, we had children and we want to raise them right. But now they'll go off to school or university and come back full of ideas. 'Oh, Dad, I'm a lesbian! Meet my girlfriend!'" Some hoots of laughter at this. "I don't want that for my children. We've lived like this for hundreds of years and it hasn't done us any harm. That's all I want, to carry on the traditional way."

The atmosphere was more animated. Eyes were brighter.

"You're right, my friend," said Grom. "But the tide is against us. People who've decided what's right and what's wrong want to smash all of that to pieces, destroy it, so the places we live in are nowhere places with no identity and no belonging. They want to rip the heart out of our communities." He looked around as he said this, at the cracked plaster and boarded up windows. "And they're determined. There's nothing so arrogant as a well-educated self-important member of the elite stuck in their own bubble. If we want to stem the tide, we have a lot of work to do. They're all against us. We need to unite. The people at this camp are from many different countries but it's the same everywhere. We're all on the same side with this."

"What about the politicians? What about Kornai?" a Hungarian said. This was met with dismissive noises and gestures, particularly from other Hungarians.

"Kornai's a fraud," said one of them. "He talks a good talk but he doesn't mean any of it! He just says it to stay in power. He's not even a practising Christian! He took up churchgoing when it suited him."

"Yeah, he doesn't have any guts," said another. "He talks tough about the EU, but he takes their money, doesn't he? Siphons it off for his friends. He's not going to do anything for real if he's in their pockets. He's just a crowd-pleaser."

"So what are we going to do?" That question cut across the grumbling. The man asking it was in his forties or fifties with a lean, hard face. He was speaking Croatian. Having gained everyone's attention, he continued. "What are we all here for? What's going to work? Not some stupid thing that gets us dismissed as nutters. And I don't want the secret police following me everywhere. Some of us have had that already."

Grom was appraising the guy. "You're right. It's got to be something that will make people sit up and take notice. Something that will change things. You bring some experience to the table, by the sound of it?"

The man's eyes slid across to Fairchild. "It's show and tell time, is it? With this guy here?"

"You don't trust him?" said Grom.

"He's not one of us."

"He has reason to feel the way you do. He's been cheated and betrayed. We don't all have to be the same, do we, to come from the same place?"

"What about you?" another one piped up. "Why are you so interested in this? They said you were Russian."

Grom didn't correct him. "I worked for the government for years, the Kremlin. Assessing the security threats. Rounding up the dissidents. Imposing order. But I wasn't listened to. I went to the highest people and said look, you can see where the world order is heading. Yes, Russia is huge but where is the wealth? What about NATO? They're against us, I said, and slowly they're winning. We need drastic action. But I was turned away again and again. There were too many vested interests, even in Moscow. Cowards who simply wanted to skim something off the top and keep their heads down. Too scared of causing offence. Too scared to even name the enemy, let alone fight back. We need people to question what others decide is right and legal. People who are brave enough to fight and prepared to be first, to lead and wait for others to follow. People who are prepared to risk something, to give something now for the sake of the future. That's what I've been waiting for."

Another respectful silence. Everyone, as Grom intended, was asking himself: What would I risk? What would I give? Questions started forming on some faces; Grom wasn't rushing them.

The hard-faced man came in first. "What are you risking, then? What are you bringing?"

"Money," said Grom, simply. "Resources. Lots of it, if I can make my argument. Other people's money, which is why it's a risk. But I can find sympathetic business backers and persuade them. They've realised, some of them, that tearing down borders and having huge mega-markets has its downsides. Always forced to compete with the lowest-paid, lowest-skilled workers in the world. Only managing survival-level economies of scale by making products so anodyne and multinational they could have come from anywhere. Global markets mean cheap tat. Why should we be forced to accept substandard foreign goods made by half-wits happy to live on a dollar a day when people right here can't find work? We have friends, believe me, and we can find more. I just need to persuade them to put their trust in us. And if you think there's no risk involved in that, think again."

The interpreters' voices died out into silence. Grom could read a room; he knew they were unsure. "Let me show you what I have already." He nodded to a couple of the men, who got up and dragged forward a wooden crate. Several more were stacked up behind. Fairchild hadn't noticed them before, or assumed they were more abandoned detritus. In the glare of the lamp, the men prised open the lids. They pulled out a number of long bulky heavy-duty cases. Fairchild felt his pulse quicken; he knew what these were. Grom took one on his knee and opened the lid. He picked up the main chamber of a gun and held it up.

"Semi-automatic. Russian-made. What the army is using right now." With a fast, sure hand he assembled it. Everyone was staring. Grom put the case aside, stood and aimed into a corner of the room. There was absolute silence. He lowered the weapon.

"No firing today. Plenty of time for that tomorrow, out in the woods. These are yours, guys. For the training camp. You need to take yourselves seriously. You need to know what power you have and be prepared to use it, before it's too late. Take a look." He nodded towards the crate. "Pick one up. Feel the weight of it. That's what power feels like."

The cases were passed round. People took them tentatively and opened them up. They were brand new; Fairchild could smell the synthetic padding. Most didn't try to piece the weapons together but picked up a component and turned it over in their hands. One or two knew what they were doing, or thought they did. Someone passed one to the lean-faced man: "You want it, Marko?" He shook his head, arms folded to show how unimpressed he was. Grom was watching all of this very carefully.

Fairchild slid over to him. "There's live ammunition in those cartridges?"

"Don't be such a fusspot. They have to learn to trust each other, don't they?"

The noise in the room increased as the conversation buzzed. There was some laughter too. "Don't be tempted, boys!" said Grom. "They're all counted. You'll get to play with them again tomorrow. I'm just showing you now how serious I am. So, the question is, how serious are you?"

A few more minutes and Grom nodded to the helpers to collect them all up again. That took some time, during which conversations were going on, including between the different nationalities. Grom held his hand up. The room quietened. "Questions? Questions, please."

There were a few, mainly about the guns, how they were used, where they were from exactly. To that one Grom smiled. "That's never a good question to ask."

"So what do you want from us?" someone asked.

"Courage," said Grom. The room was so quiet Fairchild could hear an owl hooting outside. "Character. Strength. Determination. It's down to you now."

There wasn't a man in there who wasn't affected by that. Eyes were down; a lot of thinking was going on. Grom made subtle moves to end the meeting. It was masterful persuasion. First build the why; the how comes later.

Grom ignored Fairchild and dealt instead with all the people who wanted to talk to him. Eventually they started to drift away. Fairchild sensed eyes on him again. If he was really expected to be trusted by these people he'd need more than Grom vouching for him. The aftermath lasted an age, and then Grom seemed on the verge of leaving with a couple of them. Fairchild managed to pull him aside.

"You're not going back to Budapest?"

"Oh no, I'm here for the duration. It's a kind of boot camp. Tomorrow some psycho is going to take them all into the woods for special manoeuvres. They lap up all that pseudo military stuff." There wasn't a trace of the sincerity he displayed earlier.

"You don't want me here?"

"Not unless you need to learn how to shoot."

"Then why did you invite me?"

"To show you, my boy. So you're in the picture. You want to know the plan, don't you?"

"What plan?"

"All in good time." He started turning away.

Fairchild was learning nothing. "What did you mean before, about Hungary? There's something here, isn't there? Something my parents didn't want me to know."

"There certainly is."

"You said you'd tell me—"

"Okay, okay, keep your hair on. One thing at a time. Look." Two of the men were waiting for Grom at the door. "I have to go. János Mészáros. Go talk to him. He'll put you in the picture."

"Who's he?"

"Look him up. I have to go."

Grom had already turned away. He joined the two waiting men and they left.

Fairchild was the last to leave. He went back to his car and set off back to Budapest. He already knew how to shoot.

Chapter 18

Tas was already in bed when Bálint got back home. But he wasn't asleep. He heard the door, then he lay on his side and listened to Bálint moving around the place, trying to be quiet but not succeeding as usual, lights on and off, getting a glass of water, bathroom and then slipping his clothes off into a big untidy pile on the floor and sliding into bed beside him.

"You're cold."

"You're warm." Bálint wrapped him in a full-body embrace.

"Ouch! Not any more!" Tas turned onto his back. Bálint sniggered and buried his head somewhere under Tas' armpit. Tas raised his arm to see the man's face. "So, how did it go?"

A grin was plastered all over Bálint's face. "Good. It went good."

"You made a plan?"

"Yes. Oh, yes, we made a plan."

"What kind of plan?" Bálint had the kind of look Tas and his sisters and brothers had when they came home from doing something they shouldn't have done.

"A good one. A really good one!" His eyes were dancing.

"But what is it?"

"I can't tell you."

"Why not?"

"It's a secret."

"Secret? Why? What's the point of that?"

"It won't be a secret when it happens, will it? Just before. We don't want someone mouthing off to the authorities or something."

"I won't do that."

"I know you won't." He planted an enormous kiss on Tas' bare shoulder. "But it's best you don't know. It'll spoil the surprise, anyway."

He made to make another kiss, but Tas pushed the hair away from his face to look at him. "Is it dangerous?"

"Dangerous? No."

"Is it illegal?"

Bálint paused. "Probably."

"So you might get in trouble?"

A slight hesitation. "Nah. I don't think so. Not for very long, anyway." Bálint's hand started roaming along the top of Tas' thigh.

"You could lose your job."

The hand slowed. The solemn face was back. "If this bill goes through we could lose everything. But we can't live in fear. We have to be proud. Like you said. It's the only way."

The hand was on the move again, making mischief and derailing Tas' chain of thought. "It'll be okay." Bálint was speaking right into his ear now, his warm breath tickling. "It'll be more than okay. It'll be brilliant! Fabulous! Perfect!"

Bálint and his crazy ideas.

Chapter 19

Grom was evil. Grom was an unapologetic manipulator of human emotions and behaviour, twisting people to serve his own selfish and spiteful ends. Grom had Fairchild's parents abducted and killed. Grom was a man Fairchild loathed. Which was why it so incensed him that he was sitting in his hotel room waiting for the man to call him, like some lovestruck teenager mooning about at the end of a phone line.

Clearly Grom was stringing him along. Whether or not he had a role for Fairchild in this scheme he was cooking up, Fairchild had deliberately been sidelined. At the disturbing event in Ózd earlier, Grom seemed to be trying to undermine Fairchild, not bring him in. Was there anything in this Mészáros idea, or was it just some wild goose chase to get him out of the way? Damn the man. And damn this country with its impenetrable language, and damn his parents for hiding secrets in it.

He'd pushed everyone away, determined to wade this river of blood alone, but now he needed help. Who to call? Who had he alienated the least?

He texted Zack, on a number most people didn't know about: *Call me, please.* It was two in the morning in Budapest. God only knew where in the world Zack was. Fifteen minutes later, Fairchild's phone rang.

"Well whaddaya know? A call from the dark side. I thought you'd be too busy plotting to take over the world."

"I'm well, thanks, Zack."

"More's the pity."

"So, how are you? Where are you?"

"Who wants to know? You, or your new sociopath buddy?"

"Just making conversation."

"Oh, excuse me! Of course, you're British. So let's be polite and pretend nothing's happened. Wanna talk about the weather as well?"

This wouldn't be an easy conversation, he'd realised that. "Look, Zack, you know me. You know I'd have a good reason for going in with Grom. Don't you?"

"I don't remember you sharing it with me any time."

"I didn't want to get anyone else involved. This guy brings whole new meaning to the term guilty by association. Anyway, I thought you'd probably figure it out by yourself." Zack wasn't immune to flattery, and besides, it ought to be true of a guy with his experience in intelligence gathering and special ops – stateside in his case.

"Yeah, well, I figured you must have cut some deal with our friends the Wong Kai in exchange for that Fire Sappers information they fed you."

"There you go. It turns out that Darcy Tang had a dossier on them herself. She holds a grudge against them. They stole electricity from her for their crypto mining operations. A lot of it. I was the person who could bring them down, she felt."

"Bring them down? That's your gig? Bring down a highly successful and ruthless group of anonymous international hackers? She doesn't ask much, does she, the lady?"

"Exactly. While their head honcho Milo was still around I might have had a chance to get in through him."

"But our own cuddly Agent Rapp put paid to that by shooting him twice in the chest."

"And that was the end of that idea. Until Rose happened to mention that Grom was involved with them too."

"Interesting. You used information from your favourite MI6 officer to go behind their backs and get in with the bad guys?"

"And I'm sure she hates me for it. But given we needed the info, I didn't have any other option, apart from waiting for Darcy Tang's henchmen to catch up with me in a dark alley somewhere. But you're missing the point. We're actually on the same side here. You're still involved with Rapp's taskforce?"

"'Fraid so. That's why I'm stuck in Washington. We're getting nowhere. Does this call mean you've got some useful intel?"

"Not much, I'm afraid." Fairchild gave a quick précis of Grom's info on the high command, the involvement of Bogdan, and the Ózd gathering that evening.

"Bogdan? You think that's his real name?"

"Nope. And you already knew we were in Hungary, didn't you?"

"Yeah, we got that far. That's where your MI6 friend is, too."

Fairchild's stomach did a somersault. "If you mean Rose Clarke, I think she'd take issue with that description. But that's all I've got. He's holding me off big-time. This extremist group is just getting started. I don't think they'll be putting anything into action any time soon, though Grom clearly has something in mind. I've no idea how I fit in. He's playing games with me."

"Of course he is. That's what he does. And he doesn't trust you. I wouldn't either, if I were in his shoes."

"I need your help, Zack."

A sigh. "Okay, well, you've given us something, so I guess I owe you."

Fairchild hesitated. This part was more personal. "He told me something which made me rethink everything." He recounted Grom's question about learning the language, the nursery rhyme and the name Grom gave him. Zack was as impressed as he usually was with Fairchild's family revelations.

"There's one language on the face of the earth you haven't mastered, and you're reading something into it. Right. And you think you've heard some jingle on TV before. Yeah, I can sense a great conspiracy brewing."

"There's something here, Zack. It's real."

"Who's the guy?"

"Some kind of academic, according to the internet. Historian. Who he is to me, or who he was to my parents, I don't know. But I've got to follow it up."

"Could be another one of his games."

"Yes, it could. Or it could be for real. Walter knows more than he's ever told me, that's for sure. The problem is—"

"The problem is, you don't speak the lingo and you don't know anyone in town for reasons previously explained."

"So I could really do with some local help. On the quiet. Someone who'll do a bit of interpretation and can be trusted to keep their mouth shut. Someone who doesn't mind falling down a rabbit hole."

"Doing what?"

"Stepping into the unknown. Didn't you read when you were a child?"

"Not really."

"Do you have any friends here at the Embassy, Zack? Or at the base?"

"What base? There's no US base in Hungary."

"Sorry. I assumed there were. I thought they were everywhere."

"Hey, you're asking me for a favour, remember?"

"I said sorry. So can you help?"

A pause. "We'll stay in touch? You hear anything useful through your psycho traitor buddy, you'll pass it along?"

"As long as you can be discreet."

"Fairchild, this is me you're talking to! Discreet is my middle name. But I'll have to pass on the intel."

"Just don't mention my name, okay?"

"I never do anyway. You're an embarrassment at the best of times."

"Thanks, Zack."

"No promises. But I'll see what I can do."

Chapter 20

Rose endured a long slow day waiting for nine o'clock to arrive and wondering if this was a big mistake. She had a creeping feeling that history was repeating itself, that she was falling into the same trap again. But, another part of her brain reasoned, the circumstances of the meet seemed safe enough, although daytime would have been more reassuring. She was more prepared for a trap than she'd ever been before. Danny would be with her. And after all, she'd persuaded her superiors to let her come here to Budapest. What was the point in being on the ground in Hungary if she were just going to sit in front of a laptop all day like she could do back in London?

She met Danny at Széll Kálmán Square and they walked up the hill together. Narrow roads lined with stone walls wound upwards, cut through by murky tree-lined flights of steps with gutters that smelled of drains. Behind, a night time view opened up of the city suburbs, lights spreading into the Buda hills. At the top they reached the Castle District, a wide, flat area incorporating several impeccably restored eighteenth century streets, a large church, and a hideously ugly hotel. It looked like a period drama film set, apart from the hotel. Plenty of tourists wandered around, mainly along the length of the Bastion with its squat decorative spires, ornate arches and stone walkways that might have been at home in Disneyland.

They were early. Maybe that was a mistake, the two of them standing there like targets. But better early than late. They filled the time with chit-chat – expat life, schools, exchanging Service experiences and anecdotes. It was refreshing to talk relatively freely about the frustrations of a life of secrecy. Over the wall where they stood, the city of Budapest spread before them, the wide expanse of the river curving through, bejewelled bridges, lamp-lined boulevards and clusters of taller newer towers. It was beautiful, but what place didn't look beautiful from a distance at night, when all the grime was obscured? It pricked at her a little, standing here looking down at this view; it reminded her of something but she couldn't pinpoint what.

A step made them turn. They did a double-take; it was just a boy, standing in front of them in a football shirt, looking polite if a little grubby. "Please, follow me!" he said in accented English. They exchanged glances and Danny indicated for the boy to lead on. He moved swiftly through the populated areas so that they had to hurry to keep up. They headed down the hill, below the Bastion, into the labyrinth of streets on the steep slope to the city centre. He turned into a narrow passageway of steps between buildings.

Rose turned to Danny. "You know the area? Does this go anywhere?"

"This bit is new. Recent infill."

They left the street behind, and most of the street light as well. Half way down the boy headed into an alley that curved round the back of some buildings. It was too narrow for both of them – Rose went ahead, Danny was behind. The boy put on a spurt and disappeared at the end, leaving both of them on their own and hidden from anyone else.

They looked at each other. "No," said Danny. "I don't like it. We go back."

"Agreed."

But before they could take another step, a shadow appeared behind Danny, two of them, right on him. He stepped back, ready, but it was too late. They knocked him to the ground. Rose made to leap forward but couldn't. Her arms were pinned on either side. Another two guys were on her as well. She struggled to pull away. A sharp pain stabbed her knee and she staggered. One of them had kicked her. They dragged her round the back of the building.

It was dark: some kind of service road, no street lights or windows. The men were masked with hand-made balaclavas. They were solidly built and gripped her arms so hard it hurt. She'd been trained for this, she reminded herself. She got ready.

They were pulling her along clumsily. She shifted diagonally and butted one with her knee, jarring him enough that he lost his grip. The other rounded on her but she kicked back, turned, and rammed a fist somewhere soft. He yelped and doubled up. The first guy grabbed her shoulder and got a face full of elbow, then a punch. He fell back, holding his jaw. She was free to run – but then two more came powering in, the two that had come up behind them.

Danny! Where was Danny? She charged straight at them, but they were already at speed and shoved her to the ground. One of them pushed her onto her back and knelt on top, his knee in the small of her back. The other shoved her face straight down into the stone path. She felt sick. Her nose was wet. They weren't taking any chances now. They hauled her up and pressed her against the wall. All four of them crowded round her, angry eyes through the jagged cut holes of their masks.

"So what do you want?" she said. One of them drew a hand back and slapped her hard in the face. It stung, and knocked her cheek against the wall. It was followed by a punch in the jaw, and another in the eye. One of them muttered something to the puncher, in a language Rose didn't catch. The speaker stepped forward. Eyes curious, he smoothed her face with his fingers. The hand continued, over her chin, down her neck and chest, slowing as it traversed her breast.

Oh, hell, thought Rose. Not this. Please, not this!

The man stepped closer. She tried to pull away, but the other three had her tight, and gripped even tighter when she tried to push back. The fourth man's hand was burying into her clothes now, seeking her skin and finding it around her stomach, his palm flat against her navel. Still it descended. Rose tried again. The wall blocked her from gaining any impetus. Her struggling seemed to please them, amuse them.

She shouted: "Danny!" One of them clamped a hand over her mouth. She bit his finger. He withdrew it with an exclamation, turned it into a fist and rammed her mouth. The back of her head thudded against the wall. That sick feeling again.

The hand was inside her underwear now, creeping down slowly, and under. Then it stopped. Abruptly, it went into reverse. He pulled it out and raised it in front of her face, turning it back and forth as if he were showing off a trophy. *Look where I've been!* Then he said something else to the others and walked off, away from them all.

Rose felt the grip on her arms slacken. The guy she'd bitten took a step back and rammed her face again. She slumped. Another punched her in the ribs. She curled, expecting more. But instead she heard footsteps receding as they all made off into the dark.

Her chest ached with every breath, her head throbbed and her face felt wet and swollen. *Danny. Where was Danny?* She wanted to lie there but forced herself, using the stones of the wall to pull herself up bit by bit. Moving was painful but she limped along, leaning on the wall. As she neared she saw a figure, also leaning on the wall, hunched over just as she was, a bizarre mirror image.

"Danny!" She'd have run over to him if she could. He'd come to a halt, his forehead resting against the wall. "What happened to you?"

"They grounded me. I was totally out for a few minutes. I heard your shout. But I've…" He was looking beyond her down the pathway.

"They roughed me up then they split," said Rose. She realised her blouse was hanging open. The guy must have ripped the buttons off.

Danny was staring. "Rose, did they—"

"No!" Rose buttoned her coat over her top. "Christ, I thought they were going to, there were four of them and I couldn't do anything! But they just stopped and walked off."

"Something spooked them? A noise, someone coming?"

"No, nothing! They didn't even run off. They walked. This was all set up, Danny."

"Course it was. Let's get out of here. Back to the street. Come on."

She stared back down the pathway, not really believing what had happened. "Come on," said Danny again. "We don't want to hang around here."

"They won't come back," said Rose. "They've done their job. They've done whatever they were paid to do. But what was the point of it?"

"Scare us, maybe?" Danny was making his way down the steps, slowly, both hands on the railing.

"What are we supposed to be scared about?" To get down the steps, Rose forced her legs to do things they didn't want to do. She put her hands in her pockets and felt something. "Hang on."

"What?" Danny stopped and looked back. Rose got the thing out of her pocket. It rested in the palm of her hand. She held it out for Danny. It was a portable zip drive.

"What's that?" he asked.
"I've never seen it before."
"Where did it come from?"
Rose shook her head. "No idea."

Chapter 21

Fairchild heard from Zack in the form of a text message telling him to be on a particular street corner at a particular hour of the afternoon. He walked there, taking in every detail on the way, dipping into shops, peering through windows, scrutinising every sign. The more time he spent in Budapest, the more he found memories triggered, odd familiarities. *Tejföl*, the Hungarian variant of soured cream, was in every convenience store. It was one product amongst thousands, but that word, he'd heard that word before. And there were others. No wonder his parents hadn't wanted him to even set foot in the place.

The street corner turned out to be a pleasant spot, a small square tucked under trees with a statue on a plinth, a gaggle of electric scooters and cafes with outdoor seating that extended down the street. Opposite, the brick façade of a very new-looking church loomed high. He'd only been waiting there a couple of minutes when a tall woman in leggings with a brightly coloured stripey scarf strode up to him, smiling.

"You're John? I'm Gabi. I hear you need some help."

"Good to meet you." They shook. She was dressed like a student but looked a little older, mid twenties, maybe. She had an exaggerated swept fringe that hung across one side of her face, dangly earrings and a heart-shaped tattoo on her neck.

"Not what you expected?" she said, noticing his hesitation.

"I didn't know what to expect. Let's sit somewhere and talk."

"Sure. I know a cool place."

She led the way into one of the bars, a light roomy space smelling of coffee and pastries with cartoon-like murals of city scenes on the walls. "Looks like some student place but it's really an institution here. My mother used to work here. In fact, it's where she met my father. So it's because of this place that I exist. You saw the name? Know what it means?"

Fairchild shook his head.

"*'Tilos az A'*. The A is an unfinished word. It's a kind of translation from your Winnie the Pooh. There's a sign in it, yes? It says *'Trespassers W'*. They don't know what the W is. Tilos means forbidden. So it's kind of the other way round. But that's how the sign would read in Hungarian. Drink? The hot chocolate is really good here."

Her command of English was excellent. She ordered the drinks. "So, I guess you want to know something more about me. I'm a grad student. A linguist. All students here speak English, that's no big deal, but I also speak German, Russian, French and Spanish and I'm learning Italian. My thesis is in German literature."

"And English language children's books?"

"Hah! No, everyone knows about that one. So, I've been a student since I was eighteen. I live in a house with a lot of other students. We're all very poor." She grinned.

"I see. So a little work on the side is of interest to you."

"Maybe." Their hot chocolates arrived, a celebration of cream and marshmallow and chocolate sprinkles in a long glass with a straw.

"How did you get involved with the Americans?" he asked. "I assume this invite came via the US Embassy."

"I just went in there one day and asked if they had any work. They said no to start with, but I was at my most charming and eventually they said there might be something occasionally. They did a load of background checks and here

I am. Mostly it's kind of unofficial. Cash payment. And I have to forget everything straight away." She sucked her straw.

"Sounds perfect. What did they tell you about me?"

"Nothing. I don't need to know, unless you want to tell me. As long as you're okay. Safe, I mean. They tell me they know you."

That was Zack's influence. "I'm safe, I promise. I have friends at places like the Embassy but I'm not one of them. I do my own thing. I'm a businessman, mostly. But I need some help. I'm a linguist as well." He proved the point by switching to German. "But I don't speak Hungarian. I'm doing some family history. I lost my parents when I was a child. I think they had some Hungarian connection but I don't know what it is. I've been given the name of a guy, some academic, but I don't know why or what the link is."

"What's his name?"

Fairchild told her. A broad smile spread across her face. "János Mészáros? The historian? *That* János Mészáros?"

"You know of him?"

"Of course! He's the leading authority on Hungarian history. He's pretty famous. He's written a load of books on all the key events. 1956 especially." Her German was just as good as her English. "So, you want to meet this guy?"

"I do."

Her face fell a little. "You know, you don't really need an interpreter for this. Probably he speaks good English. If not, then Russian. You speak Russian?"

Fairchild obliged by switching to Russian. "It's a little more complicated than that. He doesn't know me. I don't really know what I need to ask him about. I don't know where he lives or have any contact details. So, it's a bit more than translating. I need someone to find him and set up a meeting with him. Persuade him, if persuasion is necessary."

"You want me to do that?"

"Can you?"

She considered. "Yes, I think I can. The historians at my university would be a good place to start. But there's one condition."

"What's that?"

"I come with you to the meeting, whether you need an interpreter or not."

"Why?"

"Because I want to meet him."

They exchanged details and Fairchild left it with her. She phoned him the next day. "Mészáros lives in Pécs, near the university. You know where Pécs is, right?"

"Sure, right in the south."

"He's retired. Pretty old by now. But he still does occasional talks and interviews. If I approach him, we'll probably have to go to Pécs."

"That's okay." Fairchild had been thinking about this. "We'd need a car and a driver. Can you organise that?"

"A driver? That's so expensive. Anyway, there's no need. I can drive, if you can't."

"The money doesn't matter. And there is a need, because on the way there you're going to teach me Hungarian."

This produced a peal of laughter. "I'm happy to try, but I hope you don't end up disappointed. It's a very difficult language. And Hungary is a small country. Only a few hours to Pécs."

Fairchild knew that already. "Let's see."

Chapter 22

Gabi was right. By the time they got to Pécs, in the back of a large Mercedes with leather seats and a uniformed chauffeur up front, she'd only managed to cover the very basics of how the language worked and some everyday phrases. But it was a start, and would make it much easier for him to progress on his own.

She also brought her own János Mészáros books. The one about the 1956 rebellion was long and detailed. Fairchild flicked through the text and despaired of ever being able to read it. The black and white photos from the time showed crowds of young people with banners, then fewer, with weapons, then Soviet tanks in streets pockmarked from bullets and shells.

They arrived mid-morning at the guy's house, as agreed. He came to the door, thinner and frailer than the photo on his book jacket, but alert. Gabi introduced Fairchild. If Mészáros spoke English, he didn't seem inclined to use it. He said something to Gabi.

"He says, do you know Hungary? Have you been to this area before?"

"No, and no," said Fairchild. "I've sadly overlooked this part of the world."

"Then he's suggesting we go for a walk. Up there. He wants to give you a bit of context."

The street was right on the edge of Pécs. Behind the house, a modern single-storey building, rocky hills thick with forest rose up and curved around the town like the sides of a bowl. That was where Mészáros was pointing. "Why not?" said Fairchild.

Mészáros led them up a clearly defined path, his pace slow but steady. Gabi had the biggest challenge; her block heels weren't designed for hiking, but she kept up with him and managed to hold a conversation at the same time. Fairchild, slightly behind, got the benefit of an occasional explanation.

"We're talking about the university. He's saying it's one of the oldest in Europe." More chat between the two of them. He'd forgotten how language, or the lack of it, could cut you out.

They reached a peak and took a path along the contour of the hills, with Pécs below them, its town centre a mass of brown and orange roofs, and more hills beyond. Fairchild took off his jacket. It was a cloudy day but he was sweating from the steepness of the walk. A few birds tweeted. On a weekday morning no one else was around.

"He's saying Pécs was held by the Ottomans for a hundred years," said Gabi. "Of course there's the big mosque and a few others, some buildings here and there, but not much given how long they were here. In one street in the centre you have a mosque, a church and a synagogue."

"That's not so unusual. Plenty of places in Europe have that."

Mészáros looked at him but didn't comment. He understood, Fairchild thought. The man came to a halt at a viewpoint. Pécs lay clustered in the base of a nest, green sides rising up all round.

"*Szép,*" said Mészáros.

"Beautiful," translated Gabi.

"*Igen.*" Yes. He'd managed to pick up that much. The historian smiled and launched into some narrative. Gabi interpreted.

"When older people talk about 'szép' Hungary, they mean the Hungary before the First World War, that of the Austro-Hungarian Empire. It was Habsburg-controlled but Vienna made some concessions to keep the rebellious Hungarian nobles on board. They re-created – invented, he says, maybe – the kingdom of Hungary with all its traditions, and the Emperor was crowned." Mészáros was pointing in different directions. "It extended that way into what's now Croatia, there, Serbia, there, Romania. To the north, Slovakia. A little to the west, Austria. It was over three times bigger than it is now. In the Treaty of Trianon in 1920 Hungary lost four fifths of its area and over three million of its people. The price of defeat. But it's not forgotten."

Fairchild nodded; he'd picked up on this from his reading, but not on how current it still was in the Hungarian psyche. There was more to come.

"The problem is, Hungarians live in all these places. There's over a million Hungarians in Romania. Half a million in Slovakia. Two hundred thousand in Serbia. What is a nation? If a place is mainly populated by Hungarians, that should be Hungary, right? But what about all the non-Hungarians in these areas? Or the non-Hungarians within Hungary? Nationalism only really works if people of the same nationality live in the same place. But they don't. In 1848, the rebel forces defending the Hungarian revolution included large numbers of Germans, Polish, Croats and Serbs. The Habsburg army which defeated them also included Germans, Polish, Croats and Serbs. Everything here is mixed.

"We were never good at dealing with minorities. It was our problem back then, and again in the Second World War. The bargain we struck with the Nazis in exchange for our 'szép' land was not very 'szép'. Now the government is trying to talk down the Hungarian role in the war and the Holocaust. This is our story – we suffer defeat, we recover and rebuild, and we rewrite history."

He paused, and motioned for them to follow him. Further along he stopped and turned to the west.

"Walls go up and walls come down. Over there, between Hungary and Austria, was a fence. It was there for twenty-eight years. In 1989 it was opened up by the Hungarian government. That brought the wall down across the whole of Europe. When we joined the EU we joined the Schengen agreement. No border there at all now. Or with Slovakia or Slovenia. No borders! That's a good thing, isn't it?"

He waited for Fairchild to respond. Fairchild shrugged. "It depends." He was borderless and countryless himself. It made no odds to him.

"But now there's a new wall," continued Gabi, following the old man's words. "Along here." He was pointing to the southern border. "It went up in 2015 between Hungary and Serbia to keep immigrants out. Then it extended to Croatia. For a time, Slovenia. There was talk about Romania too. So maybe borders aren't such a bad thing. If it's what people want. Back in 1989 we celebrated when the wall fell. But that was a long time ago."

Fairchild thought about the people at the Ózd meeting; they would have approved. "Hungary wasn't the only country that put up borders."

"He says that's true," said Gabi.

They turned back and made their way down to the house. Mészáros appeared to have the place to himself. He took them into a wide room at the back with a wall made entirely of glass that looked out on an elaborate sloped garden. He brought tea and a bowl of sticky fruit-flavoured sweets.

"Can we ask about my parents?" Fairchild said as soon as they were all seated.

"Sure!" Gabi explained to Mészáros what Fairchild had told her of his family history. "Their names?" she asked.

"Edward and Elizabeth. Fairchild."

Mészáros showed no sign of recognition. "He's asking what you can tell him about them," said Gabi.

"Very little. They lived in Vienna for a time. It was a place they came back to frequently. I wasn't aware that they ever came here. I've only just learned about a connection with Hungary."

Mészáros didn't appear to have an answer. "You've been to Vienna?" Fairchild prompted.

"Of course. Very often." For the first time he spoke directly to Fairchild, in English. "But I don't know those names. I'm sorry."

"What about London?"

"Yes, London, of course!" He had some standing in his field. It was natural that he'd travelled.

"What about before the change? In the sixties or seventies?"

"Then, no. Only afterwards. After the wall came down."

Fairchild's parents were already dead by then. He couldn't think of anything else to ask. He sat and stared at the backs of his hands. What was the point of it all? Stupid of him, to take Grom's bait and come here. The man was probably laughing at him right now. Maybe Fairchild was mistaken about the nursery rhyme. He'd been so sure. That could have been Grom again, putting ideas into his head, turning him about so he didn't know what was going on.

In the silence Gabi reached out and touched his knee. "Do you mind if I ask him something?"

"Sure, go ahead." It needn't be a wasted journey for both of them. Gabi made her request, whatever it was. *Igen,* said Mészáros, then something else. Gabi seemed impressed. With a few prompts from the young woman he launched into an extensive narrative. Something occurred to him. He asked her something. Another *Igen*, from her side. He got up and went into another room.

Gabi turned to Fairchild. "I asked him about his role in the 1956 rebellion. He was right in the middle of it all, a student in Budapest. He's talking about how they crept out at night and stole weaponry from the Soviet troops."

"That was pretty courageous."

"Then he said he had more photos. One of their group kept a photo journal of the whole thing. There's a lot more than in his book."

Mészáros appeared again with two thick photo albums. He handed them to Gabi and carried on talking. Gabi leafed through the small black and white images, listening and occasionally interpreting at the same time. Looking at them upside down, Fairchild saw under-exposed shots of hands holding up candles or lighters. Small groups of young people sitting round tables. Piles of leaflets being run off a printing press. Scenes of celebration, rows of grinning faces. Scowling Soviet soldiers being driven off in the backs of vans. Triumphant young fighters brandishing a motley collection of weapons.

"You want to look?" Gabi handed Fairchild the first one while she turned to the second. He went back through them more slowly. "You can see there the first stage, the success," she said. "The second one will be different."

Mészáros still had plenty to say. "He's talking now about how difficult it was getting these photos out," Gabi said.

"They had to smuggle the film canisters over the border. The photographer was killed in the crackdown."

A pause in the narrative, then it started up again. "Most of the organisers were rounded up. He's saying he escaped himself by leaving Budapest and hiding out in a village. Many people crossed to the west. Hundreds of thousands." She was turning the pages of the second album: more happy rebel fighters in various poses, then distant hurried shots of tanks in streets. One or two of huddled worried faces, then no more photos. She handed it over.

"He's saying it wasn't all for nothing. Hungary had a more free and tolerant version of communism. Goulash communism, you've heard of that?" He nodded. "Some movement was allowed, some business activity. The history always mattered. In 1989, the reforming communists announced that 1956 was a popular uprising. That was an important change. Under communism it had always been described as a counter-revolution. More rewriting of history." She said something to the historian, then explained to Fairchild. "I told him he should publish all of these. People my age, our parents talk about 1989, our grandparents talk about 1956. We still care about this." The man seemed doubtful.

Fairchild was going through the second album. Something caught his eye, one of the group shots. It was taken in a large room that was being used for storage. Wooden boxes were piled up, and in the midst of them, looking down into one of them, was a group of people. Seeing his interest, Mészáros pointed and commented.

"The boxes are full of guns and ammunition," said Gabi. "Donated from the local police stations that were sympathetic."

But Fairchild wasn't looking at the boxes. He was looking at one of the people, a woman with long dark hair, staring into the box, unaware she was being photographed. He pointed. "Who is that?"

Mészáros peered at it. "Ilona," he said without hesitation. "It's Gulyás Ilona. Ilona Gulyás."

Ilona Gulyás. The name meant nothing to Fairchild. But the face did, the eyes. Then he remembered something he should have thought of earlier. He got out his wallet, took out a small battered photograph and passed it to Mészáros. It was one of the three of them, standing awkwardly outside some gothic building. They were dropping him off at school, he thought. They weren't big fans of photos. He always had this one with him, but had forgotten about it.

Mészáros stared at it and frowned. He spoke directly to Fairchild. "Ilona and Viktor? This is them?"

"That's Elizabeth and Edward. That's my mother and father."

Chapter 23

Mészáros picked up Fairchild's photo and held it to the light. He examined it for some time. Then he looked at Fairchild. "I don't understand. It's them. Viktor and Ilona."

Fairchild's mind was racing as fast as his pulse. He pushed the album back towards Mészáros, noticing that his hand was trembling. "Do you have any photos of Viktor?"

Mészáros browsed and stopped a few pages later. "Here." He turned the album back to Fairchild. In the image, a young man leaned against a tank, smiling at the camera. He was holding a gun, casually, as if it were no big deal.

Fairchild looked up at Mészáros. "Do you mind?"

"Please."

He got both photos out of the album and lay all three pictures on the table. The other two watched in silence. The room felt uncomfortably hot. Fairchild's brain was refusing to process what was lying right in front of him.

"Who are they?" he asked. "These people. Viktor and Ilona. What can you tell me about them?"

Mészáros reverted to Hungarian and Gabi interpreted. "Students, like me. They came from the east of Hungary, near Debrecen. They knew each other before they came to Budapest. Grew up in villages near each other. Childhood sweethearts. Both really clever, super-intelligent. They got on so well with each other that people wanted to be around them. They were fun, always in the middle of things. Viktor was studying politics and economics, Ilona—"

"Languages," Fairchild finished.

"That's right."

"So what happened to them?"

"They fled. Crossed the border in '56 like so many other people. They were already known to the police and would have gone to prison if they'd stayed. Or worse."

"And then what?"

"*Hát...*" Mészáros used that curious little word Fairchild had heard before when people hesitated or weighed something up. Gabi took up the flow again.

"They started a new life. I heard from them occasionally. By letter only. Delivered by hand by people we trusted. It was like that with everybody else, too, from '56. They didn't say much about what they were doing. They travelled a lot. They seemed happy enough, from what they said. I know they got married at some point. Viktor made a kind of joke of it. Don't ask when or where! I think there was something about the secrecy that he liked, though there was a reason for it all."

"What reason? They didn't have to hide once they were out of the Eastern bloc."

"The Soviets pursued people even in the West. They had their assassins. Their spies could have caught up with them. I think Ilona and Viktor missed Hungary, for a time at least. But they found other things and places to interest them. They were explorers, really. Sometimes they asked about particular people, who was where, who was still alive. But the letters stopped. We heard from them no more."

"That was around 1980?" Fairchild asked.

"Yes, about then."

"Did they ever mention a child?" He tried to keep his voice steady.

"I'm afraid not."

Fairchild sat back. Why? Why lie so utterly, so completely? It was all possible, of course. Their oh-so-English sounding names would check out perfectly, if he'd ever thought to investigate them, their legends immaculate. As a family they never took him to their childhood places — there was never time, they were always abroad somewhere, away. They had no family: all dead, they said, and they were only children of only children.

"I knew nothing of this," he managed to say. "I thought they were British. I thought I was British."

Mészáros asked a quiet question. "Do you know what happened to them?"

"They were killed."

Mészáros nodded. "I thought so. They caught quite a few of us over the years."

"It wasn't about the rebellion. It was something else entirely. To do with their work."

Mészáros took a moment to absorb this. "In some ways that's more tragic. They evaded Moscow's retribution but something else got the better of them. It's a tragedy, really. The Soviets weren't stupid. They could see the potential in those two. It was obvious Viktor was a future leader."

Gabi paused and asked Mészáros something. He laughed sadly and replied with something that made her blush.

"What?" asked Fairchild.

"I asked him why only Viktor had potential. Why not Ilona? He said she was just as capable, but in those days, well, it would be different now."

"And then?"

"And then he said that I should make the most of it. Use my own potential."

"Quite right." Fairchild's eyes went back to the photos.

"But it's so sad," said Gabi, "that they completely abandoned their nationality. They didn't have to hide that they were Hungarian, did they?"

She turned to ask Mészáros the same question. He shrugged. Fairchild could see it. If they'd decided on a Service life, a British background would make things much easier. Most people couldn't have pulled it off. They'd have needed help setting it all up, but it made sense. Their talents would have been used, as well as their connections here, and they got protection and an opportunity to help destabilise the Soviet regime they'd fought against.

It was impressive. They were basically living under cover the entire time. With him they kept up the pretence. Their version of his background – his entire identity – was a fabrication, elaborate and utterly convincing. Except for a few moments when, alone with her son, his mother sung lullabies to him in Hungarian. And he would never have known, never have picked up on that, if it hadn't been for Grom.

"So, John," Gabi was smiling tentatively. "Welcome to your country! It's not so bad, really, being Hungarian."

She was right. He'd gained something here. He'd discovered who he really was. He'd found a home, possibly. But it was going to take a hell of a lot of getting used to.

"Do they have any living relatives?" he asked Mészáros.

"Yes. Cousins out east," said Mészáros via Gabi. "I'll give you their details. You must go and see them. They'll be delighted that Viktor and Ilona had a son. Those two always planned to have a family."

The old man went off and came back with a piece of notepaper on which was written a name, address and phone number. Fairchild stared at the mass of consonants and accents. Family. His family.

"Give them my regards," said Mészáros.

Chapter 24

They were busy planning it for ages, but Bálint still wouldn't tell Tas what was going on. "Soon!" he kept saying. "It's really soon, I promise. You'll love it!"

Then one Saturday he said that he'd have to leave Rebellion early and go with a couple of other people. "It's got to be done at night, this thing."

"Why?"

"You'll see, Tas. You'll see in the morning. Just stay at the club when I've gone. You can get a taxi back with Andor, can't you?" Andor was a regular at the club, there every week.

"I guess." Tas wasn't happy but at least it would be over, he supposed.

It wasn't much fun, that Saturday night. Bálint was playing the fool as usual but Tas knew he was putting on an act. When they all disappeared he almost cried. Bálint was having more fun without him. Was he losing him? Eventually Andor took pity on him moping around and they left early.

He didn't get to sleep for ages, but then he did, and suddenly Bálint was getting into bed beside him.

"You're back!" Tas turned and reached for him, overwhelmed with relief.

"I'm back, little boy, I'm back. Just like I said, you little worrier, you. Hey."

Tas couldn't help it, he was gripping on like his life depended on it. There were tears on his face, he knew it. Bálint stroked and murmured and said all the right things, like he always did. "It's done now, anyway. Finished. Over. No more worrying, okay?"

Tas grabbed one of his huge hands. "What's this?" He could feel something scabby on the skin.

"Paint. It'll come off."

"Paint?" Tas held it up. He could see blotches, some dark, some pale. "Oh, Bálint, what have you been up to?"

Bálint grinned and kissed his ear. "You'll see tomorrow. Want to go to a rally?"

"What kind of rally?"

"A political one. For the election. For Kornai."

"You hate Kornai."

"This one will be different."

"Different how?"

He kissed him again. "You'll see."

Next morning Bálint made breakfast. That never happened. He was feeling guilty for worrying Tas. Tas didn't mind – he liked to be treated. Pancakes with honey and tejföl and lots of coffee, and then they went out and got the Metro to Kossuth Square. Bálint was all pent up like a child waiting for Christmas. Loads of people were about when they got there, and lots of police. They were lined up all the way down to the parliament building. Bálint saw some notices, printed in black and white, pinned up on the lamp posts.

"What do they say?"

"The rally's been moved. It's in Heroes' Square now. They're trying to turn people back."

"Oh, I see." But Tas didn't really see. It was such a milling mess. Tas got nervous in crowds. It was okay at Rebellion. Everyone there was all right. But here, already he'd felt a couple of cold stares. "Should we go up to Heroes' Square, then? Why are people still going that way?"

"Because they've heard." Bálint's eyes had a strange glow. "Wow." He was looking at the people who were heading towards Parliament. The police officers kept stepping up and pointing them back, but they didn't seem interested and pressed on all the same.

"What's happening, Bálint?"

"This is brilliant! Come on!" Bálint stepped up his pace and Tas struggled to keep up. They were coming to the end of the street. The square and the Parliament building were in front of them. People were straggled in groups right across the open space. No rally was going on but something was. In the street it felt like they were walking in a growing tide of people. Tas glanced behind. So many heads! He felt breathless all of a sudden.

Then, in front, a bunch of police trooped across the street. They faced the crowd. Someone pulled a line of tape across. The people at the front stopped. The people behind kept going. Tas and Bálint were squeezed up between them.

"What's going on now?" Tas couldn't see a thing.

Bálint peered above heads. "They're closing the square!" There was such a look of disappointment on his face. He wasn't the only one. Everyone around was muttering as well.

Tas was feeling more and more pinned in. "Should we go home now?"

"No!" Bálint was snappy. "No, we're not just going home! That's what they want! But they can't do this! Come on." He grabbed Tas by the hand and edged forward through the gaps.

"Are you sure?" Tas didn't like the way Bálint had to push, though he was trying to be respectful.

"Yes, I'm sure. You want to see, don't you?"

They got to the front. It was like Bálint was possessed or something. He reached out and grabbed the tape to duck under it. Tas let go of his hand and took a step back. He didn't mess with the police.

Three of them came over straight away, blocking Bálint. "You can't come in. The square is closed."

"Why?" demanded Bálint.

"Public safety." Tas could see other people listening, the crowd lined up along the tape.

"Is there a threat?"

An officer squared up to him. "It's for your own security."

"What's the threat?"

The officer didn't answer. Bálint pointed beyond him. "I see people in the square, standing and talking, walking around. How is that a threat to security?"

"There are too many people."

"There's loads of space. The square's nothing like full."

"More are coming."

"There was going to be a rally here. You must be prepared for a crowd."

No answer.

"Did you see any weapons? Did anyone make any threats?"

No answer to that either.

"This is a public square. You can't just close it off for no reason."

"I told you the reason."

"That's not a reason. It's just an excuse. Is there anyone here who's not in Kornai's pocket?"

That got them angry. A load of them were looking at him now. Tas shrank back even more.

"That's a serious allegation. Who do you think you are?" said one of them, red in the face.

Bálint whipped out his ID card and held it up. "This is who I am. A citizen of this country. This is my city. That's my Parliament and that's my square. And unless you have a good reason I have a right to go there."

Mr Redface folded his arms and stared. He wasn't budging. Then Bálint did something that made Tas' mouth fall open. He pulled the tape up to his mouth and ripped it apart with his teeth. It fell to the ground on both sides. The crowd cheered and pushed forward. Within seconds the tape was underfoot and people were streaming past. The police were looking at each other, no idea what to do.

"Come on!" Bálint grabbed Tas' hand and they rode the surge into the square.

It was clear where everyone was going – not to the Parliament at all but the patch of lawn off to the right, in front of the statues. There was something different about them but Tas couldn't make any sense of it behind all the bobbing heads.

Bálint was grinning like an ape. "Look at all these people!" His pace didn't let off. They squeezed through to the front. There, up above them, were the big white statues of the important men with their beards and their robes, lined up looking very thoughtful and clever. But today they were different. Very different.

Tas raised a hand and pointed to the one in the middle. "He's *pink!*"

From head to foot, the huge statue was a bright, glossy pink. From left to right, each of the guys in the row behind was a different colour of the rainbow, from red and yellow at one end through to purple and blue at the other. They were completely covered, and paint pooled out around their feet as if each was covered in a body-hugging veil.

"Wow!" Tas turned to Bálint. "I love it! You did this?"

"Shut up, you fool!" Bálint looked round. "You want them to cart me off? I had no idea it was going to be this huge!"

Everywhere, people were holding their phones up and getting selfies on the steps. Some were climbing around the statues themselves, doing silly poses. Someone had thrown a big cloth clown's hat onto one of them. It missed his head but hung on to his ear, resting in the crook of his neck. A woman was talking into a microphone with a camera in front of her, pointing back to the crowds.

"It's on TV!" breathed Tas.

"Yeah, it's amazing!" There was a hint of nervousness in Bálint's voice but he shrugged it off. "Come on! Let's say hello to Lajos."

"Who's Lajos?"

"Who's Lajos? You don't know? The pink guy! Lajos Kossuth! You don't know who he is?"

"Not really."

"Okay, well, he did some things."

"I guess. Otherwise there wouldn't be a statue of him." That made Bálint laugh.

They sat on the plinth by the feet of Pink Lajos, as everyone was calling him, and someone took a photo of them there with Tas' phone. The paint wasn't quite dry and people were getting handprints in the different colours and slapping it on each other.

"I've been goosed by Lajos!" someone shouted, running past and bending over to show the two handprints on his backside. There was a roar of laughter. It was a party. But the police didn't like it. They were coming now, a line of them stretched across, sweeping the square, directing everyone out.

Bálint eyed them. "Time to go. How about the park? Margitsziget?"

It was one of their favourite hangouts when the sun was out. They walked there along the river and over the dog-leg bridge, and down to the roundabout with the musical fountain and the scooters and the cycle-rickshaws for hire. And they got corn on the cob from the street stall and munched it walking to the tip of the island, and Tas worked out on the outdoor gym and Bálint sat picking his teeth. And then they went and got candy floss and sat on the grass eating it and getting it all over their faces like you always did. And they lay on their fronts in the sun and watched the joggers and the tourists and the families, and made silly conversation and laughed a lot, and stayed there all afternoon until they felt like going home.

Chapter 25

Rose was with Danny in his office for the conference call with Rapp and the task force. Danny's people had started to analyse the information on the zip drive, and had passed it to Rapp's team for their input. Rapp, her absence of bonhomie apparent even from the other side of the Atlantic, did some introductions. Zack was there and a number of techies, that was about it. The senior figures whose heads had appeared on screen from time to time seemed absent today, a sign perhaps that interest in this initiative was waning. A pity, in Rose's opinion, given the intel they'd just got.

Rapp got things started. "Okay, this zip drive. Rose, can you talk us through that? Where it came from, particularly."

"Sure." Rose summarised the note and what happened at the meet. She played down the violence of the attack, though it was impossible to completely overlook given the dramatic grazes on her face and a black eye that was changing colour by the day. Danny had no visible injuries, though his concussion had led to an overnight stay in hospital and he should still have been resting at home.

Rapp picked up on it. "So it was an ambush?"

"It seemed like one. But an attempt to scare, nothing more."

"Why do that then push a load of intelligence onto you?"

"We have no idea. It makes no sense to us either."

"Then we can't really trust the intel, can we?"

"Have you seen it? It's basically an in-depth study of the interactions between extreme right-wing groups across Europe. It's a who's who and a what's what of all these organisations and their main players, and how they've evolved over the past ten years or more. It dovetails perfectly with what we know from other sources, doesn't it, Danny?"

"Absolutely," said Danny. "It seems sound. But it gives us a lot more, links we didn't know about, people we suspected were involved but we didn't have it nailed down. We're verifying as much of it as we can right now. So far so good."

"Some of the names I've seen before," said Rose. "A pan-European group called Crusaders was active a few years ago. They've disbanded but some of the key players are still active, including a bomb-maker called Marko. That charmer made the bomb that killed ten in Sandhill in the UK, so we're especially interested in him. He went underground but now he's resurfaced in Hungary. The drive also tells us that these groups are much more connected than we thought. We need to change our assumptions. Right-wing extremists are not just resentful loners."

Danny came back in. "There's reference to some paramilitary training in the north east of the country by the Slovak border. That's a regular event. It's happened every year for a few years now. It's officially a legitimate event for those interested in survival skills and so on. But we suspect a lot more goes on behind the scenes. Hungary is increasingly viewed as a natural home of this kind of white supremacist thinking that comes out of extreme nationalism. Kornai has encouraged it to a certain degree, though he's distanced himself from the fringes."

"Any mention of Fire Sappers?"

They all knew the answer to Rapp's question already.

"No," admitted Rose. "There's nothing that ties any of this in with Fire Sappers."

"Then the intel is irrelevant."

Rose had anticipated this. "Except that Fire Sappers themselves gave a clear steer that they're toying with right wing ideology."

"They did," said Rapp. "Anything recently?"

One of the analysts came in. "Some of their language expressed political views for a few days before the end of last year. Since then they've continued with the same kind of bragging tone they had before."

"Right." Rapp was good at asking questions she already knew the answer to. "It was just a blip. Someone trying to leap into the power vacuum after Milo, and failing. I don't see how this new stuff is helping us. We need to know how the group is organised and who's making the big decisions."

Rose let her impatience show. "Maybe we'd know more about that if Milo was in our custody, and hadn't been shot and killed in Japan."

Rapp didn't flinch. She'd survived an enquiry into how she'd handled that, so a biting aside in a conference call wasn't going to faze her.

"So, anyway." This was Zack coming in , possibly to avoid the UK-US relationship being soured any further. "We do have a little more on the organisational side. One of our people told us Fire Sappers have something they call a high command, a group of selected people across the world who make decisions. So Milo wasn't the top dog after all. They have a pack of 'em. When he was twisting the arm of those Japanese hackers, he was probably carrying out their orders."

"Where's that from, Zack?" Rapp wasn't pleased.

"Source outside of the team. Stateside." Without his trademark shades, Zack's eyes were a picture of innocence.

"And I'm only finding out about this now?"

"It just dropped. Fresh intel. I only just heard it myself."

"That's the most definitive piece of new info we've had in a long time. How reliable is it?"

"Uncorroborated so far, but I'd say pretty reliable."

"It makes sense," said Rose. "In Japan Milo said that he was persuaded to go out there, that it wasn't really his decision. We thought it might have been Grom's influence, that he was trying to get rid of Milo so that he could step in himself."

"Speaking of whom," said Zack, "we also have positive confirmation that our favourite former Russian spy is definitely involved, or would like to be."

"Khovansky?" That was Rapp. Khovansky was Sutherland's name the whole time he was working for the FSB, and was the ID he was known to this team by. His real identity MI6 was keeping to itself, having no wish to showcase its former traitors on an international stage. Zack knew all about it, though. Whatever else the studiously loud American was, you could rely on his discretion.

"Yup, that's the guy. Like I say, he's involved. Or, more like he wants to be and is pushing the alt-right angle to them, but still needs to persuade this high command of the wisdom of the idea. Sounds like he jumped the gun earlier. Maybe persuaded someone to do something unauthorised then had to backtrack. He has the support of at least one former FSB sidekick going by the name Bogdan."

A frosty silence. "This is all new, Zack," said Rapp.

"Sure is! As I say, we're doing some checks. Suggest you Brits do the same." He was unapologetic for undermining Rapp by not giving her a heads-up – but then he'd never had much time for Rapp and had too many friends within CIA and military intelligence for her to push him out of the team. This source of his was intriguing, though. Very intriguing.

"So, according to these reports, Khovansky is actively involved with these far-right groups?" Rose asked.

"Very much so," said Zack. "And, he may even have something in mind."

"A target?"

"Yeah, but it's too early to know what or when. He made an appearance at some boot camp, which sounds like the thing you mentioned earlier, Danny."

"That's interesting," said Danny. "Totally backs up our concerns about those events. They're perfect for bringing people together – recruitment, training, planning, everything. We've appealed to the authorities to close it down, but they've resisted. Sounds like it's time for another try."

"Sounds to me like this info needs verifying, otherwise we could all be on a wild goose chase." Rapp was narked her meeting was being taken over. But she had a point. All the information they'd discussed so far had dubious origins to say the least. "Let's come back to it when we know what we can actually rely on. Zack, we'll talk afterwards about this source of yours."

"Sure." That would be a fun conversation.

"Right. Let's move on," said Rapp. "What do we have from the code analysis?"

They had nothing from the code analysis. Reviewing lines and lines of hacker code trying to find patterns and clues to identities and commonalities produced patterns in the sand that seemed to shift constantly and relate in no way to actual people. It had been the same since the US team had started tracking the group months ago. They had nothing new at all except the zip drive and Zack's nuggets. If they could take it seriously, Grom had his sights set on Fire Sappers. It was exactly what they were most afraid of, and exactly why this task force had been prioritised. But Rapp was pushing back on it. Maybe Rose could get Danny to pass the drive to the serious techies at GCHQ, to search for hidden clues as to where it came from. It might make the intel less questionable.

Listening only in part to the meeting, Rose's mind returned to the incident at Fisherman's Bastion. That alleyway, the guy with his hands on her, the look on his face. It had stayed with her, crept into her dreams, jolted her awake in the small hours. But that was normal, she told herself; it would fade in time.

She shuddered suddenly, shifting in her chair.

"You okay?" Danny mouthed at her.

"Fine." She settled herself but her heart was beating fast. Some trauma was natural. But it was more than that. It was staying with her because it reminded her of something. She'd just realised what it was.

There'd been another alleyway, one in Beijing. Years ago now, so long she'd almost forgotten, or wanted to forget. But deep down she remembered it all. A woozy, unreal feeling, a cobbled street at night, floating by the side of a lake. Cold stone on her back. Hands pushing her against the wall, holding her up. And she remembered whose hands they were.

They were the hands of John Fairchild.

Chapter 26

Fairchild asked Gabi to phone his cousin, but in his presence. He sensed the long silence at the other end of the line, heard the scepticism in the man's voice. The name János Mészáros seemed to count for a lot; Gabi (following Fairchild's suggestion) asked the man, whose name was Tamás, to speak to Mészáros directly to confirm what she'd said. Tamás did – and called back within a few minutes, wanting to speak to Fairchild and inviting him in halting English to visit. So Fairchild did, though he didn't take Gabi this time. He'd grappled some more with the language. They'd get by somehow. And this was family.

"So, now I forget everything?" said Gabi, after they'd settled up.

"Please. And thanks for your help."

Fairchild changed trains in Debrecen onto an infrequent local line. Out here the infrastructure faltered; two hours took him little further distance-wise. He spotted rows of makeshift housing tapping into overhead power lines, shoeless children playing in muddy puddles on barely surfaced roads. Coming into the village of his cousins – his family village, he supposed – he saw square single-storey houses painted pink, white, yellow and tan. Chimneys and pointed roofs nestled behind varieties of wooden fencing set back from neat grass-lined streets. A white church with a spire sat opposite one or two shops, a bus stop with no buses and a few parked cars.

Tamás was there to meet him, along with Nina, his wife. Their handshakes were warm, their smiles curious. His too. They drove him to the edge of the village, to a white painted house with a garden behind that stretched out of sight. At a glance Fairchild saw rows of vegetables, fruit trees, goats, geese and what looked like a pig pen.

"It's the Hungarian way," said Tamás, following his gaze. "We grow and make what we can. But we don't live from this. Actually, I'm a vet. I trained in Budapest then came back home to live. Sorry for my English. I don't need it too much these days."

"It's fine," said Fairchild, and attempted a little Hungarian. Pathetic, really, but they smiled indulgently.

"You can practise here," said Nina, choosing wisely to revert to English. "The children will love to teach you. You can learn a lot in a few days."

"Days?" Fairchild had assumed he'd only be here for a few hours.

"Oh, you must stay. We have so much to show you." Tamás was studying him. The Hungarian was a similar age to Fairchild, probably a little younger, but Fairchild could see his own mother in the man's face. It weakened him; he felt like a child standing here blithely accepting the hospitality of strangers.

"It must be difficult," Nina said. "Learning so much about yourself so suddenly."

"Yes." They were still standing in the garden alongside the house, separated from the road by a slatted wooden fence. It was quiet. The air was very still. A dog came out of somewhere, tail wagging, sniffing around Fairchild's feet. Some kind of spaniel. Fairchild bent down to pat it and it licked his face.

"Miksa!" Tamás chided.

"It's fine." Fairchild rubbed Miksa's head and the tail wagging accelerated.

"We kept some lunch for you," said Nina.

In an unevenly-floored kitchen featuring a range and a heavy oak table, Fairchild ate some kind of warm meat-and-potato stew while the others did most of the talking. Tamás practised in the village. It had always been his ambition to return. Budapest was fun for a while, but not a place to live. Such a place could never be home, he said. Nina worked in Debrecen but happily moved out here and helped out sometimes running the veterinary practice. They knew everyone around here who had animals, which sounded like pretty much everyone. They had three children who would be home from school shortly.

They were both curious about Fairchild, but hung back from asking. Fairchild explained what he could. They nodded when he described his international upbringing, his boarding school, and his parents' constant roaming; it seemed alien to them. He described himself as an entrepreneur, a business investor. They seemed impressed that he had holdings ranging from electronics to cleaning firms across every continent, but had nothing to ask about it.

"So where is home?" asked Nina.

"Nowhere. I own property in a number of places."

"Not UK? London?"

"I never go there at all." He didn't say why, and they didn't ask. Then the conversation turned to his parents. Fairchild described them as diplomats and gave them Mészáros' explanation for why they changed their identities.

"My dad spoke about his sister quite a lot," said Tamás. "She was so bright and could speak every language, it seemed to him. But they lost touch. I only met her once."

"You met her?" Fairchild hadn't expected that. His parents fled Hungary in 1956 and died in 1980. Tamás must have been born sometime in the early seventies. "Where?"

Tamás rolled his eyes. "It was all so complicated. Out west somewhere. Near the Austrian border. My dad went over there a few times. It was all very secret, we had to follow all these instructions. One time he decided to take us along. We went to some room in the middle of the night. Afterwards my mother refused to let him take us again. No more, she said. They're too young. You want them marked out for life? Ilona made her choices. *Hát*, she was probably right. It all seems so distant now. These days you can just walk across. No need to show ID, even."

"What do you remember about her?" Fairchild asked.

"She seemed kind. Sparkly eyes. Asked us a lot. It was my brother and me. You have to meet him too, he lives nearby. She brought us some things from across the border. We were hoping for sweets and chewing gum, but it was biros and pencils, good quality stationary for school. A big disappointment!"

They both chuckled, Fairchild thinking of her zest – obsession, at times – for learning. "That sounds like her." He tried, in a few words, to summarise his memories of them. As he thought he remembered more and more, tiny things that the enormity of loss seemed to obscure before. Now, with the passing of time and all things being known, now that he sat and thought about it, the smoke cleared and pieces came back. His mother's voice, the perfume she wore, an old raincoat she had for years. His father in the kitchen lost in steam and smells, cooking some elaborate foreign dish he wanted to try. The games they played: poker, chess, mahjong. Books, always books, reading and learning. The way they were with each other, a moment of tenderness, sneaking a kiss when they thought he wasn't looking.

"They were always devoted to each other," said Tamás. "We all knew Viktor. Marked for great things, some thought.

My dad wasn't so sure. Back then, though, it was about toeing the line. Viktor was too much a rebel. After '56, the police came here looking for them, I was told, but they realised nobody here knew anything." He looked grave. "János told me they died."

Fairchild didn't want to burden them with truths they wouldn't welcome. "In the course of their work, they offended someone powerful. They were trying to do the right thing, but years later he caught up with them. I only found out the circumstances a few years ago. I was ten when they disappeared. I suppose my life must seem rootless to you, but I was searching for them, you see. I was looking for answers. But even now, every time I find some, they seem to generate more questions."

Tamás and Nina exchanged a look, one that he couldn't interpret. "It's hard to know what to think about all this," said Tamás. "She was such a distant person anyway. It's a pity my parents have passed away. My dad would have been glad to know there was a reason they fell silent. He thought they'd decided the old Hungarian family wasn't good enough for them any more."

"I don't think so." Fairchild told them about the nursery rhyme. "They hid their identities to protect themselves, and me as well. And they often spent time in Vienna. That must have been to try and meet up with family when they could. I think they missed their country."

"No need now for anyone to hide away," said Nina. "Everything is different now. Nothing to be scared of any more."

"Yes," said Fairchild, but without the same conviction.

"They would like Hungary how it is now. You think so, Tamás?"

Tamás shrugged. "Maybe. Who knows?"

"I would like to get to know my country," said Fairchild. The words sounded strange to him. "I have a lot to catch up on."

"Of course!" said Tamás. "You must stay for a while. Meet your other cousins. And here are some now!"

Running footsteps preceded the door flying open. But on seeing a stranger sitting in their kitchen, the three animated faces became guarded.

"Oh, they're shy!" exclaimed Nina. "No need for that here. Come in, all of you. Meet your cousin, John Fairchild!" She repeated it all in Hungarian for them, but stopped when she got to his name.

"My name isn't real," said Fairchild. "It was made up. By them, I guess."

"John is a real name," said Tamás. "That's János in Hungarian. Or Iván, in Slavic."

"Iván." Fairchild had gone by this name before. "And my given name?"

"If they married, Ilona could have taken Viktor's name, or used her own, or both. *Hát*, you choose. You can take Ilona's name if you want, our name."

"Gulyás?"

"So, this is Iván," said Nina, introducing him to the children. "Gulyás Iván. Great aunt Ilona's son. Your cousin."

Fairchild played it back, hearing it again. Gulyás Iván. That was his name.

Chapter 27

They were watching a movie when the police came. Curled up on the sofa with the lights off, their big TV screen was sending flickering reds and blues all over the walls. The police didn't just knock. They banged the door so loud it sounded like they were going to punch a hole in it. "Police! Police! Open the door!"

Bálint jumped up and stared into the hallway. His eyes were wide.

"What is it?" said Tas, stopping the movie. "What do they want?"

Bálint put his finger up, telling him to be quiet. He wasn't moving. He was standing there like he didn't know what to do.

The banging started again. "Open up! We know you're in there! We'll break down this door if we have to!"

That made Bálint move. "Stay in here!" he said, and went to the front door. Tas crept to the door of the living room to listen. Bálint opened the door. A man asked his name and he told them.

"We'd like to come in."

"You can't."

Tas peered round the door. Bálint was standing fully in front of the doorframe. Behind him were two men in police uniform, big guys, bigger than Bálint. Much bigger than Tas.

"It's late," said Bálint. "What do you want?"

"Tired are we?" said one of them. "Busy painting all day?"

"Look, either say what you want or leave us alone."

"Oh, it's 'us', is it? Interesting. Wife and kids in here somewhere?"

"None of your business."

The second guy gave Bálint a mighty shove. Bálint staggered back and the man pushed past him into the hall.

"Hey! Are you deaf? I said you can't come in!"

"Funny, I thought he said come right in officer," said the second guy.

"Me, too," said the first.

"Who do you think you are?" said Bálint. "You can't just walk into someone's home! We've got rights, you know!"

The second officer spun and punched Bálint in the face. Bálint fell to his knees. The first one stepped inside and closed the front door behind him. Tas must have gasped or something because the second guy looked round and saw him.

"What do we have here?" he said. "This is what you call a family, is it? Your boyfriend?"

Bálint was holding his hand up to his face. "What if it is?"

The man stood right in front of him, looking down. "People like you are a disgrace."

Bálint stared back. "Me, a disgrace? When did I go barging into someone's home and assaulting them? What have I done?"

"What have you done?" said the first man. "Seriously? You deface our most important monument, and you think that's nothing? Don't you care that people fought and died for this country?"

Bálint's head was down but he was listening. "What makes you think I did it?"

"Oh, so you know what we're talking about, then."

"Of course I do! It's on every news channel in the country! It's all over social media across the world! Everybody knows what you're talking about."

"Get him up," said the first man. The second one got behind Bálint and pulled him up under his arms. The first man swung like he was throwing a hammer. Bálint's head jerked back. Spit and blood sprayed out. Tas thought he was going to throw up.

"Proud of it, are you?" the first one said. "You people make me sick."

Bálint was breathing heavily. "It wasn't me," he said. Tas didn't dare move a muscle. The men looked at each other.

"Really?" said the first.

"If you think it was me you need to prove it."

"Prove it? You mean, like having paint all over your hands the next morning? Did you think no one would see?"

Bálint was silent for a moment. "I could have been painting anything."

"Like what?"

"A shed."

"A shed? You live in a flat."

"A friend's shed."

"You can show us this shed, can you?"

"Yes."

"That'll be interesting," said the first man, "but it doesn't explain why you're on CCTV in Kossuth Square on Saturday night." There was a silence. "Does it?" Another silence, except for Bálint's ragged breathing. The second guy came to stand in front of him, arms folded. "And then you show up the next morning bold as anything, showing us your ID card with paint all over your hands! Do you think we're a bunch of cretins or something?"

The second officer drew his arm back and punched Bálint in the stomach. He gasped and fell to his knees. Tas knew his mouth was hanging open. He couldn't move.

"That's for the clown hat," said the puncher. "Kossuth Lajos and his supporters weren't clowns. They fought for the nation."

Bálint was on all fours, clenched up. "That wasn't us. That was someone in the crowd who showed up the next day."

"Ah, so the rest of it was you, then, was it?"

Bálint sat back and tilted his head, eyes closed. His mouth was ringed with blood. He didn't say anything for a bit, then: "Are you arresting me?"

"We certainly are. You're coming with us." The officer drew out a pair of handcuffs.

"No! You can't take him!" Tas didn't mean to say anything but the words escaped from him like birds from an opened cage. They both turned to him.

"Stay out of it, Tas," said Bálint.

The second one, staring curiously, reached out and switched on the light. Tas drew back, blinking. "Are you Roma?" said the policeman. "Seriously?" he turned back to Bálint. "This is what you keep at home for your perverted amusement? This filth?"

"He's got nothing to do with this."

"No," said the first officer. "No, it's you we're interested in. And your hooligan friends. Get up! On your feet, now!"

They pulled Bálint up. The first officer reached for the door.

"You can't take him!" Tas couldn't help himself.

"Tas!" It was a reprimand. Bálint was meek now, pale as they manhandled him out.

"But what do I do?" Tas could barely breathe.

"Talk to Andor. Tell Andor. And don't worry. Okay?"

He was out of the door now and turned back to look at Tas.

"Okay, Tas? It's all okay."

The door slammed shut.

Chapter 28

Budapest's downtown campus of the European University of Humanities appeared closed at first glance. Rose managed to attract the attention of a security guard who came to unlock the unmarked glass door. She only had to name her destination for him to let her pass. For mid-morning during termtime in one of the most prestigious academic institutions in its field it was, to put it mildly, quiet. After wandering around inside an inner courtyard for some time, she found the building she was looking for. No buzzer or camera, and the door just opened when she pushed.

Inside, she headed down a corridor, checking the door names as she passed. Her feet echoed on the shiny floor. The air was musty. She stopped at a narrow office with windows looking onto the corridor. It was a small space, two desks piled with files and papers, the walls covered with noticeboards, flipchart pages and post-it notes. But the sign on the door, printed on a desktop printer and stuck up with drawing pins, told her she was in the right place.

Someone was working at the far desk, engrossed in a laptop. Rose recognised her immediately, though her hair was shorter, lighter and straighter, and her face somehow harder. And she was older, of course. The woman sensed a presence and looked up. When she saw Rose, her expression said curiosity more than anything else. She got up and turned a key to open the door.

"Come in, Anna. Do I still call you that?" She was speaking Croatian.

Rose walked in. "Do I still call you Tihana?"

The woman seemed to flinch slightly as she took her seat and pointed Rose to a chair. "My name is Zsuzsanna."

"How long have you been in Budapest?"

"A while."

"You had to leave Croatia?"

She gave Rose a bland look.

"What is this place?"

"It's an NGO. Non governmental organisation."

"What do you do?"

"We provide assistance to people who are fleeing from war zones. Advice, translation services, support to access state aid."

"You help asylum-seekers? Refugees?" That would explain the coyness and the security.

"We try. Our budget gets smaller every year. Government is looking for ways of blocking our work, but they want to use the funding for their own purposes. We could close any time. Like this university."

"You're not part of the university?"

"Not really. They had spare office space. A lot of it."

"What about the art history? You're not lecturing?"

"I don't do that any more." Her voice was clipped. She closed her laptop. "I was one myself. That's why I do this. I'm an immigrant."

"Croatian citizens can live and work in Hungary. They're both in the EU. That's different."

"Is it?" There was something accusing in Tihana's – Zsuzsanna's – manner.

"Is he still looking for you?"

"Who?" No expression. She'd become the ice queen. Before, she was warm, human, kind. Before she met Rose, that is. Or Anna.

"Your husband. I assume you're still married."

"I'm a Catholic."

"Do you know where Marko is?"

A faint smile. "Still, even now, you're more concerned with him than with me. I should expect that, I suppose."

"It's not like that. I want to know why you passed me the zip drive. It was from you, wasn't it?"

Zsuzsanna's face tilted up, a gesture Rose remembered. She did it when she didn't want to share something out of pride, or shame. When she wanted to keep something to herself. Tihana had done far too much of that.

"We analysed the meta data," Rose said. "The information within a file that describes the file itself. There were reports and spreadsheets based on templates created by this organisation. All I had to do was look up the full name and address."

Zsuzsanna drew her arms around herself as if cold, and stared ahead.

"You sent the note, didn't you?" said Rose. "With the meet point at Fisherman's Bastion. How did you know I was in Budapest?"

That half-smile again. "I saw you. I saw you in the street, by the Opera. I thought I'd never see you again. But you were just walking along, talking with someone." That must have been Penny Galloway. "And I thought, why would I not see you? We're all still in the world, aren't we? You're not hiding. You didn't have to run for your life in the middle of the night. You didn't have to change your name, or the way you look. Really, you're just the same. Older, of course, but we're all older."

"So why did you give me this information?"

A sigh. "When I fled from Marko I just wanted to put it all out of my mind. But I couldn't. The things he'd done, the people his bombs killed, the women and children. He was an evil man. I knew that from the start. I stayed with him because I couldn't think how to get away. But then I had to. So I managed."

"We could have helped you with that, Tihana."

A flash of anger. "My name is Zsuzsanna. And it was you who put me in that situation in the first place."

Rose had been through this in her head a thousand times. "You were married to him already when we met. You were already in that situation."

"You made it worse. You forced me to spy on him."

"You wanted to. We were saving lives."

"You blackmailed me! What choice did I have? If you'd told him about the abortion he would have killed me."

"He could have done that anyway. You chose to stay. To try and manage the situation, somehow. Besides, with the money we were paying you, you could have saved up and left. And it wasn't difficult, what we were asking you to do."

"So it's my fault, what happened? That's what you're saying?"

Her hoarse tone took Rose back to that midnight meet at the viewpoint in Zagreb, Tihana standing in front of her beaten and bruised, incandescent with rage, refusing all offers of help. The view at the Bastion was similar, but now it was Rose who was beaten and bruised.

"That's not what I'm saying. Marko is an evil man who did bad things, to you and plenty of other people. You and I helped curtail that for a while. I'm sorry you feel you weren't a willing participant, but it didn't work out great for me either. I lost my job." Rose looked for some reaction in the woman, but her face had frozen over again. "Do you know why I lost my job?"

A possible sign of life. "I heard about it. He put a bomb in a mosque. In England. He did. Not me."

"That was what we were looking for. That was why I asked you to check the laptop that evening. To find out where the attack would be."

She looked down at her hands. "I was doing exactly that when he walked in and caught me."

But you stayed there too long, thought Rose. You didn't follow the instructions. You only had to find the sites they were using and tell us. We could track the content. Instead, you sat there reading all that filth, and he came back and found you. Rose had seen the state of the flat after Tihana had limped off and Marko had fled underground. The man was capable of some terrible things. What happened to Tihana was not Rose's fault. But there was no point in saying that now.

"I'm sorry he hurt you," she said.

"You got your job back," said Zsuzsanna. "So it seems."

"I did, but it cost me. Where does it come from, the information on the drive?"

"From me. I study these people. I can't help it. I hate everything about them, their fear-mongering, their sense of entitlement, their lashing out at anyone they can blame. You used to be interested. Back then you were. Maybe not so much now, I don't know."

"We're interested," said Rose. "But we have to know where it comes from. It's all just your own research?"

"I don't have any secret sources. I go on the dark web. You told me how. Weeks, months, years of looking. I put everything on there. I don't know why any more. I can't change anything. But maybe you can. This is what you do, isn't it? Take it, use it if you want. What can I do with it?" She seemed cut off, sitting here disillusioned in this empty office. But it didn't stack up.

"Look at me, Zsuzsanna." She hesitated, but she did. Rose's injuries couldn't be missed. "When we went to the meet point, we were ambushed. Led off into a side street and attacked. Quite seriously. My colleague spent a night in hospital." She scanned the woman's face. No reaction.

"You think that was me?" The ice queen again.

"After the attack I found the zip drive in my pocket."

"I paid someone to slip it to you. A pickpocket I caught once, a Roma kid. I told him to drop it into your pocket in the crowds at the Bastion. Nothing else. That's all."

A silence fell. Rose waited.

Zsuzsanna remained calm. "I'm sorry that happened to you. Some people target the tourists up there. It gives the city a bad name."

"Why didn't you come yourself and give me the drive? Why the secrecy?"

"I wanted to keep out of it. When you came into my life before, in Zagreb, it wasn't good for me. I didn't want another experience like that. I just wanted to pass you the files. And to know I had the right person."

"So you were there, then? That evening? To ID me first before your pickpocket made the drop?"

She shrugged. "What does it matter? You have it. If you want to use it, use it."

"I'd like to know who jumped us, that's why it matters. It could have been a lot worse."

"I'm sorry to hear that. Life can be traumatic at times. I have work to do." She opened up her laptop.

Rose got up. "I'm glad you got away from him. Found a new life."

Zsuzsanna looked up. "This is a life, is it?"

Rose turned the key and opened the door. "Thanks for the info."

Walking back through the empty corridor, she heard the key turn as Zsuzsanna locked the door behind her.

Chapter 29

The children lost their shyness pretty quickly. They went with their new cousin Iván every afternoon to walk Miksa. Their passage through the village became a language lesson, pointing and comparing English and Hungarian. Door, road, car, house. Then shop, bread, money and how to count it. It was as useful for them as it was for him; even the youngest was learning English at school. Running, skipping, jumping, shouting, they had plenty of energy to demonstrate verbs. Then onto adjectives: quick, slow, hot, cold, wet, dry. The village provided a wealth of vocabulary lessons with its horse-drawn carts, front gardens bursting with spring flowers, market stalls on the village green, and the tiny *vegyes* shop that stocked everything under the sun.

Generally, Fairchild only had to hear something once to remember it. So much that they exploded into hoots of laughter if he ever forgot anything and had to be told again. They became well known in the village, with folk stopping to talk to them. Day by day, cousin Iván understood a little more of their conversation.

He helped Nina outdoors. Spring was the time for tidying, sowing and planting. In the herb garden they tamed the mint and rosemary and made space for onion and garlic shoots to appear. In the salad bed they sowed lettuce, spinach, rocket and radishes and put up protection against the roving goats and chickens. In the polytunnel they planted tomato, cabbage, peppers and chillies. They'd plant them out when summer came, Nina said. They worked side by side, knees on the damp soil, Fairchild following her instructions. He liked the sounds of the animals, the smell of the earth, the satisfaction of the task.

"Do you ever feel like leaving?" he asked her once. "Getting away from here and seeing the world?"

"I've travelled," she said, straightening, picking dirt off her hands. "We've been all over. London, Paris, Barcelona. Portugal. New York. But we come back here. We always come back here."

"And the children? Will they stay?"

She smiled. "They can stay, they can go. It's up to them. They will do as they like." They went back to the peppers and the chillies.

A long-standing bathroom project made some progress; along with three other men Fairchild helped carry the old bath out and the new one in. Tamás and he spent evenings prising tiny mosaic tiles off the walls. When finished, Tamás said, the grey walls would gleam with new white tiles and the cold stone floor would be warm underfoot.

They slaughtered a pig. Not for him, they insisted; it was the last chance before summer and they wanted to stock up. The cousins came over from their village, relatives of Viktor – he'd met them before and they'd stared at him curiously but found little to say. Half the village came too, and the *pálinka* glasses were first raised before the morning mist had cleared. With five other men, he helped heave the bellowing pig to the slaughter room, and stood while it was stunned, slit, and pushed onto its side to bleed out. They singed and blackened the creature's skin all over with a blowtorch, burning flesh combining in the air with the smell of blood. Someone passed him a knife to join the multitude engaged in transforming its huge bulk into buckets of flesh and organs. For hours they sat and chopped, wet fingers numb with cold. This would all be packed away in freezers across the village. All that was left by the end were two pools of blood on the ground.

He got used to the cockerel that cried out randomly at all times of the day and night. He learned to recognise the tinny music of the gas van, and became accustomed to the ferocious barking and snarling of all the dogs behind the fences, following him in a chorus down the street. On the first warm Saturday they went swimming in the lake, the kids running down the grassy bank to splash amongst ferns and lily pads, screaming as they hit the water, which was still too cold but would warm up as the year wore on. Afterwards they lay on the grass eating deep fried garlic *lángos* loaded with tejföl and grated cheese, throwing scraps to a grateful Miksa. In the summer, they said, they came here every week, sometimes more.

He wandered the village on his own when he felt restless, and got to know every street. *Eladó*, said a sign on a long pitched-roofed hut. For sale. It was more of a barn than a house, with creepers starting to obscure the windows. Chicken wire fencing marked out a generous square of overgrown land. Plenty of space, on the edge of town. Quiet. Needed a lot of work.

"You should buy it," said Tamás one night, when the three of them sat at the stove. Fairchild's pálinka paused mid-air. "The Szabós saw you looking at the place. Hard to keep secrets here. Zoltán says the roof is fine. It's sound."

Fairchild drank his pálinka without commenting. Tamás shrugged. He and Nina carried on tapping on their keyboards catching up with news and friends. Fairchild, as usual, wrote down all the words he'd learned that day, checking the spelling, and studying them. He would try out sentences, learning the intricate grammar, developing a sense of what sounded right and what didn't. And he would read. First, everything they had in the house in English or German, then moving on to Hungarian – children's books, then history and biography though he missed much of the meaning. A pair of bilingual dictionaries became his companions. Sometimes he would glance up to see Nina or Tamás looking at him curiously. They'd never say why.

Sometimes the place made him think of a village in Siberia where he spent some time one winter, nursed back to health by a babushka named Olga, following Grom's very first attempt on his life. He could have stayed in that village. It was what he was good at, after all: blending in, becoming part of a place. But this was different. This was Hungary. This was home. This was where he was from, after a fashion.

He'd been here for weeks. But he could do what he liked, couldn't he? He checked for messages: nothing from Grom. He'd passed everything to Zack in any case. They had a team on it. They'd be following up. Then there was Darcy Tang. But this wasn't forever. Just for a while. Just until he got his head around things.

He found the hut for sale online. The price was easily affordable. He thought of Rose, picturing her suddenly in a pair of wellies and a muddy old anorak, chasing chickens in the rain. He sniggered. Tamás and Nina looked up.

"Nothing," he said. They smiled and went back to their screens.

They seemed comfortable, having him here. He'd stay a little longer, he thought. There was no hurry. The world could manage without him.

Chapter 30

Andor picked Tas up in his car after work and drove him to the prison. "He's being held on remand."

"What does that mean?"

Andor's lips were tight as he drove. Tas had never seen his car before. You only saw people from the club on Saturday nights. It was a big dark thing with leather seats and an air freshener smell. Andor was in a shirt and tie. "It means he has to stay in prison until his case is heard."

"How long will that be?"

"No one could tell me that." They were in the outskirts of the city. Tas had never been to this part of Budapest before.

"Does he really need to be locked up before they even hear his case?"

"For what he did? No! But they want to make an example of him. Government, police, judiciary, they all work together, you know that, right?"

Tas didn't understand. Andor sighed and gripped the wheel. "Bálint did a foolish thing, Tas."

"But people liked it! There were crowds!"

"Exactly! He embarrassed the government. He embarrassed Kornai. And picking on Kossuth Lajos, that was just asking for trouble."

"Why? The guy's dead, isn't he? He won't mind."

"He's symbolic of our great country." Andor didn't sound like he meant it. "And it's election time, on top of everything else! Kornai's fishing for something to target. The common enemy! Threatening our way of life! I mean, the timing of it." He was shaking his head.

"But you can help him, right? He said to call you."

Andor glanced across. "He needs a lawyer."

"You're a lawyer."

"I'm not the right kind of lawyer. He needs a defence lawyer. A criminal lawyer."

"Bálint's not a criminal."

"No. Well – not really. But he'll need a pretty strong defence, believe me."

Andor turned into a road that led up to a cemetery, and pulled in. "It's back there on the main road. Fences, barbed wire, you can't miss it."

"You're not coming in?"

He hesitated. "Tas, there's a limit to what I can do here. I can look things up, maybe make a couple of calls. I've brought you here, haven't I?"

"But—"

"Listen. You get on the wrong side of these people… you know I have kids, don't you? I was married before. I pay for them. So I need this job. I need to stay clean. I'm sorry. It doesn't take much these days."

"But who's going to help him?"

"Like I said, he needs a defence lawyer. He needs to ask for one, if he hasn't already."

"What about the other people? The ones that organised it all with him?"

"But none of them showed up the next morning with paint on their hands flashing their ID into the faces of police officers, did they? I'm sorry Tas, but really, it was a foolhardy thing to do."

"But it was on TV! All over the world they were talking about it! Does no one care at all now? Someone must."

Andor sighed. "There's Amnesty International. They may be prepared to take it on. They might see it as a significant case, with all the political context."

"It is, though, isn't it? All this stuff Kornai is doing? That's what the whole thing was about! Will you try, Andor? Will you speak to them?" Andor pulled a face. "Come on, Andor, we have to do everything we can, don't we? He's a friend. He's one of us."

He shifted on his seat. "Okay. Okay, I'll give it a try."

"All right. Thanks."

Andor didn't want to look at him. They sat there for a moment. Tas twisted and peered through the back windscreen. He couldn't see anything except an enormous road.

"There's a tram stop over there," said Andor, nodding towards the other end of the road. "Call me later if you want, okay? I have to get back to work."

Tas got out. Andor drove off. Tas trudged up to the prison gates, trying to look braver than he felt. Everywhere were men in uniform, bulky with vests and weapons. Their glances were cold as he gave them the prisoner's name, and they sent him to a bare room that smelled of disinfectant where he sat for ages, but eventually they told him to go through and sit at a booth. On the other side of the glass a door opened. Bálint walked in, dressed in baggy grey prison clothes. The look on his face made Tas' heart burst. He was happy and sad at the same time. All the tension cracked. He knew he was crying.

"Hey, little boy! How are you doing? Are you trashing my flat while I'm not around?" Bálint was smiling but the edges of his mouth were trembling.

"I miss you so much! It's so quiet! I don't know what to do!" Tas was clenching his fists, trying not to sob, but couldn't help it. Two of the guards exchanged glances and smirked.

"Look at me, Tas, look at me." Bálint's big brown eyes were concerned. "Don't do that. Don't. It's all fine, okay? It'll all be fine. Just relax." He was saying calming words but the worry was marked on his face. Tas took some deep breaths. He'd try and be strong, for Bálint.

"Good. Good." Bálint nodded. He was sitting opposite now, behind the glass. "So you spoke to Andor?"

"He told me you were here. He brought me here."

"Can he help me? Did he say that?"

"He said he's the wrong kind of lawyer."

"But does he know someone? He must be able to find someone."

"He said you need to ask for one."

"Yes, I did that, but the person they got… He can't find someone more sympathetic? You know, Tas, one of us?"

Bálint looked so worried. Tas had to be upbeat. "He said he'd ask these international people as well. Because it's been on the news and everything they might want to take it on. A significant case. With all the politics and everything."

"That sounds good. Oh, Tas, it would be so good to get out of here." His voice wavered.

"Are you okay in here?" Tas lowered his voice. He knew the guards were listening.

"It's okay. It's okay, really it is." The words sounded positive but Bálint's voice was resigned, really quiet like he was super-tired. "Don't worry about me. I'll manage. As long as there's a plan to get me out."

Tas felt lost. "I don't know what else I can do. Tell me what to do, Bálint."

"Just keep speaking to Andor, I guess. Ask if there'll be a trial, or a plea, or I don't know what. I don't understand these things."

Tas reached up and touched the glass with his fingertips. Bálint did the same on the other side.

"No hands on the screen!" The shout from the guard made them both jump. Tas drew back as if he'd touched something hot. There was a hint of a smile in Bálint's face, that naughty smile.

"Don't worry, little one," he said again. "This will all be over soon. I'll be home before you know it. You'll see."

Chapter 31

Instead of sitting around getting nowhere at the Embassy, Rose had decided to spend the afternoon sitting around getting nowhere in her hotel room. It was a change of scene at least. The days were passing; outside were the beginnings of blossom in the trees and more warmth in the sun. It was just another reminder of how much time they were losing. Her laptop was in front of her as she sat up on the bed leaning back on an arrangement of cushions, but she was running out of ideas. Grom was up to something, she knew it – they all did, thanks to Zack's mysterious source – but they were no closer to finding out what, and in the meantime his source seemed to have fallen silent.

It being election season, Béla Kornai's face was visible even more than usual. The TV was showing a local news channel with English subtitles, and the man was being interviewed by a journalist who'd chosen not to be especially challenging. Kornai was giving what appeared to be a very long response on Hungary's relationship with the EU and reputation in the world.

"Of course they criticise," he was saying. "But more and more people in Europe are willing to say that they're with us now, that they don't want liberalism, that there's nothing wrong with traditional conservative views, knowing who you are and where you're from, and wanting to live a particular way. In Poland, Slovakia, Croatia, Serbia, Austria, even Denmark and such places, just like Belarus and Russia, people are rejecting these so-called international values. There's nothing wrong with our values, but they're under attack, with money coming from stateless billionaires to generate propaganda."

The journalist found the temerity to ask about immigration.

"We're not against people coming here, if they'll fit in. Why do Muslims want to come here anyway? This is a Christian country. I know Hungary is seen as a home for people who think like us. I say if Germans, Italians, Scandinavians want to come here to live amongst like-minded people, they're welcome, if they share our values. They know we're prepared to defend them."

What could people be persuaded to do to defend those values? That was the danger. Kornai may see this as no more than political rhetoric – electioneering – but words, particularly where there was blame and resentment, could be twisted by those with a more bloodthirsty agenda. This had been discussed. But the view at the Embassy was that Kornai would not, at this time, be open to an appeal to tone down his rhetoric, even from his own security advisers. His ratings had dropped and he had to ramp things up, not the opposite. Besides, it was the job of politicians to 'speak the truth', he would likely respond, and the job of the security services to keep people safe. Kornai was skilled at distancing himself from the fringes, the extremes, anything that could get him into real trouble. At times he'd even claimed that giving 'illiberal' views a platform prevented those that held them from feeling oppressed and going underground.

The interviewer moved on, and a shot was shown of Pink Lajos and the other recently-defaced statues in Kossuth Square. "What would you say about the response?" she asked. "They attracted a lot of attention, visitors, social media. There's a petition to keep them the way they are. How many thousands have signed it now?"

Kornai dismissed this with a wave of the hand. "Some kids might think this is funny but they take so much for granted. People had to fight to preserve the Hungarian nation. It was almost destroyed but for people standing up and being prepared to give up their lives. They will grow up, most of these young people. But we have to show them the way."

"So the statues will be restored?"

"They will be restored. And the people who did this will be punished. You know, one of them is a schoolteacher! People like that, in our schools, filling our children's heads with nonsense about our history and these alien values. This is why we're pushing this bill through. It's wrong for these liberals to be allowed to indoctrinate young people. We need to protect our children. Believing in Christian things like marriage, there's nothing wrong with that."

"So, no more Pink Lajos?"

"Absolutely not."

Rose switched off. She didn't envy that schoolteacher and whoever else was involved. Kornai's righteous anger might be exactly what his campaign needed.

In the meantime she had her own problems. The info on the zip drive didn't relate to Fire Sappers in any way. While valuable in itself, the immediate threat was Grom, his involvement with the hackers and potentially with these extremists too, bringing together hatred and a willingness to deploy violence with practically limitless resources. But nothing on the disk made that connection.

Why did Zsuzsanna, as she'd have to get used to calling her, give her all this? It just didn't scan that the incident at the Bastion was a random attack. Either Zsuzsanna was lying, or this whole thing was more complicated than it looked. Was Zsuzsanna trying to lead her somewhere? Was she working with other people? The woman was clearly bitter. How far would she go to punish Rose for what happened back in Zagreb?

One place Zsuzsanna had managed to lead Rose was into her own subconscious. She'd been thinking more and more about the Beijing incident she'd almost managed to forget. When she and Fairchild had first met, her job was to tail the man. He didn't want to be tailed. The result: he'd spiked her drink in a bar, led her to some alleyway, quizzed her about what she knew, and abandoned her. Not exactly top-notch behaviour. In time, when they were somewhat more reconciled, he'd apologised, and sounded like he meant it. She'd put it out of her mind, or thought she had. But it was starting to seep back.

She'd kept her distance from John Fairchild because, she told herself, she didn't trust him and didn't like his aimless mercenary existence, doing work for whoever paid him. But she was starting to dig a little deeper now. Maybe that episode was shaping her attitude to him more than she thought. She wanted to believe she could put traumatic experiences behind her and move on. Was she kidding herself? What if she hadn't moved on at all but was carrying it around with her, its poison silently contaminating her?

Enough of this. Any more thinking along these lines and Walter would be pushing her into another counsellor evaluation. She needed a better grip on where Zsuzsanna was coming from. Zsuzsanna knew more than she was saying. Rose checked the clock; she had time. She got her things together and set off for the university.

But she discovered when she got there that time had run out. The NGO office was unoccupied, the door open, nothing inside except a couple of desks and an empty filing cabinet. Maybe Kornai had got his way and closed them down, or maybe the whole thing was some kind of front. Either way, Zsuzsanna was gone.

Chapter 32

In time, the tomatoes sprouted. The peppers shot up but the chillies were slow. Lettuce and rocket shoots formed tiny rows of green across the salad bed. Vocabulary moved on to abstracts, the children asking difficult questions. *Why aren't you married? What's your job? How long are you staying? Are you going to live here?* In the evenings Fairchild tackled the subjunctive using communist-era grammar books unearthed from a loft somewhere in the village. Hand drawn illustrations depicted a world of wholesome but modest living with all the benefits offered by state socialism: a flat, a job, a bus to get to work, holidays in various Eastern Bloc countries. But the images haunting his own life could no longer be banished, he was realising. They returned more often, day as well as night. Darcy Tang. Gregory Sutherland. Rose Clarke.

He and Tamás did one big push on the bathroom tiles, hacking off a few more each evening until the walls were clear for the next phase, which was already delayed. Tamás promised to return the favour and help Fairchild convert the barn, if he bought it. But Fairchild didn't.

He asked if they had anything personal that belonged to his parents. Tamás brought down a dusty old box full of toys wrapped in newspaper: trains and trucks, dolls, a tiny sewing kit, a miniature vanity set with a brush and comb, a mirror with a glittery frame and some tiny lipsticks. His cousins brought him a Bible that belonged to Viktor – it was the one he took to church every week, they said. Fairchild opened it and fanned through the pages. It smelled of incense.

He packed the sewing kit, the vanity set and the Bible. On their final walk through the village, people came out to shake him by the hand. The Gulyás family piled into one car to go to the train station. *When will you be back?* the children asked. He said that he didn't know but would be sure to visit, making full use of the subjunctive. He got it wrong on purpose so they could delight in correcting him, and they were still smiling when the train pulled in.

They passed him apples and slices of poppy roll wrapped in napkins through the window for the journey. They waved. *Köszönöm*, he said to Tamás and Nina. Thank you. It seemed inadequate. But it didn't matter. They gave freely; they were family.

Something pulled at his heart, like a sapling wrenched from the soil, when the train started moving and he lost sight of the platform and the Gulyás clan. He would wither and shrivel, he thought, back in Budapest, back in the city.

After the train had gone, Tamás turned to Nina on the platform. The children were already scampering back to the car.

"You think I should have told him, don't you?"

She angled her head. "I don't know. Maybe."

Tamás looked back at the train tracks. "He has nobody. No family, no home. *Hát*… everyone needs a home."

Chapter 33

Tas was getting used to the visits now. He was allowed an hour three times a week. It took him another hour to get there, but that was okay.

"What about work?" Bálint asked.

"I cut my hours. They didn't want me to but never mind." At the warehouse they liked Tas. He was a worker and he was strong, could lift and carry all day long. So his boss shrugged and said okay.

Tas was feeling happier this time. "Hey!" he said as soon as Bálint sat at the booth. "Guess what? The Amnesty people want to take this on! They say it's a landmark case. Human rights and all that stuff."

Bálint nodded a little. He was pale and his eyes couldn't seem to rest on anything. "That sounds good. When can they get me out of here?"

"I don't know. Andor's looking after things. He says the authorities are trying to stop the lawyers seeing you. But they can't do that."

"Okay."

"That's good news, isn't it?" Tas wanted to see him smile. "All those people, see? Everyone liking the statues? And that bill they want to do, the Amnesty people say it's important. They can get people interested across the world, with all the publicity."

There! A little bit of a grin. A tiny sparkle in the eyes. "I'll be famous, then?"

"Yeah, maybe."

"Maybe I can hang on a bit longer, then." The smile faded.

"Is it that bad in there?" Tas was almost afraid to ask.

"It's not like home." Bálint's voice was gruff and his face crinkled for a moment.

"Home's not like home," said Tas. "Not without you."

"You keeping it clean for me?"

"Of course!" Tas drew himself up with pride. "You know me."

Bálint was going to say something but stopped.

"What?" said Tas.

"Listen. If anything happens to me—"

Tas' heart dropped like a stone into a pond. "What's going to happen? What do you mean?"

"I just …" He seemed to run out of words.

"What are they doing to you in there? You know, the Amnesty people said they have to treat you okay. You have rights. You said so, remember?"

"I thought I did, little boy." His brow was ridged and his eyes sad. "I thought I did."

Tas could have punched a hole through that screen to get to him. "But you do! And they'll help! They said they will!"

Bálint nodded slowly. "Yes, yes. But just in case—"

"Just in case what? Just in case nothing!" A guard was looking at him; he was talking too loud.

"Under the bed, Tas." Bálint spoke so quietly it was just a mutter.

"What's under the bed?"

"You know that old box that's always been there?"

Why was he talking about a box? "The one that's locked? You said it had old stuff in it."

Bálint gave a smile but it was there and gone, brief as a shooting star. "That lock never worked. You didn't look in there, ever?"

Tas shook his head. He'd never thought to doubt Bálint's word.

"Take a look. If you need to."

"Why would I need to?"

"If it doesn't go to plan."

"It'll go to plan, Bálint." Tas held his hand up to the glass, so close the guard peered – but he wasn't touching it. Bálint did the same. "You'll get out of here soon. Then it'll all be back how it was. This will all be over."

Bálint gave him such a look of love that he melted inside and his eyes felt wet. "You promise, little boy?"

Tas turned his raised hand into a kind of salute. "I promise."

Chapter 34

It felt unreal being back, as if the village had all been a dream. In his hotel room, Fairchild spent some time examining the tattered old Bible, the glittery little mirror and the sewing kit – tangible, physical remnants of a past he'd known nothing about. Then he wrapped them, slipped them into a sealed and padded envelope which he placed into a cardboard outer layer, and took them to the lobby to be sent special delivery to an address in Vienna.

His inbox and voicemail messages he largely ignored, except the latest one, a brusque invitation from Grom to his hotel suite. And now here he was, Grom standing at the door holding a whisky glass, Bogdan tapping sulkily at his keyboard, an action replay of when Fairchild was last here. Only now he, Fairchild – Gulyás Iván – was a different person.

"Look who it is!" said Grom cheerily. "We were wondering if we'd ever see you again, weren't we, Bogdan?" Bogdan's momentary glance belied this claim. "So, what have you been up to?" Grom indicated an armchair. On the table next to it a gin and tonic already sat. "Had a break? A bit of me-time? Getting to know this wonderful country? Or a mixture of all three?"

Fairchild sipped his gin. Grom knew, of course; that was why he wanted Fairchild in Hungary. How Grom knew was an unsettling mystery. But he'd already decided not to engage with the man about it.

"You wanted answers," said Grom. "Don't blame me if you don't like them very much. A thank-you would be appreciated." Fairchild raised his brows. "Be honest with yourself, John. How much of that would you ever have unearthed if it weren't for me? And you think that's all they've been hiding?"

Fairchild put his drink down and looked at the ceiling.

"Fine, fine, give me the silent treatment. In any case, that's not why I invited you here. While you were gone, things have moved on. The situation has developed."

"I'm sure it has." This was what he'd come here for; this he could talk about. "When I last saw you, you were disappearing out of a door with a group of disaffected right-wingers, telling me to go back to Budapest. Shooing me away, practically. That's hardly a great basis on which to congratulate yourself on your transparency. You think I can't see how you're stringing me along? What kind of dissembling half-truth are you going to peddle tonight? It serves me right, I suppose, for believing you might be prepared to be less secretive than Walter and all the others. It was all a smoke screen, wasn't it?"

Grom pursed his lips. "I'm sorry you feel that way. Actually, I was about to invite you to witness a meeting."

Bogdan stood and placed the laptop on the main table, arranging the leads.

"What kind of meeting?" asked Fairchild.

"The high command." Grom's expression was completely serious.

"Right."

"Yes, right. You can leave if you want, but we need to get online." Grom glanced at his watch. "Are we ready?"

"Yes. Starts in ten minutes," said Bogdan.

"Let's get there. Show them we're keen."

Bogdan hit a key. "Connecting. We're in the lobby."

"Come, come." Grom got up and moved to the table, beckoning Fairchild over. The screen was set up for a video conference. "To forestall your disappointment, it's not the convention to show your face at these. Avatars only. For mutual protection. But the voices are real. We have to know people are who they say they are."

"So what's your avatar?" Fairchild asked.

"Grom," said Grom. "It's—"

"Russian for thunder. Yes, I know."

Grom's mouth registered amusement. "I may as well. Only a certain type of person knows me by that name. No actual role for you in this, I'm afraid. But few people have witnessed it. Consider yourself lucky to be in the room."

"Honoured, I'm sure." Typical of Grom to be arrogant enough to use a known nomenclature as an avatar. Fairchild sipped his gin. He wasn't going to give Grom the satisfaction of showing what a big deal this was. If it was for real, of course. It could all be some hoax for some purpose yet to be revealed.

There was a short pause. "Is anything happening?" Grom asked Bogdan.

"Just waiting."

"So what's this meeting about, then?" asked Fairchild. "Since it's so important."

"It is indeed important," said Grom, straightening the collar of his jacket, even though no one was going to see it. "I'm going to be making my pitch. This is my final chance to persuade Fire Sappers to back my plan. They bought into it before, of course, but then they got cold feet. They won't this time."

"Why not?"

"Because it's a much better plan. Power, John, and how to manipulate it. Power's the key these days, in the world that we live in. Do you understand what I mean?"

"Not really."

"You will." He cleared his throat. Either he was acting nervous very convincingly, or this really was a big deal.

A dialogue box came up. Bogdan clicked, and after a pause the screen filled with profile pictures. Five of them, plus Grom. The images gave little away: a mountainous landscape, a beach hut, a silhouette of a tree. The names were also unremarkable – combinations of letters and numbers. Fairchild memorised them, though. He could extract another favour from Zack with these, at the very least. There was a background crackle; the audio was on.

"So," said a voice. "Now we have Grom here again. It's my turn to chair this time, so I welcome you on behalf of us all. I can assume, I think, that you don't need reminding of the rules?" It was a man's voice, speaking English with a French accent. The language was as formal as any you'd hear in a board meeting. If Fairchild had to guess, he'd say the speaker operated at senior level in business. Perhaps this group weren't hackers themselves but investors of some kind.

"You can be assured on that front. The rules are for everyone's benefit in any case. I don't want to know you any more than you want to know me." Grom managed to tone down his British accent; it would be difficult to be sure where he was from just hearing his voice. "So – straight to business?"

"Please."

Grom straightened in his chair. "Gentlemen. Fire Sappers is a formidable organisation. You are using the expertise of those at the forefront of hacking technology to amass large sums of money. The unique management methods you employ give you substantial control over operations, enabling you to plan strategically in a way that most other groups aren't even attempting. Your global reach is vast. You work with existing criminal gangs in many parts of the world to co-ordinate cyber and physical attacks and enforce your authority over the network. And yet, you have limitations. If I'm not much mistaken, Fire Sappers is sitting on a mountain of stolen crypto currency that's worth, at today's values, billions of dollars. Of course while prices continue to rise you're wise to hold onto some of this, but I fear you may be holding back from realising the value of these assets. This is your Achilles heel, is it not? If you're going to be traced, it will be through your crypto earnings and how they are spent. And let's be honest, spending millions and millions of dollars isn't as easy as it might sound. It's actually very difficult without drawing attention to yourself. I feel that I can help you in this regard. As you know I operated in Russia. In keeping with the zeitgeist of the nation, naturally I creamed a little off for myself."

It was impossible to know how this was being received with no physical cues, but it sounded like Grom was hoping for amused smiles at this point. The 'little' he creamed off amounted to hundreds of millions of dollars' worth.

Grom continued. "For years, I successfully extracted this money and held it secretly, beyond the reach of my Russian colleagues and their counterparts in the West. It wasn't just sitting somewhere either. I can assure you I made full use of it when I wanted to. What's the point of stealing it otherwise?"

A yellow light came on. A participant wanted to speak.

"Go ahead," said the Frenchman.

"So, Mr Thunder, if I can call you that?" A smattering of laughter generally. "From what you said last time we spoke, you fell out of favour with Russia. Did they not pursue you for this money you stole?" The voice had a staccato clip to it: Chinese, maybe, or Korean.

Fairchild watched Grom's reaction. If the speaker knew that much about Grom, maybe their prized anonymity wasn't all it was cracked up to be.

"Yes, they did," said Grom, "and I'll admit that they successfully managed to track a lot of it down. Not only that but covert operatives from other nations also engaged in a pursuit of my assets. Of the original amount, I only have a fraction left. But that doesn't have to be for nothing. I know their capabilities now. I know how they did it. Let me tell you, it's not the legitimate authorities you need to be afraid of, my friends. It's the people who will come after you with no regard for the law. I admit I broke every law on the books amassing this fortune of mine, and the Kremlin did the same to get it back from me. But I have access now to that expertise. My technical team has studied their every move. No one is better placed now to hide money, not only from authorities, but from those who have no authority. I have the skills on my team. The Russian-trained hackers are the best. Together with what I know about the laundering and tracing of money, it's a powerful combination."

Throughout this, Bogdan sat still, eyes on the screen, hands on his lap. Did Grom's technical team consist of only one person? Fairchild was yet to find that out.

Another yellow light. "Yes, please ask your question," said the chair.

"That's an intriguing idea," said a voice. "But our earnings as you know are held entirely in crypto currencies. The world of decentralised finance is quite different from dollars and rubles. There are particular challenges with the record-keeping, the immutable chain. You can't just take cash out in the same way."

The voice had a Spanish tinge to it — Central or South American, Fairchild thought. He was talking about the blockchain, the network of nodes holding encrypted data which assured the uniqueness of records and enabled the concept of virtual currency.

"It is indeed different," said Grom. "But many of the principles are the same. It's all about breaking the ownership links, obfuscating through transfers of ownership and asset trading. Using mechanisms like exchange rate fluctuation to present a movement as a loss. Fabricating transactions, buying assets that don't really exist. And you should know that some of my own earnings were held in crypto format. I have to boast considerably more success holding onto those amounts than the more traditional holdings."

This time Grom and Bogdan exchanged glances; Bogdan, then, had some involvement in the financial side as well as the hacking.

The Korean came back in. "From my side, subject to some proof of competency, this sounds interesting. But it is a very different offer from what you came to us with previously. I thought you were trying to embroil us in politics. As I'm sure you recall, I wasn't convinced of the merits of that."

"Indeed," said Grom. "And I want to let you know that I've considered your feedback on that score. I did, however, continue forging links with the groups I spoke of earlier. Now, I've come to the conclusion that the benefits these groups can bring to Fire Sappers is even greater than I thought. I appreciate your reluctance to take a political stance. You were right on that. I was wrong. There's no need for you to do that. You can take all the advantages and leave behind all the downsides."

Grom, admitting he was wrong? This truly was a big deal. Fairchild's restless sub-conscious was causing him discomfort. Grom had invited Fairchild in to witness this, the very heart of his ambition. He was putting his vulnerabilities on display like a dog rolling onto its back to be petted. Why?

"Well," said the Frenchman, "we're all keen to hear about these advantages, I'm sure."

Grom continued. "I've spent weeks with these people. They're angry people. They feel hard done by, discriminated against. And who are they angry with? Who is it who's taken what's rightfully theirs? Who are these secret networks, these forces working together to threaten their way of life, destroy their identity and their birthright? Jews. Muslims. Blacks. Roma. Gays. Women. Intellectuals. Europeans. Bureaucrats. Internationals. Liberals. I'll tell you who it is. It's whoever we want it to be.

"Forget about political debate. When it comes to hatred, the kinds of feelings that make people justify carrying out random acts of violence, there's no logic. It's pure emotion. We're all built the same way. I've spent my life pushing people's buttons. I know what works. I know how to generate that anger and direct that fear, build a narrative of resentment that would make anyone prepared to bloody their hands. Okay, maybe not anyone. But these people are ripe for it. You should hear them talk, see the expressions on their faces when you hand them a weapon. *They* are a weapon, gentlemen. I can target them wherever you like. At whatever best suits your interests. And no one need know of your involvement."

A pause. No yellow lights. The chair came in. "So, your thoughts, colleagues. I know you will have some. Ah! Yes, please."

A yellow light had come on, a new one. "We don't want to blow anyone up. Why do we need a weapon?" The speaker sounded American.

182

"Causing death isn't the objective," said Grom. "What these people want to cause is terror. Terrorism, the violent disruption of everyday life, the destruction of the status quo, in order to sow fear. At least – that's what they think. But there can be other motivations."

"Such as?" The American again.

"Think about this. If you knew that everything was going to come to a stop, that there would be general panic and chaos, if you knew in advance exactly when and where this would take place, what could you do? How could you draw advantages from it? I know what you do, gentlemen. I know you have the imagination and knowledge to leverage that chaos for your own ends. Even if it were only for five minutes. Sure, it can look and sound like terrorism, but that could mask other things, could it not?"

The American again. "So that's what you're offering? Five minutes of chaos?"

"As a proof of competency, as a taster, if you like, that's what I'm offering," said Grom.

He sat back in his chair and waited.

Chapter 35

They wouldn't let Tas in this time. He'd gone all the way there and they said no visits. They wouldn't even tell him why. You're not next of kin, they said. Next of kin? Tas felt a coldness seep through him. But still they said nothing, and then, when he wouldn't leave, they threatened to throw him off the premises.

He phoned Andor. Andor said he'd make some calls. He phoned back. "Where are you?" Tas was walking around in the cemetery. "Stay there. I'll come to you."

Andor's car came through the gate half an hour later. Tas got in. Andor stopped the engine and turned to look at Tas. "I'm sorry, Tas."

"What?"

Andor's eyes were pink. "Bálint. They found him in his cell."

"Found him?" His heart was pumping.

"He'd got a razor blade from somewhere. Slit his wrists open."

Tas couldn't understand. "He's dead?"

Andor gave a single nod.

Tas felt panic. "No, he can't be. It's a mistake! He's still in there! He must be!"

"They found his body, Tas. In his cell."

"It must be someone else. It can't be him!" Andor didn't say anything. How could he just sit there? "How do you know this?"

Andor sighed. "They wouldn't tell me anything. So I phoned his parents."

"His parents?" Tas had never met them.

"They told me."

"They know it's true? They saw him?"

"They'll go to identify him."

"When?"

"Later today. Tas, I'm so sorry."

It just didn't add up. "They're saying he killed himself? He wouldn't do that!"

"Are you sure? He was pretty depressed, wasn't he?"

"Of course he was depressed! He was in prison! But we were going to get him out. You said that! You said that, Andor!" Tas couldn't breathe. The car was tiny and hot.

"Yes, I know, I thought that too, that maybe... but we don't know what it was like in there. What he was going through. I guess he just couldn't take any more."

Tas was shaking. He felt sick. No way would Bálint do that. He wouldn't leave Tas on his own. No way. Andor had it wrong, staring at him in his suit and tie. He was lying!

He couldn't stand it. He got out of the car and ran. Andor called after him. He got out and tried to catch up but Tas raced away, down a long straight path, gravestones all around. He ran without looking back until he couldn't run any more. A suffocating wave overtook him. He sank to the ground.

Bálint was gone. He was gone. Tas would never see him again. He closed his eyes and clenched his fists and screamed at the sky.

Chapter 36

Fairchild phoned Zack as soon as he was back in his hotel room. After the usual security rigmarole, Zack was on.

"Who the hell is this?"

"Sorry. I was busy."

"Busy? Is that all? I thought you must have been swallowed up by a sinkhole or something. You know, a place where they don't have mobile signal."

"I didn't have anything new for you. And I was making some discoveries. Personal ones."

"Oh yeah? Like what?"

"Later. Something more important first. I've just been with Grom." Fairchild gave Zack a summary of the high command meeting and Grom's proposal to them.

"How did they respond?"

"They were interested. But we didn't get on to discuss details."

"Details? You mean, like, some idea at all what he's actually planning?"

"That would have been ideal, but in the meantime I can give you the online handle of each of these five commanders, or whatever they call themselves. If you're interested."

"Okay, that's pretty good, I guess. Shoot."

Fairchild reeled off the five IDs as they appeared on screen along with his own estimate of where they were from in the world. "As for the plan itself, it's going to be something dramatic. Theatrical. The high command being his audience. And soon, probably. Grom is showing no signs of leaving town. So I'd get here if I were you. Bring Rapp and line up whatever resources you can. I'll keep digging but he could shut me out any time. I don't know why he's let me in this far."

"Must be a reason."

"That's what's bothering me."

"I'll pass it along anyway. Rapp will bite. Nothing else is coming up. So what's this other thing? This discovery of yours?"

Fairchild told him the news about his parentage.

"Christ." Followed by a stunned silence. "Christ, I mean that's quite a—"

"Yes, it is. Listen, Zack, can you do me a favour? I need to speak to Rose. But I can't contact her directly."

Another pause. "You want me to set up a meet between you and Rose Clarke?"

"Well, I can't just call her, can I? That'll set off alarms all over the place. She thinks I'm with Grom now."

"Well, you kind of are."

"Temporary situation."

"But she doesn't know that."

"Right. She may not even want to meet with me. We'll have to take that into account."

"You want me to trick her into meeting you?"

"You know what I mean, Zack. I can't exactly send her a dinner invitation in an embossed envelope on a silver tray, can I?"

"Why do you want to meet with her, exactly? She's part of Rapp's team. Everything you just told me she'll get to hear about anyway."

Fairchild got off the bed and stared out of the window. Zack was being annoying. "It's not just that. It's something else."

"Look, Fairchild. You're upset. You're vulnerable. Everything's been turned upside down. I get that. So take my advice. Avoid the woman, for now. She's never had your back, has she?"

Fairchild couldn't answer that.

"Don't put yourself out there. Not right now. Leave it a while. Get on an even keel again. Figuring out this Fire Sappers thing, that's the priority. As you said, she probably doesn't want to see you anyway."

"You're refusing to help me?"

A sigh. "Yes, I am. Because I'm your friend and you don't need her right now. Okay?"

"Well, I can't make you, I suppose." Fairchild was already thinking about other options. "I'd better go."

"Wait! How do I get hold of you if I need to?"

"You could call."

"I never thought of that. But what if everything goes wrong with your psycho guy? What's your emergency get-out? You already said you don't know why he's letting you in. It could all be a trap."

"I don't want to risk it, not now we know there's something going on."

"Just knowing where you are would help. What if he gets suspicious and calls it all off, slips away again? We need to be ready to move in fast. I can speak to the tech people over there."

"Zack, seriously, that's a bad idea. If he cottons on I'm wearing a tracer or whatever you have in mind, it'll be a disaster. Just get here, okay? I'll keep you in the loop."

The call didn't exactly end well. Zack was being a pain in the butt. Fairchild didn't need avuncular advice. Zack always had a problem with Rose but it was time the man got over it.

He phoned Gabi. "It's John Fairchild."

A long pause. "I'm sorry, I have no idea who this is."

"Yes, yes, very good, following instructions to the letter. But I need your help again."

She perked up. "Oh, okay! That's cool. But don't you already speak perfect Hungarian?"

"More or less. But this isn't translation. It's something else."

Chapter 37

"We may finally have caught a break." Danny's announcement, as he leaned on the door frame of the Embassy office Rose was using, was extremely welcome.

"Thank goodness for that. I thought we'd be chasing our tails forever on this one."

Danny came into the room and sat. He was, finally, fully recovered from the attack. Rose felt better too, but some grazing on her face was still visible.

"Rapp called with a heads-up," said Danny. "A source is saying that a link between Fire Sappers and the far right groups is confirmed. Your chap Khovansky is brokering. There's some plan which could kick off soon."

"What kind of plan?"

"That's the bit we don't know. But it's likely to have a Hungarian connection. Rapp and her team are flying over here as I speak."

"Really? They're taking the source seriously then. Is it the same one Zack was talking about in the last meeting?" Rose had thought a lot about who this source might be.

"She didn't say. Still, nice to be kept in the loop." He was still sore about Walter spiriting Rose away. Rose didn't blame him.

"So what now?"

"As soon as they've touched down, we'll meet. So stand by. In the meantime – possible lead on the zip drive analysis."

"Great! It must be my birthday."

"One of the messages on the drive contains a partial postcode here in Budapest. Out east. It covers a big area and normally wouldn't help us much, but that patch has been on our radar before. A few years ago a premises there was flagged up as a storage centre and workshop for a neo-Nazi group. The group itself is long defunct. But the same people could still be around operating in a new guise."

"That's worth a look."

"It is. But we're rammed here until Rapp arrives. I can't spare anyone."

"I'll take a look. Check it out from a distance. Any satellite data?"

"I can request it, but it'll take a while."

"I can watch it for a few hours, see if anybody's going in or out."

"You sure?"

"If we think this is urgent, we should get onto it. We can set up proper surveillance once the team's in place."

"Okay, then. But watch your back. Remember, all the data on that drive is suspect since your Croatian friend did her vanishing act."

"Yes, and I haven't forgotten how we got it either. I'll be careful."

"I'll send you the address. Oh, hang on." Danny's secretary had appeared behind him. "Apparently someone's asking for you downstairs. A woman."

"A woman?"

"You think it's her? Your NGO person?"

All attempts to trace Zsuzsanna had so far failed. Like Danny said, the woman dropped the drive with them then disappeared. Highly suspect. "Who is she asking for?"

The secretary answered. "Rose Clarke."

"That was the name?"

The woman nodded. Rose looked at Danny. "Zsuzsanna calls me Anna. Unless she knows a lot more about me than

I thought." She remembered their conversation: *Do I still call you that?* "I'd better find out."

The woman in the waiting area wasn't Zsuzsanna. Much younger, funky haircut, brightly coloured scarf, big smile. She introduced herself as Gabi. "May I have a few moments of your time?"

"It depends what it's about."

"It's about a mutual friend."

Chapter 38

The flat was horribly quiet. The silence went on for hours. It seemed to speak to Tas, laugh at him. Everything here, the prints on the walls, the lamp shades they'd chosen together, the rug Tas got as a gift, the sofa that still smelled of Bálint, it was all saying to him, you fool. You thought you could have all this. You thought some Roma village nobody could get away with this.

He stood up. His muscles were stiff. He'd been sitting for he didn't know how long. It was light, now. He should be at work. He hadn't eaten or drunk or checked his phone. But it didn't matter any more. None of it mattered. He didn't want to think or feel. It was over.

The silence was shouting at him. He picked up the remote and switched on the TV. It burst into life, some news programme. He didn't care. He just wanted noise. He wandered into the kitchen. He started tidying up, taking a glass off the drainer to put it away. He opened the cupboard. Bálint's favourite coffee mug was sitting there. Blue and white stripes. It had a chip in it, but Bálint still insisted on using it.

Tas grabbed it and hurled it to the floor. It smashed into pieces, scattering everywhere. A pain gripped him. He clenched, gasping, staggering. The floor crunched underfoot. He slammed into the counter, his head and arms crashing down on the cold surface. He took heaving breaths. He heard himself moaning. It sounded like someone else. His head felt light. He stumbled into the bedroom and fell face down on the bed. He sobbed and sobbed. He thought the blanket would smother him. He hoped it would.

He jerked awake. His mouth was dry, buried in a pillow. The TV was still blaring. How long was he asleep? How could he sleep? He moved to get up and a wave of blackness hit him. He lay back on the bed, face up. The ceiling was blank and white.

Bálint's face came to him, the last time they spoke. *Under the bed, Tas.* Suddenly he wanted to reach out, touch something of Bálint, embrace what was left of him. He got on the floor and pulled it out, this old box that he'd dusted and vacuumed around a hundred times. Tatty old thing. When he pressed the catch it just opened. He lifted the lid and made some sound that wasn't a word.

The case was full of cash. Dollars. Euros. Forints. He reached out a trembling hand and touched it to check it was real. He picked up handfuls of it, neatly bundled. High values. There must be thousands worth in here. Tas flicked a few of them. He could smell the ink of old banknotes. How long had Bálint been stashing money in here? He smiled. So Bálint had a bit of Roma in him too. It was Tas who told him the Roma didn't trust banks, hid all their money in corners and crevices. Tas had thought nothing about money. But Bálint always had more than he did; this flat was his place.

He picked up a wad and weighed it in his hand. An act of love. Bálint always looked out for him. But that made the pain come back, the pain that crushed him inside. He had to move. He got up and went into the living room.

The TV was showing some election thing. Béla Kornai was standing on a stage, talking in a microphone to hundreds of cheering people. Behind him stood a row of young people, grinning and cheering, more girls than boys, all pale and fresh, the faces of Hungary. As he watched this man, this man Bálint hated, the one who had caused the whole thing, he looked down at the cash in his hand and had an idea. An idea that might quell the pain inside, give him a purpose, make things more bearable, maybe even make things right.

He sat and watched, the money on his knee. Thoughts shifted around in his mind, forming a pattern. A sequence of events that would lead to a moment. It drew him in and he could see himself walking down a tunnel, following that sequence, making that moment happen. It wasn't light at the end of this tunnel, though. There was only darkness. But that was okay.

He checked the time. He showered, dressed, ate, cleared up, swept the kitchen floor, and went to work.

Chapter 39

Rose got off the tram two stops early. The route followed one of the main arterial roads out of Budapest, terminating by a cemetery and a prison. The road was a mix of retail and industrial, and was on the shabby side. Bargain outlets sold cut-price groceries and cheap clothes. The commercial blocks were run down with peeling paint, patched-up walls and broken signage. Some were entirely abandoned, with missing window panes and forecourts sprouting weeds and bushes.

At the address Danny gave her, an informal market occupied a space between buildings. Its offerings – stackable plastic boxes, bumper packs of cigarettes, brightly-coloured stuffed toys – attracted a good crowd. As Rose approached, her neck prickled. She recognised this feeling of unease, mainly from her time in Moscow. She stopped and tracked round, looking up and down the main road, but saw nothing except shoppers with carrier bags trudging from stall to stall. She veered into a discount electronics shop and watched passers by above the gaudy adverts in the window. Nothing. But still. Danny's words of warning were in her mind. She also knew to be wary when Grom was in town. He'd caught her this way once before.

She browsed the stalls. She already knew from Danny's team that the entrance to the workshop was at the back. Eyeing the yard behind the parade as she examined a variety of mobile phone covers, she saw exactly what she was looking for. At the end, a commercial building extended out, giving it a right-angled view of the doors along the back of the shops. What was more, a number of boarded-up window panes told her it was unused. Perfect.

She emerged from the market and walked past the shop fronts down to the next block. She ducked into a shop selling nothing but bottles of carbonated soft drinks packaged into bundles with shrink-wrapped plastic. Not much browse potential, but it gave her some space to flush anyone out. She waited, came out and glanced round: nothing. She walked swiftly back the way she'd come, then when she was finally sure no one was looking, made a sharp change of direction to go up the side of the old block and round the back.

She was ready with her lock-picking gear but the door was so rotten she could elbow it open. She slipped inside and closed it. Pausing by the door, she listened: sounds from the stalls outside, nothing else. She crept in, found the stairs, went up and settled by the window with the best view of the grey steel door below. It was a cold musty spot, but she was well prepared and even had water and energy bars. She watched the flow of shoppers and traders and heard no sounds from within the building. Maybe her instincts were off after all.

Five hours later the water and energy bars were gone, and it was starting to get dark. The market stalls were all packed away. No one had been anywhere near the grey door. They needed to be watching round the clock but she wasn't going to stay up here all night. Aside from not wanting to freeze to death, there was somewhere else she needed to be. She was just starting to think about leaving when a dark van pulled up and stopped right outside the place. When the driver jumped out to open up the back, it was just about light enough to see his face. She took a sharp breath.

It was Marko. Marko who made the bomb that shattered the Sandhill community and took ten of their lives. Marko whose wife used to be called Tihana. Marko who followed his wife to Zagreb when she tried to get away from him, who beat her to a pulp when he found out she was informing on him. And now here he was, in Budapest, the same city where she was harbouring herself under a different name.

Of course Marko was still involved in all this. Crusaders was long defunct, but the anger didn't just go away. What brought him to Budapest? Did he know his wife was here? Surely not. She'd know about it if he did. Was Marko involved in whatever Grom was planning? That was all too possible.

She watched him open the steel door and unload a wooden crate from the back of the van. It was clearly heavy. Another guy appeared from the other side of the van: overweight, dirty jeans, shaggy hair. This one rang no bells. Between them they carted a number of crates inside. There was no chance of catching sight of the contents. They went in and closed the door. A few minutes later they came out again, locked the door, locked the van, and set off together on foot towards the main road.

Rose scrambled into action. She thought they were going to drive off, but she'd got lucky. They crossed the road to the tram stop. She kept her distance, only approaching as the tram pulled up. She followed them onto the tram and they rode it to the city centre, Blaha-Lujza tér. From there she thought they were heading for the Metro but they went straight past, across Rákóczi út and into one of the narrow streets leading off it. This was the part of Budapest where much of the nightlife was – the Jewish Quarter.

Crossing the street to follow them, she turned, that prickling feeling back again, but once more saw nothing amiss and had to hurry on to keep Marko and his companion in sight. They were moving ahead with some purpose, talking to each other only occasionally. It was darker now; the shapes of people passing were turning indistinct. They came to a city square, a mass of mature trees, grass around a circular flower bed with a central statue. The two men came to a halt. Marko had a lot to say suddenly, pointing and gesticulating all over the place. The other guy lit a cigarette and nodded occasionally. He seemed happy to stand and chill, but Marko, worryingly, was on a mission. He beckoned the other on and they headed west. The narrow streets were lined with restaurants, cafes and bars. She caught glimpses of courtyards beyond heavy wooden doors. She glanced up at a large mural of a woman's face, and almost got run down by someone on an electric scooter. Marko was still pointing as he walked. Then, without warning, they both disappeared into a doorway.

Rose approached. The doorway was in the centre of a frontage shrouded in plastic sheeting, with some official looking notices fastened to the outside. A renovation project, maybe. She could see or hear nothing within, no voices, no footsteps. If she went any further and they were there, she'd be committed, with no play except beating a hasty retreat.

She stepped in. The doorway led through the width of the building into a courtyard with an overgrown central garden. She could see nobody. She crept through, her feet making no sound on the stone floor. Where it opened out, she stopped. She had a full view of the courtyard. The plastic sheeting covered the frontages right round, blocking every possible exit. But the courtyard was empty.

Something made her turn. In the street outside, someone was standing in the road watching her. As she turned, they took off.

Gotcha! She sprinted out, catching a glimpse of the moving shape before it rounded a corner. No wonder she hadn't spotted him before. It was just a kid, a boy. She ran after him and almost missed him turning off again. Now they were both in a street busy with people. Rose dodged pedestrians and danced round motorbikes. He was having the same trouble. She was gaining on him. They came out on a busy road. The boy launched himself across the six lanes of traffic just as the lights were changing. As she got there the traffic was in full flow. She stepped out, dodging as best she could, horns blaring as cars braked.

By the time she got to the other side, the boy was gone.

Chapter 40

It was Saturday. Tas went to Rebellion as usual. Only of course it wasn't as usual. Everything was different, but he did the same things they'd have done together. Dressed up, a little mascara – not much, only enough so people could see he'd made the effort. Rebellion was their home after all. Their village.

The same crowd was there. He got a lot of hugs and ruffled hair. He couldn't think of much to say to anybody, and they didn't know what to ask. Andor was around, hovering miserably. He came over, told him some stuff about funerals and autopsies. Tas was only half listening. Someone put a drink in his hand. Even that tasted different, syrupy and sweet. Wherever he went the conversation dried, like they didn't want to have fun with him there. That was okay. They could do that after he'd gone.

The ladies opened the floor show as usual, glittering and shapely and smiling, their hands wild, their jokes shocking. Belly laughs filled the small space. Tas stood at the back, his warm drink in his hand. He watched the room and saw who was at the tables, but didn't meet anyone's eye. He didn't want them to invite him over.

The ladies started their first number, a cheeky one. They posed and preened and got a lot of whistles and cheers. Tas put his drink down, slipped out and made his way to the dressing room. The door was unlocked, the room empty. He could hear the music and laughter next door, as he quietly found what he wanted.

He stashed it in his jacket pockets and closed the door behind him. He went home; no one saw him leave.

Chapter 41

Gabi stuck her head round the door. "She's here."

Fairchild wasn't expecting it. His heart made some crazy movement in his chest. He didn't think she'd actually show up, not really. And now he felt completely unprepared.

Gabi withdrew and Rose walked in. Blond hair, longer than he remembered. Blue eyes, looking at him. Scratches on her face. Speechless, he watched her glance round.

"Nice place."

"Gabi organised it. We can't meet in public right now."

They were in a downstairs room of what Gabi called a *romkocsma* – a ruin bar – in the far reaches of a basement whose vaulted corridors ran the entire length and width of the vast derelict complex above. A glitterball threw specks of light across graffitied walls, a scuffed coffee table, tasselled lamps of all sizes, and a motley collection of furniture. A rolltop bath filled one corner, a battered gymnastics horse another. On the walls were clown masks, mannequin parts, car number plates and empty picture frames. Exposed pipes brought a modicum of heat to a fat radiator fixed sideways onto the wall. The lighting gradually faded from pink to blue and then back again. There was a smell of stale beer. Music thumped upstairs. Through a glassless window, flickers of light came from some old newsreel projected onto a wall.

Fairchild was on a sofa sagging so low it was practically on the floor. Rose went for a stool. "I don't think I'll fall asleep in here," she said.

So she remembered how he'd snuck out on her in the Tokyo piano bar. He didn't think she'd forget. "Sorry about the sudden exit that time. I had to—"

"Oh, I get it. You had to use information I'd given you to go behind my back and find a way to get in with Grom. As well as the contents of an MI6 file you were passed in good faith by people who considered you a friend. I can see how you'd be in a hurry to get on with that, as soon as you had what you needed."

It was unfair, but not entirely so. "It wasn't like that. I wasn't pumping you for information about Grom, or anything else for that matter."

"No, I know. I told you of my own volition. Don't worry, I blame myself. It won't happen again." She sounded weary for a moment. He wanted to protest but didn't get the chance. "Why did you do it, anyway? I know Walter's a devious operator but is he really worse than the guy who killed your own parents?"

At least she was asking. That much was positive. "Remember Darcy Tang?"

He let her bring up the memory. "The mafia grandma? The one whose nephew you shot?"

"Our relationship did improve after that. When you and your brother went missing, I went to her for help. It was Tang who put us onto the shipping company and gave us Milo's identity. But she wanted something in return."

"Like what?" She'd softened a little already.

"Fire Sappers. She has a major problem with them. They stole from her. She decided I was the one who could get inside and bring them down. While Milo was alive, he might have been a way in. But with him gone—"

"Grom was your only entry." Her face puckered with distaste. "Couldn't you have just walked away? Or told her you couldn't help?"

"I'd have ended up with a price on my own head. I've put plenty of noses out of joint over the years, but not someone of that calibre."

"You could have told me." Her eyes were accusing. He knew this was coming.

"I felt I'd dragged you into this enough, this thing between me and Grom."

"I don't need protecting."

"It isn't about protection. It's about not throwing you to the lions. Think about Georgia. That happened because he associated you with me. You shouldn't have had anything to do with it."

A shadow crossed her face. "I don't think about Georgia."

"I do." That made her eyes narrow. He could say things to her now that he wouldn't have done before. He felt different. He was fed up of games. He wanted her to know how he felt. But did she want to hear it?

"You're Zack's source, aren't you?" she said. "You're feeding him information about Grom."

He didn't deny it.

"You really don't know at all what he's planning?"

Fairchild thought back to the conversation at the Gellért. "He said something about power. Power's the key these days, in today's world. Something like that."

"Sounds like him. Typical Grom rhetoric."

It sounded at the time like Grom meant something more by it. But Rose was probably right.

"It's a dangerous path to tread," she said. "Trying to please everybody at the same time. Does Grom really trust you?"

"I don't think so."

"Then why is he letting you get so close?"

"He must have a reason but I haven't figured it out yet."

"Watch your back. I'm not the only one who can be thrown to the lions."

Fairchild may have shrugged. She took exception. "He's nasty, Fairchild. Don't let him persuade you that he isn't. He's tried to kill you before. And if you get a chance to put a bullet in his head, don't pass up this time."

"I won't. But until Tang's happy, I need him. Unpleasant though that is."

She frowned. "How did you explain it to him, this change of allegiance?"

"I said I'd had enough of all the lies and needed the truth. About whatever Walter et al are hiding."

"And has he furnished you with the truth?"

"He certainly has." He said it straight. This was what he really wanted to say to her. He told her about the Hungarian nursery rhyme, the revelations of János Mészáros, his cousins in the village. He watched it sink in, on her face. She knew what a big deal it was.

"You're Hungarian?"

"My parents were. So, yes, in a sense, I am. More than anything else."

"They never told you."

"To protect me. To discourage me from coming here."

"To try to stop you and Grom from ever finding out about each other. Didn't work, did it?"

"Ultimately, no. But whatever happens next, I'm glad I know. It feels – different. Knowing where I'm from."

"Okay. I get that." It sounded like she really did. "Grom is still a shit, though. Don't forget it. He had a reason for leading you to all that. Probably not a nice one."

He hadn't managed to say what he wanted to say. Now she changed tack. "I've been privy to some revelations of my own. You'll never guess who showed up in Budapest, specially invited by Walter?"

Something dropped into place. "Penny Galloway?"

Her eyes widened.

"I went to see her," he explained. "I found out she was posted here years ago, so I drove over there to talk to her. The place was all locked up. So she was here all the time."

"Walter brought her here to give me the story of what happened in Berlin."

"Berlin? What happened in Berlin?"

"The thing they don't like to talk about."

And Rose then told him what happened in Berlin, a sordid story of manipulation and bungling and consequent loss of life, all covered up to protect reputations and enhance personal influence. The story was new but the taste it left behind wasn't.

"So," said Rose, "because Walter wants Salisbury to stay in post, but Grom keeps slipping away and is now becoming ever more of a danger, Walter has determined that Grom has to go."

"Go?" She said it so matter-of-factly he didn't pick up on her meaning to start with.

"Yes, go."

"Walter's put a kill order on Grom?"

"It can't be official because Salisbury would never agree to it. Too scared of what might happen if it failed. So he's just let me know that if the opportunity arose…"

"He wants you to do it?"

"Don't sound so outraged. I'd be more than happy to. Though it's not my area of specialism I'll make an exception for him. I can't go crawling over rooftops with a long distance rifle but I'll settle for something closer and dirtier, should the opportunity arise."

"I see."

"He did also say that the same principle might be extended to yourself." Again, her tone was so light it hardly sunk in.

"To me?"

"If it were indeed true that you and Grom were working together."

He couldn't make it add up. Walter, wanting him dead? Whatever the circumstances, that was a punch in the gut. Walter was practically his parent from the age of ten. Admittedly Fairchild had behaved like a rebellious teenager throughout – and ever since. But dead? "Well. I guess I pissed him off one time too many."

Rose noticed how strained his voice was. "It's the overall threat of the situation he's responding to. You and Grom, what you could achieve together if you really did decide you were with him, doesn't bear thinking about. And this vulnerability with Salisbury just amplifies it."

"He really thought I'd join Grom?"

"You do sound terribly cynical sometimes."

He did, he knew. But was his reputation really that bad? "What about you? Did you think I was with Grom?"

He examined her face as she pondered her answer. "No. I didn't. Not really."

He felt weightless suddenly, floating. Her voice was smooth as she carried on. "With Walter it's all about self-blame. He thinks he messed it up with you and feels responsible for all of this."

"But if all this is because of the link between Grom and Salisbury—"

"Why not get Salisbury out of the game? Believe me, I made that point. The guy could be persuaded to step down,

I'd have thought. But that might mean a career end for Walter as well."

"So it's every man for himself, then."

"See? Cynical. And it's every person, not every man."

She was so calm, so grounded. He felt all at sea, riding crests and troughs. She could anchor him, he was sure. And now he finally knew how it could feel to be on solid ground. He needed to say something. But how to choose the words?

The door opened: Gabi's head again. "So, guys, there's a massive queue outside. Like, a hundred. They're saying they need to open the basement."

"Can't it wait for a few minutes?" Please go away.

"There's an office upstairs. I can take you now."

But Rose was getting up. "I should go anyway."

He stood, trying to think fast. How could he delay her? But she was at the door already. She turned and put a hand on his arm. There was uncertainty in her face for the first time.

"We are on the same side now, aren't we?" Her eyes told him how much she needed his response.

"Always," he said.

He saw relief there, a lessening of tension. She gave his arm the smallest squeeze before stepping away. "Let's stay in touch. Directly." She caught Gabi's eye. "No offence." The Hungarian shrugged. Rose looked back at him. Then she was gone.

Gabi raised her shoulders. "Sorry. That was bad timing, I guess."

He should be angry with her but he couldn't stop smiling. "It's fine," he said. "Really, it's fine."

Chapter 42

Tas was about to go out when the knock came. It was late, dark already. No dressing up this time: jeans, t-shirt, jacket, scuffed old boots. A working man's clothes. Tas was a working man after all. For now at least.

It was the landlord at the door. Tas recognised him but they'd never spoken. It was always Bálint who dealt with him. "Mind if I come in?" he asked.

"I'm just going out." Tas didn't want this man inside. He didn't have time, and besides, there was something unfriendly about him, his small eyes and long nose, like a rat, his rolled-up sleeves and his stance – ready for anything.

"Oh. Well, we need to talk"

"You can come back tomorrow if you want."

This didn't seem to please him. "Look. I heard about your – friend." Tas waited. "Saw it on the news." Tas gave a slight nod. He hadn't said he was sorry. "See, it was his name on the lease. We need to normalise things, make changes, you see. Truth be told, the place needs a bit of work. You've probably noticed."

Tas didn't react. The man carried on. "It all costs, doesn't it? I didn't put the rent up, you see. A good deal for you! But what am I supposed to do? Costs go up all the time. I'm stuck in the middle."

He gave a miserable little shrug as if Tas should feel sorry for him, though his chin was still high and his mouth set. "I mean, I don't want to be too hard on you, of course. You must be upset and there are arrangements to make. I understand that, I really do. We could say a week."

A week. The word hung in the air. He hadn't said it as a question. It was a statement. A week.

Tas wasn't going to make it easy for him. "What's a week?" he asked.

"*Hát…* a week longer. In this flat. Before I take possession." He used some legal phrase but Tas knew what he meant. Bálint, at least, was respectable. Before, anyway. Someone like Tas would never have been offered the flat in the first place. Tas had nothing to stand on, couldn't do the talk like Andor or this guy here. But he knew of something that always talked.

"Is the rent overdue?" he asked, with no drama.

"The rent is due," said the landlord, with a nod, as if that were the same thing.

"How much?"

He said a figure which sounded about double what Bálint was paying.

"Wait here." He shut the door, went to the bedroom, and came back with two wads of cash. "Forint or Euros?"

The landlord's eyes glittered as he looked at the money. "Euros if you have them, I guess."

Tas shoved the Euros at the man's chest. He took it, his mouth hanging open slightly. Tas had doubled the sum he'd said, and added more for good measure. "I have to go out," he said, and shut the door.

When he opened it again a few minutes later to leave, the landlord was gone. He'd be back, though. And he'd want the same again, if not more. But that wasn't a problem. Tas' work would be done by then.

He took the Metro, then a tram. It was a line he knew, the one that went up to the prison. He tried not to think about that, and got off half way along. He crossed a busy road and went through to the back of some shops, all closed up for the night. It was deserted. He saw a grey metal door, locked up, bars on the windows. A light was on inside. Tas stood in the darkness hearing nothing except his own breathing. Was this the most risky thing he'd ever done?

Malik was a guy at work. Tas didn't know Malik very well. But everyone said that Malik was the person to go to for cheap cigarettes, discount SIM cards, cut-price DVDs, perfume and jewellery, drugs, anything else you might want but couldn't get the usual way. When Tas cornered him with his request, he was grave and gave it some thought, but didn't ask any difficult questions. A couple of hours ago Malik's text sent him here. He had no idea who was behind that door or what would happen. He readied himself. If nothing else, he could run. He took a breath, stepped forward, and knocked.

Some fumbling on the inside and the door opened outwards. A wide form filled the space, a chunky guy, flesh rolling over his belt, long scrubby hair, a beard. The guy stared, saying nothing. There was a tattoo on his arm. Tas' heart raced.

"I'm Malik's friend." He tried to sound calm.

"Okay." The man beckoned him in. The door clanged shut. The guy drew a bolt across. Their eyes met. "Not a nice area." It sounded accusing. He looked like he was twice Tas' body weight. The room was small – a workshop, electricals or something. A counter had tools on it: wire cutters, a soldering iron, a clamp. Boxes and crates were packed in everywhere. The man leaned back on the counter and folded his arms. He smelled unwashed.

"So," he said. He wanted Tas to commit first. Well, if he had to.

"Malik told me you have guns."

"Guns?" For one moment Tas felt a stab of panic. There'd been some terrible mistake. Then the guy started to laugh. His body wobbled like a jelly. "How many do you want? Yes, I have guns."

"Just the one." Tas didn't smile.

Fat guy sobered up. "What sort?"

"What have you got?"

"Most things." He wanted to see if Tas knew his stuff.

"Something small. A handgun. With a good range."

"Automatic?"

"No. Too bulky."

"Fast reloading?"

"Not if it's accurate."

That made him look again.

Tas' father turned his hand to many things to put food on the table. One of them was hunting. With his collection of knives and some old rifle he'd restored himself, he'd tramp off early and return, on a good day, with a bird or a rabbit dangling from his pouch. On a bad day he'd complain about the light or the state of the woods or the landowner, and they'd all go hungry. For his father didn't have licences or permission, and spent as much time hiding and running as he did stalking prey. His father was a poacher.

He'd take Tas with him sometimes, dragging him out in the mist of the morning, putting the rifle in his hands and making him shoot for practice when they were far enough from the village. They'd stand still for hours and Tas would hear his own teeth chatter. When his father downed an animal, he'd make Tas fire the kill shot. To make a man of you, he said. To know what it is to take a life. Tas would pull the trigger, seeing the light die in the creature's eyes, watch the ruptured brain ooze, smell the blood. Something big like a deer, they'd skin and chop it, carry the slimy chunks, heavy and cold, miles back home. In the evenings his father would clean his precious weapon, telling anyone who happened to be there how it worked, showing them all the parts, describing the different kinds that were out there and what you could do with them. So Tas knew his guns.

Fat guy's eyes roved the crates. He crossed and heaved a couple from under the counter. He prised off a lid. It was full of gun cases. Tas must have drawn a breath because the guy turned to look up at him.

"It's a good haul. A gift. From someone who wants to be our friend. For training, supposedly. But no one seemed to care where they ended up afterwards." His smile widened into a manic grin. "We can do some mischief with these, eh?"

What kind of mischief would Tas do with this man? Tas couldn't imagine. He pointed to one of the smaller cases. "That one?"

"Huh? This? Let's see." Fat guy got it out and opened it on the counter. It was a simple handgun, small and sleek, with a separate magazine. Tas felt panic. His father had an old Soviet era hunting rifle. Nothing like this. Fat guy saw his hesitation.

"You know what you're doing, right?" He picked up the gun, pushed in the magazine and pulled back the slide. "Now. Loaded. Okay?"

Tas nodded, uncertain. Fat guy reversed the process and handed him the gun. Tas repeated the steps, awkwardly at first, but after a couple of tries it went smoothly. He nodded. It made sense. "Where do you practise?" he asked.

Fat guy smiled. "We did a load of exercises up north, in the forest. Round here, I'd go for an old warehouse or something like that. Not the woods. You don't want to stick a bullet in some guy out walking his dog, do you?"

"What about a silencer?"

"A suppressor? Right here." Fat guy really fancied himself with all this. He took the long tube out of the case and screwed it onto the front. The gun felt heavy and unbalanced, and it was huge. But it would be useful.

"How much?" asked Tas. The man told him. It was a lot, but he had it with him. If Bálint had thought this money would go on a comfortable retirement, he was wrong. Tas unfolded a roll of high-value notes and handed some over. The man pocketed it, watching Tas put the rest away.

"So, what are you going to do with it?" he asked. "Horse rustling?" His smile became a smirk.

Tas was emboldened by the heavy feel of the gun in his hand. "Why are you selling this to me? To someone like me? Why do that?"

The big guy shrugged. "I have debts. No one will notice it's gone. We've got plenty more. You have to get by, don't you?"

He said it as if everyone were in the same boat. Tas disarmed the gun and stashed it and the silencer in his jacket pockets. It didn't show. He'd walk home, just in case.

"I suppose you do," he said.

Chapter 43

Walter took most of the day to return Rose's call. In the meantime Rapp and her team had assembled, including Fairchild's man-friend Zack, who was as cool towards Rose as ever. They all met in person at the US embassy. Rose updated them about the premises, Marko's presence there, and the tail which ended nowhere. That still bothered her; there was no way of avoiding making it sound like she'd simply bungled it. She was also bothered that she had no way of contacting Zsuzsanna to warn her that Marko was in town.

Rapp agreed to put twenty-four-hour surveillance on the workshop, but not the city centre location where Rose had lost them. "We don't know what we're surveying. We don't know what they were doing there or where they were going."

"Well, they weren't just out shopping," said Rose. "I could tell that much. The journey had a purpose to it."

"There's nothing on their route that stands out as a target," said Danny. "You said they didn't go near any of the synagogues."

"They didn't."

"As far as you saw," said Rapp, with her usual tact.

"Our guys can't think of a specific target there either," said Zack. "But I kind of feel we should be warning people."

Danny wasn't so sure. "It's so vague still. Might spook a lot of people and we could be completely off track. There's a reputational price. When we say something, we want to be believed."

The inaction made Rose itch. "Let's pick them up, then. Marko, Grom, the Russian. Get them off the streets. Zack, your source can point us to them, can't they?"

"Local law enforcement would want more evidence," said Danny.

"Not enough evidence for a prosecution in any jurisdiction," said Rapp. "All we'll do is let them know we're onto them so they can move off and start again somewhere else."

They were right, but a sense of menace haunted her all day. She hung around the Embassy casting about for things to do until eventually Walter called back.

"So sorry. A little busy here."

Rose had no idea where he was or what he was doing, and knew better than to ask. "A question for you. John Fairchild's parents. What can you tell me about their nationality?"

A silence. Rose could hear traffic noise in the background. "May I ask where this is coming from?" Walter's voice was the very definition of caginess.

"The man himself. Our paths crossed. Actually, he arranged it through an intermediary."

"What for?" More extreme wariness.

"Walter, it's Fairchild who's been feeding information to the team. Via Zack. He's really not with Grom. He says he's doing this to return a favour, by bringing Fire Sappers down, and Grom was his only way in. Anyway, it was Grom who brought him to Hungary and encouraged him to do some digging."

"I bet it was." Walter spoke faintly, as if talking to himself.

"Is there any truth in it? That his parents came over to the West in '56? Or is it all some fantasy of Grom's?"

She heard footsteps – Walter's, probably – and the traffic noise faded. "Since he's got there anyway, there's no great loss, I suppose." He didn't sound very pleased about it.

"You mean it's true?"

"Yes, my dear, though really what difference it makes at this stage I couldn't say. I wasn't around at the time but when his parents came to work for me I was put in the picture. They were already on the radar of the Soviet secret police. That outfit doesn't let country borders hinder the pursuit of their version of justice. It was felt at the time that those two could go a lot further with British identities. They had a lot to offer. When recruiting amongst the Hungarian diaspora they reverted, of course, but to everyone else they were solid UK-born citizens. Not everyone could have done it, but they were fired up about the regime that had just crushed their rebellion. They passed off as British with flying colours."

"But they never bothered telling their son. You knew more about them than he did."

"My dear, I'm sure they had quite a list of things they were going to tell the boy as soon as he was old enough. But they never got the chance. You wouldn't tell a child something like that. All he'd need to do was blab at school and it would be over. I really can't see what difference it makes now, anyway."

But Walter was still holding back. Why did the Fairchilds deliberately discourage their son from learning Hungarian, in ways so subtle he only realised it now, decades later? They were concealing their nationality with a care that said there was more to it than regular security.

"Grom has certainly used it to his advantage," she said. "If Fairchild feels in the guy's debt for opening up his eyes, it wouldn't surprise me. Keeping secrets like this is only going to stoke up trouble in the future. Particularly something so fundamental."

She was skating on thin ice criticising him like this, and he didn't like it. "Fundamental, Rose? Is it really? Bear in mind who Grom is. He plays games. He latches onto people's insecurities and feeds them until they can be exploited. Grom has a reason to poke this particular anthill."

"What reason is that?"

Another long pause. "Believe me, you and he would be better off leaving this alone."

"There's more, isn't there? That's not the whole story."

"It could be. It should be. It would be better if it were."

"Walter, nothing is going to work with Fairchild until he knows everything. He'll just keep digging. You know it."

"Do I? You just said he'd never have discovered this unless Grom had pushed him. He took the bait and Grom is reeling him in now. The best thing he can do is walk away and leave it alone. Otherwise he'll be following Grom wherever he wants to take him. Can you not take my word for it? Can you not believe me when I say that some things are better off staying hidden?"

He sounded genuinely upset. But it was desperation. Whatever Walter wanted to keep hidden, he knew it would come out. "You may be right, but I'm not your problem here. Fairchild is. If you want me to play a role and limit the damage, put me in the picture. I can be dispassionate. I'm not him. You know that."

A sigh. "Very well. But this is for your ears only. Don't pass it on. Especially not to him. You'll understand why. Talk to Galloway. She can tell it better than me, and it's best heard face to face."

"Penny's still in Budapest?"

"She was in no hurry to leave. I think she's enjoying the trip down memory lane."

"Can you give me her number?"

"She doesn't have one."

"She doesn't have a phone?"

"She says it's her single rebellious act, her way of not being owned. Besides, she's retired. She claims she doesn't need one."

"So how do I get in touch with her?"

Walter sounded tired. "The old-fashioned way, Rose. I'm sure you can figure it out."

Chapter 44

Fairchild was early. The drive to Vienna was only three hours and the roads were good. He filled in the time doing something he always did when he came here. The street hadn't changed much: elegant stoneworked facades on both sides, cast iron street lighting. A lot like Budapest, in fact. Mid-afternoon it was quiet, nobody much around. He looked up at the windows of the flat, the last place where he'd seen his parents.

August 1980. He ran through that evening in his mind, as he'd done so many times. The card game they were playing, his childish tantrum on losing, running down the stairs ignoring his mother's entreaties, his fevered walk through the dark streets, he couldn't remember where. His return an hour later to a silent, empty flat. Was this another game, he'd asked himself, sitting there listening to some clock ticking? But he couldn't work it out, so he'd called Walter. His life after that was transformed.

Now he knew more about them than he'd ever known before, the reason they spent so much time in Vienna, their real names, their backgrounds, what drove them. He knew where they were from; he'd been there, seen it, lived it himself. But somehow, the more he knew the more distant they became. His childhood, it turned out, had been a farce, a game from beginning to end, but it was the only childhood he had.

He was still ten minutes early but Dr Reicher saw him straight away. Reicher was a private practising consultant, and his room was more like a CEO's office than a medical facility. The tools of his trade – bench, equipment drawers, curtain – were tucked away in a corner while an immense leather-topped desk took pride of place. Only a faint smell of antiseptic betrayed his profession. Dr Reicher appealed to the type of people who wanted a medical consultation, not a practitioner who would simply dole out treatment. But he was good, and Fairchild had been on his books a long time.

"It's been quite a few years since we last met," said the doctor, offering a hand, a smile on his deceptively young looking face, no white coat in sight. "I trust all is well? Though I hardly dare ask."

Fairchild assured him, in German, that whatever breaks, bruises and burns suffered during the period were healing nicely, and declined the offer of an examination. They both knew that wasn't the reason he was here. He sat. This was just a precaution, he kept telling himself. Just to be sure. That was all. But still, he wanted it to be over.

Reicher sat as well, and centred a file on the desk in front of him. "So, first I need to explain that due to the extreme urgency of your request the cost was considerably more than it would normally be. The laboratory gave it the highest priority."

"That's fine." The doctor had already said that. Fairchild would pay whatever it cost.

Reicher opened the file. "So, you sent me a number of items from which to take samples, as well as your own." He embarked on an explanation of the process.

"I know the basic principle." Fairchild was a little short.

"Of course. I just want you to know how certain we can be of the result."

"How certain?"

"Very. There is not much scope for doubt."

He put a few sheets in front of Fairchild – tables with numbers, charts. Fairchild glanced but was incapable just then of ploughing through it. "Can you give me a summary?"

"Very well. There were numerous discrete DNA samples on the objects, and evidence of familial matches between them. But not with your own."

"Excuse me?" Fairchild thought he'd misheard.

"You are not related to any of the people whose samples we identified."

The room seemed to contract around him. Something must have shown on his face. The doctor leaned forward. "Is that not what you were expecting?"

Fairchild took a breath, feeling the need to steady himself with his fingers on the edge of the desk. "It was not." It must be a mistake. "You can't actually identify the DNA, can you?"

"We can't tie it to an actual person. As a private practice we don't have access to databases, and besides, the use of that data is strictly controlled. But we can isolate different strands and do some basic analysis. Only gender so far, but it's possible to do more on request."

Fairchild's heart was pounding. In this quiet, formal office there was a storm going on in his head. Many others must have received unwelcome news in this room. The formality might have helped. He had to focus. "So – the hairbrush, I'm interested in the person whose hairbrush it was. Also the sewing kit. Was there a predominant sample?"

"Yes, yes. The hairs in the brush and most of the oils left by fingers on those two are all one person, a female. That's all we know about her."

His mother. So he'd thought. "And I'm not related to her?"

"That's correct." He said it as softly as he could. "And as for the Bible, as you suggested there is a tradition of kissing the gospels, so that was the starting point. In fact, the book opened automatically on the first page of St Luke, but the technicians also covered the others."

"And there was one dominant sample there too?"

"Exactly. A male." Viktor.

"But he's not…" Reicher had already told him. But somehow he needed to hear it again.

"He is not related to you."

All Fairchild could do was sit there trying to make it fit, but he couldn't.

"I'm sorry," the doctor said. Reicher didn't know. With his doctor Fairchild shared all things medical and physical, but nothing else. It was easier that way.

He thought he'd discovered a home and an identity, but almost as soon as he had, it was snatched away. Instead of gaining something new, he'd lost everything. He felt a sudden hot anger for Ilona and Viktor. Who were they, anyway? They'd done nothing but lie to him.

"I have the objects you sent," Reicher was saying. "Would you like them back?"

Fairchild had to get away, out of this unbearably stuffy office. He stood up suddenly. "Burn them," he said, and walked out.

Just as he'd done that night, he tramped through the streets of Vienna without caring where he went. It hurt less when he moved, somehow stopped it crashing down on him. Across a cobbled square, past palatial gates, through some garden or other, dodging strolling couples and groups with their camera phones, he pressed on. He sank down eventually on a grassy bank. And it was here, by a lake dotted with statues of famous men, that it finally fell into place.

There'd been a woman in Grom's life. Not his wife, Grom said. But he also said that she betrayed him. Ilona and Viktor helped her get away from him. But the timing of it!

Now that everything else had been stripped away, it was as plain as day.

He sank to his knees, bent over, and vomited.

Chapter 45

As soon as Tas turned the key, he knew something was wrong. The deadbolt wasn't locked. Someone had been here. Someone with keys. Of course – he should have thought of that.

He'd been out practising. Found a good place not far from work, a disused factory in an overgrown plot where he could set up targets inside. Following a muddy track round the back, he'd found a broken fence. A few shots and it all came back. His aim was pretty good. Good enough for his needs. He figured out how to pocket the gun and the quickest way to draw and be ready to fire. By then it was getting late and he needed to move. Back to the flat to get ready. But now he had a problem.

At least the gun wasn't in the flat. Whatever else the guy had found, he wasn't getting that. Pretty obvious what he'd be looking for, though. Tas pushed the door and slipped inside. He could hear nothing. Two more steps and he squeezed the door shut behind him. He paused, frozen, every sense activated. Still nothing.

Wait! A noise from the bedroom, a soft thump. Tas withdrew the gun and attached the silencer, a move that came easily to him now. He was back with his father, out in the woods, standing, watching, listening, the hunter focused only on getting to the prey before the law got to him. Nothing else existed.

He crept to the door of the bedroom. The thief was his landlord, of course, the only other person with a key. Tas had flashed that money too much. The guy was kneeling by the bed. Bálint's trunk was open on top and the rat was stuffing notes into his bag, his pockets, every orifice he could fill. A flash of anger burst inside Tas. Bálint's case, Bálint's money, violated by this ratface robber.

"That's not yours," he said.

The landlord made some noise, jumped up and turned. "Christ!" He saw the gun and backed away. He looked Tas up and down, like he did at the door that time. "Right, so this money is yours, is it?" he said. "Earned it, did you?"

"None of your business."

"It is if my place is being used for crime. What is it, drug money? Sex work?" He sneered. Tas aimed the gun. The guy's expression didn't change. "That thing's not real." Tas didn't move. The guy was staring at it now, unsure. "You'll never fire it, anyway." He turned his attention to Tas' face, standing up straighter. "Look. Really, I don't care what you get up to in here. But if it's dodgy, I deserve a cut. It's going to come back to me, isn't it? It's my place. Let's say I take what I have on me and we'll say no more about it. I'll leave you to it. That's reasonable, isn't it? Works for both of us?"

Tas stared at him. If only that were true. But this wouldn't be the end of it. "Put it back. All of it."

"Oh, come now!" The landlord was the picture of reason. "You're not going to notice a little! You've got loads of it here! Plenty to go round."

He took a step forward. Tas should shoot him. He knew how. But he didn't, though his finger tensed on the trigger. The man was watching him. He saw the hesitation. He stepped closer.

"See, I told you! Best just to let me go. Then it's over. Okay?"

Tas lowered his gun. But he didn't budge. He wasn't ready to let this shameless thief walk off with Bálint's money. They stood staring at each other. Then the guy got impatient.

"Look, are you going to let me go or will we be standing here all night?" With his palm he pushed Tas in the chest. Not hard, but decisively.

Arrogant ratface! Did he think Tas was some scum he could just push aside? No way. Tas dropped the gun on the bed and shoved him with both hands. "How dare you! How dare you take our money! You give it back!"

The landlord made as if to take a swing, but Tas got there first. He knocked the guy's arm aside and punched him full on in the face. Ratface staggered back. Tas did it again, then in the stomach. Ratface doubled up, groaning. Tas grabbed him by the collar and shoved his head back into the wall. His skull made a cracking sound. His head bobbed back and forth. Tas did it again, and let go. The man slumped to the floor. He was out cold. A red stain marked the wall behind him. Tas went through the guy's pockets. He got every note back from him. Every one. The little shit deserved nothing.

What now? He had to split. Someone might have heard. He had to go now. Take everything with him and get ready on the way. There wasn't much time. But the rat could still come round and blab. Go to the police even, invent some story. They'd believe him, a landlord, not some queer Roma. He had to do it.

The guy's head was flopped face down on the bed, his arms dangling. Tas grabbed the gun and a pillow. Silencers weren't silent. He'd learned that when practising earlier. He held the pillow in place, aimed, and fired. A muffled twang. That was it. Easier than a deer: no light dying in this one's eyes. Blood started seeping down the guy's neck.

Quickly, now. He washed, changed, and gathered all the money and everything else he needed. He ate something, leaving the packaging on the side and crumbs on the floor. He dropped his muddy clothes in a pile in the bathroom. In the bedroom the empty trunk lay open. Feathers from the pillow settled on the bed, soaking in blood and turning red. The slumped body was still.

Tas grabbed his stuff, turned out the lights, and left.

Chapter 46

Bloody Walter. Bloody Penny Galloway. Who doesn't have a phone? Rose went to Penny's flat and tried the buzzer. No response. She hung around in a cafe for an hour then tried again. Still no answer. By now it was getting dark. Was Walter's information good? Maybe Penny had gone back to Italy. She managed another half hour of waiting, in a different cafe. At least she wasn't missing anything. There was no news from Rapp's team.

The third time she tried the buzzer, Penny answered. "Rose, dear! Come up, come up!" She sounded tired. At the flat she welcomed Rose in and offered peach pálinka. "It never tastes the same at home." Rose sipped from the shot glass. It smelled sweet but tasted bitter.

"So what brings you back?" asked Penny.

"You don't seem surprised."

"I thought you might return. It was a lot to take in."

"But it wasn't everything, was it?"

Penny's eyes were round but she didn't deny it. "Does Walter know you're here?"

"He told me to come here. Says you'll do a better job of telling it than he would."

"That would depend what it is." An elegant flick of the wrist and Penny's pálinka was gone. Rose put hers down on the glass-topped table.

"Grom persuaded Fairchild to look more closely into the origin of his parents."

"Ah." Penny sounded grave. "And what has he discovered?"

"He knows they were Hungarian. He's been out to meet the family. Rediscover his roots."

"Oh, dear." The graveness deepened.

"There's more to it, isn't there?"

Penny frowned. "Are you sure Walter wanted me to go into this?"

"I persuaded him. Fairchild will find out anyway at some point. I can be more help knowing than completely in the dark. You can call him and check if you like." Rose got her phone out and offered it.

"No, no, I believe you. You're probably right. Having got this far he'll probably uncover the whole of it anyway. Though that was one thing we were all certain should never happen."

She gave a kind of shudder and settled back. "I met Elizabeth and Edward as soon as I joined. They'd already been in the Service seven or eight years. Most people weren't aware of their past. Only those who'd worked with them directly. I was invited into the inner circle. Partly because Elizabeth – Ilona – could help me learn Hungarian. They were pretty useful, in fact. MI6 was lucky to have them. They were far more valuable as officers than they would have been at arm's length working the '56 exiles. Which they did anyway."

"And?" Rose already knew all this.

Penny poured herself another pálinka. Rose's glass was still almost full. "In '56, they nearly didn't make it out of Hungary. The Soviets caught up with them at the border. They had to run for it but it was close. There was a gunfight. Ilona was shot, quite badly. They got her to a hospital and she recovered. But."

"But what?"

"Can't you guess, my dear? She couldn't have children. Too much damage. Women are sophisticated machines on the reproduction front, but delicate. Men not so much. But she was the one who took the bullets."

Rose tried to absorb this. Somewhere outside a sound system was starting up. An enthusiastic voice was trying to excite a crowd, not far away.

"There's an outdoor concert tonight in Erzsébet tér," said Penny. "A benefit for Kornai's campaign. I saw the set-up for it earlier. He'll make an appearance himself, apparently. We'll see if that will draw the crowds. Or hear."

Rose wasn't paying attention. She was thinking about Fairchild when they'd met, how grounded he'd seemed by his news. As if something positive had finally come of all his years of searching. But this? "So, Ilona – Elizabeth – wasn't his real mother?"

"His biological mother, no. And Viktor wasn't his father. They took him in and raised him as theirs. It all fitted nicely. They would have wanted kids of their own and were just about young enough. They were British, effectively, so they raised him the same way."

This was shocking enough for Rose. She was trying to imagine what it would be like for Fairchild. "Couldn't they have just told him the truth? Been honest with him about who they were, and who he was?"

Penny looked regretful. "That's exactly what they couldn't do."

"Why not?"

"Because they made a promise. And so did Walter, before you start berating him as well."

"A promise to whom?" Walter had made no mention of this earlier. The background voice had turned to music, introduced with shouty enthusiasm, some guitar band with a lot of bass.

Penny's glass was empty again. She refilled it. "Well, if Walter says tell you, I'll tell you. You know Ilona and Viktor were investigating Gregory Sutherland, as Grom was known back then. They had some contact with his girlfriend. Poor girl. She was terrified of him. At first she wouldn't say a word. But eventually she came forward. That incident in Japan was the catalyst, I think. An agent was lost, a boy."

Rose knew about this. "Grom recruited a vulnerable young Korean who was parachuted into North Korea and never seen since. He was completely unsuited to any kind of field role. It wasn't a misjudgement. It was vindictive."

"Precisely. Well, the information she gave Ilona and Viktor pretty much made the case against Sutherland. It became clear that he was selling secrets to the Soviets. Unfortunately…"

"He found out."

"How, we'll never know. No one was more careful than those two. But he got wind of it, and she had to disappear in a tearing hurry. Viktor and Ilona helped keep her hidden. They also managed to conceal between them that she was pregnant."

Oh, Christ. Penny only gave Rose the tiniest pause to let that sink in.

"She didn't want to be. Goodness knows what it was like for her. She was all for getting rid, but the three of them came up with another plan. She would have the baby and pass it to them to raise as their own. So they did. She disappeared, the Fairchilds had a son. It was all very discreet. In the meantime Sutherland pulled his car accident stunt and fled to the USSR, unaware of his progeny. Which was how we all hoped he'd remain."

All Rose could think about was Fairchild. What would he do when he found out? After decades of hunting and digging, this was surely the worst possible outcome.

"There's a lot to be said for not knowing." Penny was studying her. "This could eat him up. Or not. What if family loyalty comes into play?"

"No. That wouldn't happen. Couldn't."

"Or even just some hesitation, some weakness? You think Fairchild would be so quick to kill him, or see him killed, if he knew?"

Rose mulled on this. Fairchild had already passed up the opportunity to shoot Grom. By a lakeside in Siberia he'd held a gun to the man's head, but was somehow talked out of pulling the trigger.

"Grom is manipulative to the extreme, we both know that." Penny's voice was silky. "He can smell any weakness and seize upon it. He despises weakness, actually."

"He confuses weakness with humanity."

"Probably."

"In any case, I assume Walter swore you to complete secrecy."

"He did." Rose wasn't going to tell Fairchild. But she wouldn't need to. He'd discover the truth himself in time.

The silence was filled by the concert, some Latin beat now, Hispanic exclamations and heavy percussion. Rose emptied her glass, tasting nothing. If she ever had a child, she was thinking, she wouldn't spare them. She would immerse them in the truth. However much it hurt or set them apart from other children, or deprived them of innocence, they would be swaddled in it right from the start. No Santa Claus, no tooth fairy, no little white lies about what Mummy did, or where Daddy was. No secrets, not one. No seeds that would grow into trees bearing bitter fruit.

"I need air," she said, standing. "Do these open?" She moved towards the balcony doors.

Penny unbolted them and opened them inwards. The concert noise intensified. The balcony was nothing more than a railing and enough space for a row of plant pots. Rose took deep breaths of the cool air and gripped the railing. Below, a procession of heads passed by, well-wrapped people heading to the square.

"Looks like a crowd," said Penny, coming to stand beside her. "Busy, busy now. What a city this is. The ghosts are still here, though. In the back streets, the tunnels, a doorway here, a staircase there. You have to hunt them out now. They're being left behind." Her voice became husky.

Something dropped into place.

"You met someone here, didn't you?" said Rose. "When you were posted here."

Penny's glance across was sharp but her face softened and her eyes returned to the street below. "I expect you're the career type. That kind of thing's a weakness, a distraction. Me, no. Marriage, kids, I assumed that would all happen. But in the end…as you said, I met somebody. Not the right somebody, though. Not the right side of the Wall."

"What happened?"

"He came under suspicion. Because of his interest in me, largely. Why else would someone pay me such attention? He must have been a double agent, of course!" The anger in her voice was new; this was a different Penny Galloway. "My instincts said otherwise. But I listened to the reasoning of others, and set too much store by it. There was never anything in it. They admitted it later. Years later. Too late by then, though."

"Too late?"

"Dead. Oh, he'd have loved all this. If you'd been here before you'd know. You can feel the freedom in the air now. His dream came true, but he wasn't here to see it."

"I'm sorry. How did he die?"

"It doesn't matter how! It was years ago. Things might have been different, that's what matters. Trust your instincts, Rose. Let them guide you. They know better than rationalising functionaries who dream up self-serving motives. Not everyone is like that. Anyway. More pálinka?"

She started to move back inside but something in Rose's head suddenly clanged. "Did you say tunnels?"

"Yes, dear. There's quite a few. Don't look so surprised. What city of any size doesn't have tunnels? Though this one is particularly well equipped. There are miles of them on the Buda side. Formed out of natural caves in the hills."

But Rose was thinking about Marko and his friend. "Are there any up there?" She pointed.

"The Jewish Quarter? There is one network that goes that way. Man-made."

"What's it for?"

"Access, utilities, aborted Metro lines, maybe. Some say there's a nuclear bunker down there but we never located that."

"You researched them?"

"We mapped them. Thought they might be useful. Did quite a bit of investigation back in the day. Got hold of some infrastructure plans and pieced it together nicely. For a while, most of downtown Budapest was powered through a substation in that quarter. We realised it was quite a vulnerability. Our logistics team even planned out how an attack might work."

"You mean, to cause a power cut?"

"A major power loss across much of the city, it would have been. Could have facilitated any number of things. Obviously it would never have come back to us. We never had occasion to use it. I'm sure they must have changed it by now. That was decades ago."

But Rose was thinking about how she'd lost Marko. "This tunnel. Is there a way in through a courtyard in the Jewish Quarter?"

Now Penny seemed curious. "That was one way in, yes."

Something clicked into place, making her blood run cold. Power. Fairchild said Grom talked about power. Maybe he didn't mean it in the generic sense. Maybe he meant it literally. "Is there any way Grom would have known about the vulnerability?"

Penny frowned. "He could have heard about it."

"That could be his plan. Getting these extremists to take out the substation. Cut the power to the whole of the downtown. It would be typical of him to use information he got on the job against us. One of the guys I tailed to that area is a bomb-maker. I was right on them until he and his friend did a vanishing act in a courtyard. They could have accessed the tunnel."

"But that infrastructure is ancient. It must all have been replaced by now."

"What if it wasn't? What if they upgraded it all but are still using elements of the original? It happens in coding sometimes. My brother told me. You have an old product that gets upgraded beyond all recognition, but it's done using add-ons. There might be original code in there that's thirty years old."

Penny was absorbing this. "When? When do you think he's going to do this?"

Rose looked down at all the bobbing heads below, passing by to Erzsébet tér, on the cusp of the Jewish Quarter. "What if it's now, Penny? What if it's tonight? What better time than with some big concert on that's pulling people to the area? He's got a ready-made audience. Or a huge number of potential victims." The whole thing was urgent, suddenly. "Look, I've got to go. I'll phone people on the way."

"But you don't know where the substation is."

"I know where I lost them. That's a start."

"No, no. That's not where it is. I'll come with you."

"Really?"

"Yes, really. I can take you right there. No one else can."

Rose wasn't going to turn her down. "Should we jump in a cab?"

"No! It's quicker on foot." Penny was inside already, reaching for a coat. "The streets haven't moved since I was here. I know the best way, believe me."

Chapter 47

Returning from Vienna, Fairchild went straight to the Gellért. His anger had built during the long drive. He was fuming as he took the stairs two at a time and knocked on Grom's door. Grom opened it himself. He didn't even look surprised.

"Ah, young John! I knew you'd show up at some point."

"We need to talk." Fairchild practically spat the words.

"Any time for you, John." Grom stood aside in a display of welcome, though his face was tense.

Bogdan, once again, was at the table typing on a laptop. Maybe he never did anything else. His face darkened when he saw Fairchild. "What's he doing here?"

"He's just in time, Bogdan! You like an audience, don't you?"

"This wasn't the plan. It's too dangerous."

Grom gave a fake shrug. "What can I do? He's family, after all." There was a mischievous look on his face. "That's what this is about, isn't it, John? Don't be angry with me. I had to let you discover it for yourself. Point you in the right direction. If I'd just told you straight off you wouldn't have believed me. *I* wouldn't have believed me. And, you know, like father like son."

Fairchild punched him in the face. Grom staggered into the table which tipped up and sent the laptop sliding. He fell to the floor. Bogdan jumped up, swearing in Russian, grabbing the laptop. "Get out!" he shouted at Fairchild. "Get out!"

"No!" Grom was on the ground holding his jaw.

"We don't have time for this!"

"He should stay. He should see this." Grom sat up. "What do you think, John? Do you want to see the culmination of our plans? The high command's proof of concept? You'll get an excellent view. Or you can just leave if you want."

Bogdan stepped towards the door. "What are you doing? You can't tell him that then let him go! He'll squeal!"

"You think you can stop him?" said Grom from the floor. "Bogdan! When did you last go to the gym? Look at how he flattened me with one thump. Still, I'm in my seventies. Not that that stopped him. But you – he'll have you for breakfast. If he wants to go, let him go. Of course he knows nothing. If he's planning on telling anyone, what can he say? We're not controlling things from here, are we? They're all out there, the nutcases. It's in place already. We're just presenting it to our potential sponsors." He was sitting up on the floor now, facing Fairchild. His jaw was already swelling.

Bogdan's face was pinched. "We can't trust him."

"Search him, then. If he wants to stay. And if he doesn't – the man's a free spirit, let's remember. He comes and goes as he pleases. Something he's rather proud of. So let's see what pleases him."

They both looked at Fairchild. He raised his arms. "Go on, then. Search." Leaving now would achieve nothing. He needed to know what was happening. And Grom was his problem, he realised that. On top of his current project, this vindictive old man had been at the heart of all of his life's disasters and torments, even before he knew of the guy's existence. Resolution would only come from facing him.

Bogdan was thorough, knowing how to check for wires and pocket recorders as well as taking Fairchild's phone and putting it on the table out of reach. The Russian sat down at the laptop again. Grom was on his feet, feeling his face and smoothing down his hair.

Fairchild sat in an armchair. "So, another video call, then?" he asked. Bogdan looked up sharply.

"All in good time, John." Having straightened himself up, Grom poured himself a drink. A bottle of single malt whisky sat on a shelf. He didn't offer any to the others.

"I'm generally known as Fairchild." He hated Grom's over-familiarity.

"Why? It's made up. They fabricated it. Not a real name." Grom emptied his glass in one gulp. "Sutherland. That's your name. I wouldn't have called you John, either. I'd have gone for – oh, I don't know, something more memorable."

"You have no claim on me." He'd always known how to get under Fairchild's skin, but his words punctured even more now that Fairchild knew who Grom was to him.

"Then what are you doing here?" Grom crossed and looked over Bogdan's shoulder. "All ready?"

"I'm doing my best." Bogdan's scowl hadn't softened.

"Like I said before, I want the truth," said Fairchild. "Like you promised."

Grom gave an exaggerated shrug. "But you know it now! You know as much as I do. Maybe even more, from the schemers who helped her disappear. I knew nothing, remember? They got into her head, filled her with lies until she blabbed about everything. I tried to find her, but she'd been very well hidden. She didn't even tell me she was carrying my child." Grom moved towards him, more intense now. "For more than forty years I had a son I didn't even know about. Do you not think that would have made a difference?"

"Bullshit. You faked your own death and high-tailed it behind the Iron Curtain to avoid a treason charge."

"But would I have done that if I'd known about you? I never got the chance to find out. You're angry about old secrets. How do you think I feel? This treason thing, they had no proof, just poisonous rumours and supposition. But I knew they had it in for me, that little cabal, Walter, the hag Galloway and your so-called mummy and daddy. I left because I didn't know there was a reason to stay. I could have fought off those charges. I would have done, for you."

On the table, Fairchild's phone buzzed and lit up. "Oh! A message!" Grom stepped back to look at it. "It's from Rose! Isn't that sweet? I thought you two weren't in contact these days. See? Are you surprised we don't entirely trust you, John?"

Fairchild couldn't bring himself to say anything. If Rose was calling, it was something important.

"You're still free to go, by the way." Grom seated himself at the table opposite Bogdan. "But you'd miss the show. I anticipate it'll be a sound and light show, as you've not quite seen it before. Well – more sound, certainly. Less of the light. When I talked about power, did you not consider all meanings of the word?"

Something clicked into place.

Grom was watching him. "Cryptic, you see. Puzzles and games, levels of meaning. I'd have taught you about all that. They tried, the two Magyar pretenders, so I'm told. Obviously they didn't do a very good job of it."

Fairchild's phone buzzed again. Bogdan rolled his eyes. Grom glanced at the screen. "Ah! Rose again! I bet she's got it. She's probably en route now to the centre of the action. The hub, as they say. Her people know where it is. They've known for decades. That's how I know. She'll be too late, of course. I do hope she doesn't get caught up in it all. That would be most unfortunate. You could go running after her, if you wanted. Bogdan and I can't stop you."

Power. Power, in the sense that Darcy Tang meant it. Power as in electricity. Grom was going to cut the power. That was his plan. And he was right; Rose had already figured it out from their conversation in the ruin bar. A voice was screaming at him to grab the phone and bolt, get to her wherever she was. But still, he stayed. Grom was the problem, the man sitting in front of him right now. Fairchild was right where he needed to be. With no means of stopping him, and no way of getting a message to Rose.

The laptop dinged – an incoming message. "They're here," said Bogdan.

Grom stood. "Decision time. Are you staying with us, or not?"

Bogdan stood and closed the laptop. Fairchild realised they were both wearing outdoor shoes. They were on the move. "All right," he said.

"Seriously?" Bogdan rolled his eyes at Grom.

"Oh, come on Bogdan, what can he do? You searched him. The phone's staying here. If friends are on the way they'll find an empty room. Come on, let's go."

An unhappy Bogdan led the way down. An unmarked car was waiting for them outside.

Chapter 48

The Metro was too risky. Tas stuck to the buses. The first took him back out to the old factory where he practised. There, in a dry corner behind some pallets, he stashed a bin bag containing some personal things, a few clothes and all the money. Then he got one to the city centre. He tried to relax. Looking nervous would be bad, though every time he thought about what he was going to do, his pulse raced. As he got closer the bus filled up. Were all these people going there? Had he left it too late? He'd just have to see.

He got out at Astoria and walked to a bar he knew. It had murals of New York or some American city all over the walls, and a dingy basement he'd been to with Bálint a few times. But that wasn't important. It had two doors, that was why he came here – one at the front and one at the back. He went downstairs to the bar. With Bálint he used to have rum and coke, or a cocktail. This time he ordered a shot of vodka and knocked it back. Then he went to the toilets. The men's was just one room, right next to the ladies. Another reason to come here. He locked himself in and opened his bag.

He got the wig out first, and fastened it in place like he'd seen the Rebellion ladies do it. They'd even tried one on him once, a long time ago. They used to dress him up like he was their doll. He didn't mind. It was fascinating how different it made him look. He got out the make-up. This had to be quick. The bar wasn't busy. But someone would come along soon. Foundation was the most important. A light shade. He applied it generously but used the sponge to make sure it was even. Then the eyeliner and mascara. Lipstick, of course. That should be enough. No change of clothes. His coat was covering everything anyway, and it was an outdoor concert.

It was his face they'd be looking at, and they'd see a lovely young Hungarian girl, out for some fun. He smiled at himself and lowered his eyes flirtatiously. Good enough.

The door handle turned. He packed up quickly, flushed the toilet and exited, signalling an apology to a surprised guy standing outside. He went out of the front and set off on foot. The noise of the band grew as he got closer. The whole park was full but it wasn't a crush. Plenty of space for a small guy – girl – to squeeze through. No gates, no baggage checks, no tickets, no ID. Sure, there were police all round. Whatever. As long as he got in, he didn't much care about getting out.

He put his phone to his ear as if talking to friends and trying to find them. He worked his way through, not catching anyone's eye. The band finished their set. Screaming and whooping all round. He joined in, still pretending to look for his friends. He kept shuffling forward, moving into gaps that opened up, edging apologetically, until he was almost at the front. A little to the side, though. He didn't want to be too noticeable. More playing with his phone like he was texting someone, while they had some filler music on to change sets.

The next act came on, a rapper, his arms up in the air. The crowd erupted. Did they know or care what this concert was for? Probably not. He wouldn't have done, before. Now the whole thing seemed false, a sham. He joined in, moving with the beat, grinning up at the stage. Not much longer now. But it seemed to go on forever.

The rapper reached a fevered finale. He went off. He came back on again and did another one. He went off again. Then the host came on.

"Budapest! Let's hear it for our special guest!"

Some cheering from the back, before they'd even heard the name. And there he was! Béla Kornai, holding his hands above his head like the rapper did, bowing to the crowd. And Tas joined in, clapping and grinning, working his way ever closer like an adoring fan pulled in by his magnetism.

The crowd quietened down. Kornai took the microphone. "Budapest! Are you enjoying the music?"

Whoops and shouts. He had friends in the crowd, though not everyone was cheering. "All Hungarian!" he boasted. "See what we can do, what a great nation this is." Another cheer, but half-hearted. "Now, I won't keep you from your music." Kornai could read the crowd. Tas squeezed closer. He wasn't going to get much time. Kornai smiled like a benevolent parent. "But I want to say one thing to you all."

Kornai waited for near-silence. Tas did one final squeeze. Now he was standing directly in front of the guy, looking up at him. "We have a wonderful country," said the man. "We have a wonderful life here, the life we've chosen." A few murmurs around. "Don't take this for granted. It wasn't always so. You know our history. You know we had to struggle to resist, that we got no help from the West. Your grandparents in '56, they've told you, haven't they? They're heroes, every one of them."

More muttering. Were people agreeing or disagreeing? Tas tried to screen it out and think only of the gun in his pocket that he was now gripping. "Hungary is special," Kornai was saying. "We're unique. Our history is important. Our history makes us what we are. The people in the statues, their stories still need to be told. They gave us our freedoms."

Tas stilled his hand on the gun. He pictured it all in his mind, imagined how it would work, made sure he had the space around him. No silencer now. There was no time and no point.

"If you think the fight is over, I tell you it is not." Kornai was pointing a finger in the air. "It looks different now. No battlefields, no tanks. But there are people out there, maybe even right here, who want to rob us of our communities and our way of life. Our safety." The man's eyes roved over the audience. Tas gasped. For a moment Kornai was looking right at him. Did he know? But the great speaker took a breath.

"There are those who tell us we have no choice. That this change is inevitable. But who are these people? They're not us! They don't belong. They have no right to tell us how to live."

He kept talking but Tas screened out the words. Panic was rising in him. He had to do this now. It was the perfect time. But it was too perfect. It was too easy. He'd just walked up to the guy and was standing metres away from him. With a gun in his hand. It couldn't be that simple. He looked around wildly for security guards to surge forward, for them to shout and throw Kornai to the ground. But nothing. A couple of guys were on the stage staring out. But they were too far away. They couldn't stop it. There was nothing stopping him now except his own beating heart, his own weak spirit.

"Let's honour their memories the way we should," Kornai was saying. "Yes, of course, have fun and play games. But politics isn't a game. It matters. Your choices make a difference."

He was wrapping up. Do it, Tas! Do it!

"Vote in these elections. Don't leave it to others. Vote for what you value, for the lives we enjoy. For our families. For our home."

Tas was back in the open field with his father, conscious of every muscle in his body, how he was standing, ready in a second to make the shot. A slight sound, a flash of movement in the grass. His father's voice: *Now, Tas, now!* Kornai was drawing breath for his final words. Tas saw nothing except the white of his shirt, like the white chest of a running deer. He heard nothing, felt nothing except the weight of the gun as he readied it.

Aim and fire. He had one chance, just one, then all was gone.

He lifted the gun, aimed, and fired.

The bullet struck Kornai in the chest. He jerked and looked up as if surprised. Everyone was frozen except Tas and his prey. Tas fired again. Another hit in the chest. The man's knees buckled and he fell.

Someone screamed. Then all was movement and noise, the crowds around him backing off, the guards surging forward, hands to their belts. Tas threw the gun down and stood, arms raised, chin up, watching them defiantly.

They could kill him now. The job was done, though he felt nothing. This was the end of the tunnel. No more light. Nothing else mattered any more.

Chapter 49

Rose followed Penny round the back of Erzsébet tér. A long grassy stretch was packed full of concert goers. The stage at the far end was barely visible. As they cut through, the music gave way to a man talking.

"Is that Kornai?" Rose said. "What's he saying?"

Penny raised her head to listen. "Hungary, values, blah blah." They kept pushing through, squeezing past people facing the other way. "Just across the big street and we're almost there."

Rose had her phone in her hand. She'd got hold of Danny with a breathless imperative to get to the Jewish Quarter. Fairchild wasn't responding. Then a sound they both recognised brought them to a halt.

Two shots. A silence, and then a scream. They looked at each other. The noise around them crescendoed to a shouting babble.

"What's going on?" Rose said. Neither of them could see anything. Penny shook her head. The sounds of shock and chaos continued. Penny tapped the shoulder of a tall man standing in a group, his face pale, hand over his mouth. He said something to her that made her jaw drop.

"Kornai's been shot," she said to Rose.

"No way!" She glanced around. "This must be part of the plan."

In front of them people stared as if lost. Some were pressing forward, trying to see. Others were turning to leave. Sirens blared and blue lights reflected off walls and windows. Flashing vans surrounded the square. Police were filing out, vested up. The sound system crackled into life, an official voice talking urgently.

"They're sealing off the square," said Penny. "Nobody in or out."

"We can't stay here. This has got to be planned. We need to get to the place." Rose tried Danny again. Her phone beeped at her. "I can't even make a call. Everyone's on their phones and the cells are blocked. Which way is it?"

Penny pointed. The crowd was thickening as people moved to leave but couldn't. Rose and Penny reached a wall of increasingly stressed people. What to do? They looked at each other again.

"Do you think you can talk your way through a line of police officers?" asked Rose.

"Yes, dear. I'm just a frail old lady getting caught up trying to go home. Can you slip through if I distract them?"

"Maybe. If there's some cover."

"The bushes over there?" Most of the park was bordered by shrubs and trees.

"Let's try." Rose paused. "Could you explain to Danny on the phone how to access the tunnels?"

"I suppose so, if I had a phone."

In a few taps Rose disabled the pin code on her phone. "I'll go to the substation, you follow and direct Danny. Give him the tunnel access points so he can get them covered off. They'll be using them as an escape route, won't they?"

"That's what we'd have done."

"So tell me where the substation is, the one they need to take out."

"Are you sure? If they're serious they'll need to be pretty destructive."

"If there's something I can do, it's worth a try."

"It's in a derelict block. In the machine room. A separate building at the back of the courtyard." Penny gave her the street name and some basic directions. "There used to be a sign, but who knows now? There's a synagogue on the same street."

"Okay." Rose gave Penny her phone. Penny handled it like someone who knew their way around a smartphone. Interesting, but there was no time to dwell on that now.

Penny moved forward, working her way towards the shrubbery. Rose followed but hung back. Somehow getting herself through the crush, Penny stepped forward and managed to engage three officers at once in an animated conversation. She hunched herself over slightly, and all three had to lean forward to catch what she was saying. Without giving them time to think, Rose sidestepped a bush and squeezed herself through greenery. She came face to face with the side of a van. Too risky to go round. She dropped to her belly and slithered under. She froze. Right in front of her face were two boots which didn't seem to be going anywhere. Not moving a muscle she waited, praying their owner wasn't going to get into the van and drive off.

They didn't. The boots walked away towards the police line. No other footwear in sight, Rose emerged and hurried straight to the main street. She heard no commotion, no shouts. Glancing behind, she saw Penny still holding forth on the police line surrounded by a small crowd of officers.

All traffic seemed to have stopped, even the trams. Beyond the main road she sped up, running through narrow streets following Penny's hasty instructions. Some way off, another blast of sirens made everyone look up. Inside, the bars and restaurants were busy, everyone eating, drinking, talking as if nothing had happened. Maybe they didn't know. Maybe they did know but didn't know what else to do apart from carry on and follow events on their devices.

She found the street. This one was quieter, though as she jogged along the sound of an amplified bass got louder and louder. She passed the synagogue. Further up, an abandoned block still had its old sign outside. But when Rose got close, what she saw filled her with horror.

Chapter 50

The car took them up a winding road and through cobbled streets into the floodlit castle complex, raised up on the Buda side. It dropped them by a wide set of steps within a square, and drove off. The place was deserted apart from a lone security guard. Grom headed round the side of the steps to an unmarked door. They walked straight past the guard, who appeared to not even notice them. Inside, two flights up led to a corridor. Grom took them into a mid-sized room set out with table and chairs as if for a business meeting. It had a stunning view of the city.

"A little favour I was owed by a member of staff," said Grom, as if Fairchild had asked. "It's as well to be invisible for this next part. Of course I don't have to explain these things to you. You know all about calling in favours and disappearing when you want to. Cut from the same cloth, you see."

Fairchild bit his tongue. Grom wasn't entirely wrong about all of that.

Grom sat. Bogdan was already at the laptop. "Okay then. Connecting. Requesting to join meeting." The Russian seemed marginally calmer as he navigated. "Waiting. Still waiting." A tense pause.

Something popped up on his screen. "What the fuck?" His swearing had crossed the linguistic barrier.

"What is it now?" Grom was edgy.

"The news, for fuck's sake!" Bogdan half-rose from his seat. "Kornai's been shot!"

Grom jumped to his feet. "What? When?"

"Just now!" Bogdan was scrolling through news feeds. "At the outdoor concert. Right in the centre of Pest. What the hell is this?" His tone was accusing.

"I don't bloody well know, do I? Someone's gone off half-cocked. Done their own thing."

"You said you controlled these lunatics." Bogdan's face was red.

"Oh, shut up! Let me see." Grom grabbed the mouse and peered at the screen.

Fairchild stretched out, recrossed his legs and scratched his ankle. "Having a problem managing the troops?" he said languidly.

Grom turned to him sharply. "And why are you so relaxed?" His eyes narrowed. He looked Fairchild up and down.

"So what do we do?" said Bogdan.

Grom's attention snapped back to the Russian. "What do we do? We carry on! What else can we do? It's all set up now."

"Is it? How do you know? They could be doing anything out there! You have no idea!" He glanced at the door. "We should run. Get away from here, now!"

"Oh, grow up! We're fine. No one knows we're here. Think of all the preparation we've done. We can't walk away now."

"Preparation? Did you prepare to shoot the prime minister? Preparation means nothing!" Bogdan pushed his chair back and stood, looking again at the door.

Grom held his arms out. "Look. I don't know which joker thought that was a good idea. Maybe it was nothing to do with us. But Marko, the explosives guy, he's sound. He'll follow through. And that's the only part that really matters now."

Grom was doing a good job of acting calm. He had to. He needed Bogdan. That much had been clear from the start. It was vital Bogdan didn't walk. Fairchild, too, was maintaining his nonchalant appearance, though inwardly a sense of dread was growing, a heart-stopping image of Rose racing towards the crux of the chaos.

Grom's voice continued, smooth as mercury. "There's still time to disappear anyway, if the thing doesn't blow. We'll know straight away. But all of this means nothing if the high command isn't watching. This is for them, remember? That's where the money is. So let's get into this meeting and put on a good face. Okay?"

Bogdan's shoulders dropped. "Okay." He sat.

Grom drew up a chair next to him. "Are they ready for us now?"

"Yes. Ready." He clicked. Fairchild saw the same icons on screen as the previous meeting. Bogdan activated the mic.

"Are you there?" It was the American's voice, loud and abrupt.

"Yes, I'm here." Grom sounded impressively calm and collected. "Apologies for the slight delay."

"What the hell is going on? We knew nothing of any assassination!"

"Gentlemen, it seems we're not the only show in town tonight. The shooting, that wasn't our people."

Bogdan looked unconvinced. The American sounded the same way. "So it's just coincidence it happened at exactly the same time?"

"Not exactly the same time. We're ahead of schedule still. Someone else must have seen the potential with this concert."

"Whoever it was, it changes everything. I for one wish to cancel this whole thing immediately."

"Agreed." That was the Korean, Fairchild thought – and his wasn't the only voice.

Grom responded. "Gentlemen, let me reassure you. That other event won't affect us. It might help, in fact. The concert was a distraction. Now we have even more of a distraction. Local law enforcement will be completely tied up with it. Our little project will barely register."

A silence. The next voice was the South American. "I'd like to hear you assure us you didn't plan this. We don't like people doing their own thing. Fire Sappers is a disciplined organisation."

"Let me say it again. I had nothing to do with this." Grom sounded completely sincere. But with him, that meant nothing.

"And your people? Could someone have gone rogue?"

"It's always a possibility. But I doubt it. They wouldn't have that much initiative."

"So much for this weapon." The French speaker now. "Sounds like it's gone off early and hit the wrong target."

"As I said, I don't think so. There's nothing to link it to what we're doing."

"Still, you've heard our thoughts. We want to abort." The American's tone was brusque.

"Abort?" Grom was clearly working to keep his voice contained.

"You heard. Send the message out, please. Abort the operation."

Grom closed his eyes for a moment and took a breath. "I can't."

"You can't? What do you mean, you can't?"

"The explosives are set. They're on a timer. There's no one near the site now. Everyone's cleared the area." Bogdan looked up. His eyes rested on Grom. Was any of this true?

"With a little more time, gentlemen, but you can see for yourselves we have only minutes left. At this late stage..."

The Spanish speaker uttered a word that wouldn't generally be heard in a board room. "You're playing games. You planned this!"

"Absolutely not. Why would I do that? I know how important discipline is to Fire Sappers. It would make no sense." That much was true. It earned him a short silence. "I don't know who was behind this shooting, but I see no reason why it would impede our operation. And besides, it can't be stopped now. We have no choice, gentlemen, but to watch it play out. As previously planned, stand by."

The American came back in. "It sounds like we have no say in the matter. We'll discuss the implications of that later. In the meantime – standing by."

Chapter 51

Above the sign that said *Elektrotechnikai* something-or-other, a string of pink lanterns blinked on and off. A retro neon sign lit up letter by letter, then flashed on and off. *Open*, it read. Two guys with security badges sat by the doors. They looked at Rose but said nothing as she stepped inside.

The ground was covered by an expanse of artificial grass. Suspended above was a large cylindrical object, an engine or a turbine, attached to scaffolding with wires. Multicoloured tables and chairs filled the central space. A bar ran up one side, its surface decorated with images of palm trees and sailing boats. Along the opposite wall hung gigantic dials with red and black hands, boards of chunky switches and fuses, and warning signs featuring text with exclamation marks and people being struck by bolts of lightning. More modern signage showed drink and food menus in bright colours.

Spotlights overhead created a pool of yellow in the middle of the courtyard. Lines of globe-shaped bulbs stretched across, their elements glowing. On the building at the back, more spotlights picked out a visual of an old-fashioned giant plug and the word *Spark*. Rose saw the same graphic on the menus now, sitting on each table.

She walked through with mounting dread. Across the back sat a separate single-storey building – the machine room. In front of its arched windows was more scaffolding supporting a Perspex roof, under which was a row of tables with checked tablecloths. Trailing plants hung down in front of the windows. And people! Around every table a group of people. At the bar, in the courtyard, coming in through the doors. A couple of hundred at least.

How long had this place been operating? It could have sprung up overnight. Did Grom know the abandoned works was now a ruin bar? Did he care? He was indifferent at best to human survival. He'd said that about her, once.

Hopefully Danny and the authorities were on their way. But she couldn't wait for that. If the shooting was planned as a distraction, this could go up any time. She scanned the walls and found what she was looking for, a giant red button in a glass case. She grabbed a beer bottle, smashed the glass and pressed the button.

Nothing. It was a prop. Decoration. Part of the theme. Great! She carried on. Tucked in a corner she found a smaller, more modern version, the wires leading out of it suggesting it was live. She smashed and pressed. A high-pitched wailing started. Bar staff exchanged glances. Customers looked round, curious. No one showed any sign of heading for the exit.

"Get the fuck out of here!" But Rose only said it to herself. She had to carry on. She hurried through to the machine room. As she passed, the bar staff were starting to mobilise, moving out into the courtyard and approaching drinkers. She could only hope they would take it seriously. She made her way round the side of the building. Boxes of bottles and cans were piled up high against the wall. If there were a way in there, no one had used it recently. She carried on. In the centre of the long wall at the back were steps up to a wooden door. The door was bolted with a rusty padlock and clearly hadn't been used for years. But the building was sound; the roof had been maintained, the windows were unbroken. She carried on, hoping no staff member would venture back here. The fire alarm, still going off, ought to occupy them.

In the middle of the remaining side was a modern metal door. She pulled. It was locked. She got out her lock-picking kit, concealed as a manicure set in her cosmetics bag, and set to work. Down the side wall she could see people moving about in the courtyard. If someone standing in the right place looked up, they would see her. Another reason to hurry.

Her pick met resistance. There was a key in the lock. That meant two things. One, at least one person was inside. Two, it was going to be near-impossible to enter silently. No matter; she had to try. A twist, and the key fell out of the lock. With her ear to the door she heard it hit a tiled floor. She carried on, making an effort to shut out the fire alarm, the shouts from the courtyard and the music, which was still going on for some reason.

Got it! The lock clicked and she could press the handle down. She stashed her gear and pulled the door open. What she saw was a long dark corridor, the length of the entire building, street light entering through the windows and patches of darkness in between. The windows ran down one side. Down the other side was a series of high metal panels, obscuring what was behind. The noise outside was strangely muted in here. That was all she had time to take in.

"Don't move." The voice was quiet. "You stay right there." In the gloom she noticed something slumped on the floor below the level of the windows. But the voice was coming from beyond that. Out of the darkness of the far corridor emerged a gun, pointing at her. And the holder of that gun was Zsuzsanna.

"What are you doing here?" Rose couldn't hide her shock. "You're not part of this."

Zsuzsanna's eyes moved to the bundle on the floor. Rose could see a face now. It was Marko, crouched on the ground.

"Don't go near him," said Zsuzsanna. "Stay where you are." She pointed the gun at Marko. "I said, put your hands on your head." Her voice was cold. Marko complied.

Rose couldn't make it add up. "What's going on? Why are you here?"

"I had you followed." Zsuzsanna didn't take her eyes off her husband.

"The boy?" asked Rose.

"Some Roma. They'll do anything for a few coins. I set you up on the hill as well. You enjoyed that, did you? I wanted you to know how it feels. Just a little."

"If that was meant to be a kind of revenge, you took it out on the wrong person. I didn't rape you. I didn't beat you up."

They were both looking at Marko now. He was unmoved. "You spied on me, you two-faced bitch." He practically spat at Zsuzsanna. "You got what you deserved."

"No." Zsuzsanna's hands were rock steady. "You owned me right from the start. You thought you had some God-given right to do what you wanted with me. Always! Even when I was just a girl!!"

"I treated you well."

"You mean you didn't hurt me when I did exactly what you wanted?" Her scorn strengthened her volume.

"I don't deserve this. You could have left if you didn't like it."

"I did leave! I ran away! But you came after me! You wouldn't let me go!" Now there was heat in her voice. This was Tihana, now, the one Rose remembered. "And all those things you did! Those unspeakable things!"

"That had nothing to do with you. I didn't involve you. You should have kept out of it."

"You were an animal. You were then and you are now. That's why I didn't want your child. *She* knew it!" A nod of the head brought Rose into the conversation. "*She* understood why I did it. But you would have killed me."

Rose could hardly breathe. She could see on Marko's face that he was working it out. Zsuzsanna had just told him her secret, the secret that Rose had used as leverage on a reluctant Tihana, the secret that so scared her that she turned informant on him and lived a dangerous lie for years.

"You got rid of my child?" The shadows emphasised the lines on Marko's face, turning him into a comic-book rendition of an angry man. "You aborted my child? And you're calling *me* an animal?"

"It was my right. But you wouldn't understand that."

"You're just another of them." He sounded disgusted now. "Rights and values, anti-Christian bullshit! I was glad when you left in the end. I saw through you for what you really were."

"You didn't follow her to Budapest?" Rose was confused. Marko's lips curled upwards. He looked almost triumphant.

"You have it wrong, Anna," said Zsuzsanna. "I've been looking for Marko, not the other way round. That's why I did all that research. I came here because I heard he was in Budapest."

"And how come I was dragged into this?"

"Like I said, I saw you!" Zsuzsanna was smiling, even though her eyes never left Marko. "I couldn't get any further with all the information I had. Years of work and it was all a dead end. But I knew if I gave it to you, you'd lead me to him in the end. You and your friends. And so you did. My Roma people brought me here. I found the tunnel and I've been waiting inside ever since." Her eyes were shining.

"Why?"

"Why do you think? I'm going to end this piece of diseased humanity. Don't think I can't. He knows I can."

Marko glanced into the corridor behind Zsuzsanna. In the shadows Rose could make out another bundle below the window. Zsuzsanna had already taken a life this evening.

"Zsuzsanna," Rose said. "Do you know why Marko is here? What's in this building, behind this panelling? It's an electrical substation. Marko here has rigged it with explosive. Haven't you?"

She turned to him. He just gazed at her. But there was no surprise, no shock.

"When is it timed for? The tunnel comes up in here, doesn't it? You were going to use it to escape." Marko smiled, cold like a reptile. "It's now, isn't it?" No change of expression. "To coincide with the shooting."

He frowned. "What shooting?"

"He's not going to tell you, Anna. He's just playing games." Zsuzsanna's grip tightened on the gun.

"Zsuzsanna, wait! Marko's the only person who can stop it."

"He's not going to stop it. Look at him! He's laughing at us!"

Rose took a step towards Marko. "There are hundreds of people out there. Just people enjoying themselves. Why do you want to hurt them?"

"For the greater good." His eyes glinted. "It's okay for you, is it? To think like that? To sacrifice people for something bigger? But when ordinary folk try it, there's outrage."

"There's nothing ordinary about what you're doing." Rose took another step. "Out there you have ordinary folk, nice folk, white Christian folk, the kind you approve of, living their lives without harming anyone, and you're going

262

to blow them to kingdom come. You're being manipulated, Marko. Someone's been pulling your strings if you think this attack is going to help your cause in any way. I know who it is, as well. An older guy. Maybe Russian, maybe British. Says a lot of clever things. Throws his weight about. Convincing." Marko's face showed unease; he recognised the description.

"Stay away from him." That was Zsuzsanna, still aiming the gun. But Rose ignored her and crouched in front of Marko.

"He's on a different agenda, that guy. Believe me. I know him. Ask yourself. Look at it again. He's persuaded you that this makes sense. But in your own mind, does it?"

"I said stay away from him!" Zsuzsanna was almost shouting. Rose lurched backwards and struck out at Zsuzsanna's arm. The gun went flying and hit the ground in the dark somewhere. Rose punched the woman in the face, hard. Zsuzsanna fell to the ground and stayed there.

Rose turned back to Marko. "Can you stop the explosion? Can you stop the bomb going off?"

He smirked. Whatever doubt she'd fostered before had evaporated. Rose grabbed him by the shoulders. "Look. Whatever happens in here, it won't go well for you. Help me stop this and I'll help you. You can claim you were manipulated. Come on, Marko. It's your best chance here!"

His smirk turned into a grin. "So you're my friend now, are you?"

"If I have to be. For God's sake, Marko, do the right thing, even if it's only to save yourself! Will you stop it? Can you stop it?"

From below their feet came a distant thunderclap. The ground shook. Marko's eyes were on Rose. "No," he said. "It's too late."

A shattering blast made her leap back. Marko's head exploded into blood and bone. Spatters covered her face. His body slumped. Zsuzsanna was standing right behind her, gun in hand.

"He wasn't going to tell you," she said.

A ripping, tearing noise split the air. The sound of shattering glass like a thousand bells. The metal plating bent towards them like it had been punched.

"We've got to run!" Rose turned for the door, Zsuzsanna behind her. A *whump* vibrated through her, then a roaring from below. She was sprinting full pelt. A metal sheet flew across her path. She tripped and went head first. Some force shoved her sideways into the wall. It all went dark.

Chapter 52

There were so many police on him it was ridiculous. Tas wasn't even trying to go anywhere. All the instructions. *Hands above your head! Feet apart!* They searched him, pushing and pulling, gripping his arms like a vice. He knew this bit wouldn't be good. He wondered about trying to run so they'd shoot him, but there were so many of them it seemed hopeless. They were discussing – arguing – where to take him, shouting at each other over all the noise. What was up with Kornai? Had he killed the guy? He didn't even know. It felt sweet, though, seeing him fall. A rich, dark feeling inside. A new feeling.

The mass of uniforms began to move. They pulled him along, surrounded. Would he go into a van and then into prison, like Bálint? Whatever.

Something changed. The lights went out. The big floodlights, the stage lights, everything. It was pitch black. The group stopped. Questions flew about. *What's going on? Power cut? Where? Even the street lights? That can't be right. Are the radios working?*

The babble of the crowd became frenzied. *They're breaking out of the square! What do we do?* In the whirl of confusion, the grip on his arms loosened. A thought came to Tas. Not even a thought, just a sense, some instinct he didn't even know was there. A force, a desire he didn't expect or plan formed inside him, underneath all the jabbering and shouting.

He twisted, kicked and bit all at the same time. Hands came at him. He slunk down low and dodged, darting into the crowd. They were right behind him. He shoved and pushed without caring that people staggered and cried out.

"Stop her!" someone shouted. It took a few seconds to realise they were talking about him. "She's the killer! Grab her!" But this seemed to make people pull away. He was faster now and knocked against them like a pinball through a machine, but no hands came grabbing. He had no idea which way he was going. It was pitch black except for flashes from mobile phones. Suddenly the crowd thinned and he was running forward, free.

"Get her! Get her!" Hands came forward to seize him, more bulky police uniform arms – but he swerved and twisted and bit. They shouted and swore. "Animal!" His head hit something heavy, a wall of flesh. A pain as his face grazed something sharp. "Got her!" Tas struggled. The hands grasped. But they were only holding the sleeves of his jacket and his hair. A sweep of his head and the wig detached. He wriggled out of his jacket and pelted away. Three or four steps and the guy realised what was going on. A frustrated shout. But Tas was quick on his feet.

Which way? Down, down to the river. Buildings loomed, unlit. Lights from cars and buses crisscrossed, making deep moving shadows. Tas kept to the dark, pounding relentlessly. The gap was opening up. But he was one and they were many. Like a fox, he was the prey now and they were the hunters, the dogs.

He turned a corner, and another one. There! An expanse of starry sky. The river. He sprinted down the narrow street. That was when he heard the first shot. Without thinking he veered one way and another. More shots, the bullets swallowed by the dark.

The riverside highway. A car was coming but Tas couldn't stop. He ran out into the headlights, clearing the bonnet by an inch as it screeched to a halt. Beyond that, the tramway.

A tram sat, stranded. Over the tracks, an iron fence. He scaled it, looked down and stopped.

Below – a good way below – was blackness. Was it water? Dirt? Rubble? There was no telling.

A shot. Another. He was a target here, silhouetted against a blue starry sky. The dogs approached, the hunters took aim.

He stood straight, and stepped out. A volley of shots burst like a firework.

He fell.

Chapter 53

There was no sound. That was the unreal thing. But exactly on cue, exactly as Grom had his audience expecting, one whole section of the cityscape in front of them disappeared. Then another, then another, then the lights in the room went out, the glow from Bogdan's laptop making a faint blue aura.

"You see?" Grom's aside to Bogdan was triumphant. But Bogdan was too busy to react. He was typing, utterly focused on the laptop. Fairchild could only see code on the screen. Bogdan was hacking something.

"So here we are, right on cue. The webcam we set up for you, what you should see is total darkness. An entire city centre blacked out. And this will last for precisely five minutes. I hope you're timing it. I certainly am."

While Bogdan coded furiously, Grom sat back in his chair surveying the dark city. He loved this, the controlling bastard. Now was his chance to restore confidence. He talked as though giving a lecture.

"Imagine what you could do if you knew in advance exactly when and where such an outage would happen, and for how long. If you were set up for it. By-passing firewalls. Entering secure premises. Altering records. Stealing data. Stealing anything. And this can be done on demand, anywhere. The people on the ground, they have the kind of programmable hatred that can be directed at anything or anyone we want. A bottomless pit, an ever-renewing well of resentment and fear. Doesn't matter what sparked it originally. Any ideology can be twisted and warped. This isn't ideology any more. It's pure emotion. But this particular grouping, this alt-right way of thinking, is particularly wide-ranging in terms of identifying the enemy. Which makes them useful to you. Of course there's no need for them to know about you. The uses to which you put their destructive tendencies will remain confidential. How are we doing?"

That last was to Bogdan.

"One minute." Bogdan was a picture of concentration.

"Sixty more seconds, gentlemen. If this were more than merely a test, you would need to be wrapping up and getting out by now, virtually or physically. Without wanting to reveal the whole trick, the destroyed hub does have a backup. Normally the explosion would have resulted in an outage of just a few seconds, but with the expertise at my disposal here, we're hacking into the municipal system to delay the by-pass for the precise period of time."

Around them, everything was still silent. Fairchild heard, very faintly, a siren going past in the street.

"Time?" Grom said to Bogdan.

"Is up." Their eyes met.

"Okay."

Bogdan tapped a button. The code screen disappeared. The lights in the room flickered on.

"We're back!" Behind Grom's supremely self-satisfied head, the lights of Budapest began reappearing in swathes. "I believe that was precisely five minutes." Bogdan had restored the conference call window on the laptop, and sat back, exhausted. "I welcome your assessment, fellows, but from our side it all seemed a success."

A thundering crunch. The door flew open. "Hands in the air! Now!" Rapp was first, gun at the ready. Zack was right behind. Others crowded in. Fairchild was on his feet. So was Grom.

"You!" Rapp was on Bogdan like iron filings on a magnet. "Hands up! Don't touch that keyboard!" She was aiming at his head. Two others came in and pulled the laptop away from him, handling it like some valuable object.

Grom was by the window, looking straight at Fairchild. "You lying bastard. This was you, wasn't it?"

Fairchild realised two things at the same time. One – they weren't windows Grom was standing next to. They were balcony doors. Two – Grom was holding a gun.

"He's armed!" he shouted, and hurled himself forward, straight at the man. Grom raised his arm. A ton of Ohio muscle shoved Fairchild sideways. Grom fired – and hit Zack full in the chest. The force knocked him backwards. Fairchild fell, Zack's bodyweight propelling him into the wall.

"Freeze! Get your hands up!" Two more of them advanced, aiming over the top of Fairchild and Zack. But Grom was already on the balcony behind the glass. One of them fired. The bullet shattered the glass from top to bottom, turning the pane into a spider-web mosaic. But the shape on the other side was still moving. Fairchild scrambled up and stepped over Zack onto the balcony. Grom was out of sight. He followed the balcony round a corner and then inward to a passageway and a door back into the building. The door was ajar. Fairchild raced through into a corridor with a lift at the end. The lift door was closing. Grom was inside. He stood, watching as Fairchild sprinted the length of the corridor. Just as he got near, the door closed and the lift started to descend.

There was only one lift but a flight of stairs next to it. Fairchild hammered down them. Flight after flight. He was descending way further than they had gone up to get to the room, but still there was more. His leg muscles were burning. The carpet gave out and the stairs continued uncarpeted. At the bottom was nothing except an unmarked fire door. He pushed. It opened. Behind it was a corridor lit with sporadic fluorescent lights. Its walls and ceiling were curved. Not a corridor. A tunnel.

He ran. The tunnel bent round and led him to a junction. Both options looked identical. He chose one and kept running. Another junction. Then another. Which way was he heading? East? The way the tunnels curved round he couldn't be sure. At the next junction he stopped. Apart from his own heaving breath it was silent. The air was musty. In every direction identical white-painted walls disappeared out of sight. This place was a lot bigger than he realised. Where the hell was Grom?

This wasn't going to work. He was never going to find him like this. He started walking back the way he came.

He stopped. He was hearing a sound, a faint tapping. The tunnels were lined with copper pipes. The sound was too light and rapid to be something mechanical. It started, then it stopped. Started, and stopped. It was the same pattern, repeated. Intermittent gaps.

It was Morse code, for God's sake. Two dashes and a dot. Dot-dash-dot. Three dashes. Two dashes. G-R-O-M. He was spelling out his own name. In the cool of the tunnel Fairchild shivered. Was all of this part of a bigger plan?

He should give up and turn back while he could still remember the way. But that tapping drew him in. He'd made a promise, to Rose as well as himself, that if he had another opportunity to kill Grom he would. His work for Darcy Tang was done. As far as Fire Sappers were concerned, Bogdan was always the person of interest; it was he who had access to the high command. Fairchild no longer needed Grom. And here he was, in a tunnel somewhere, just the two of them and a gun. Fairchild fancied his chances against the older man. Would he hesitate, now he knew who he was? No. Not for a second.

He bent to get his ear closer to the pipes. He followed the pipe that was resounding the loudest. The sound grew as he walked. Once or twice he took a wrong turn and the noise died off. He'd backtrack and choose a different path. The pattern of taps continued unabated. Grom wanted to be found. That was the worrying thing.

The pipe led him into a smaller tunnel, unpainted and unlit. Light from the lamps behind reached for a while, but this tunnel soon bent round, leading Fairchild into total darkness. The tapping was louder. He moved forward slowly. The walls were closer here and the air stale. He crept on, feet feeling the uneven floor, one hand outstretched in front, the other on the tapping pipe. How long he kept on like that he didn't know. Give up, turn back, an inner voice said to him, but he carried on, losing count of the junctions he passed.

Up ahead he saw the ghostly edge of an arch. A light source of some kind. An exit? He was starting to itch to be out of this place, but there was no new freshness in the air. He got closer, the tapping got louder, and the sides of the tunnel became distinct. Here they were not smooth and painted but rough rock, the sides of a cave. A pool of light came into view on the ground next to a turn-off. Fairchild sped up but slowed as he approached.

The tapping ceased. "Finally! I thought you'd never get here. Did you stop for a picnic on the way?"

Fairchild stepped into the pool of light. There, in the turning, was Grom, his gun in one hand and a torch in the other. "It's just you and me now."

"How do you know the others aren't right behind—"

"They're not. Are they?" Here he was again, predicting what Fairchild would do, always a step ahead. "Whatever hidden tracking device you have won't work down here, either. Way too much rock. You fooled Bogdan nicely there. What is it, the latest miniature gadget from the technical boffins? Or did you secrete it into an orifice?"

It was actually rather neatly hidden inside a band-aid on his ankle, activated by a swift touch. Fairchild had given in to Zack in the end. But he wasn't going to tell Grom all about it. "Are you trying to say you planned all of this?"

"Would it astonish you so much? Takes a lot to impress you, doesn't it?"

"You just tried to shoot me. And now you're claiming you had some other plan for me?"

"Oh, come on, Fairchild, I saw that blundering Yank coming a mile off. And before you start crying over him, those guys are coated in Kevlar so thick it won't even leave a bruise."

"You're full of shit. That wasn't even the first time you've tried to kill me. Now you're saying that whole venture with Fire Sappers was some kind of ruse for my benefit? Hardly."

"You're right. It wasn't a ruse. But I put it all at risk for you. I never trusted you. But I let you right in. I showed you everything."

"Why?"

"To impress you. To win you. To show you what I can do. You're my son! And what a son you are. Look at you. Anyone would be proud." His voice was husky. He sounded like he meant it, for Christ's sake. No one had said anything like that to Fairchild before.

He continued, his voice an echoing mutter. "I meant every word of what I said to the high command. We could have done great things. But you were more important.

273

Bringing you here, making sure you uncovered Walter's dirty secret, the truth about you and me. I know they've poisoned your mind. I had to be prepared for you to betray me. Hence the Plan B. And here we are now!"

"You planned an escape for yourself and left Bogdan carrying the can?"

"A pity, but he let his greed get in the way of his good judgement. He had eyes only on the money. Didn't question anything else."

This was a bit rich coming from one of the world's greatest embezzlers, but Fairchild let it pass. "Fire Sappers won't be pleased. If any of them get away clean, they'll hold it against you."

"They won't get away clean. Not with Bogdan pleading for leniency. Besides, the same might be said about you. It was your betrayal that caused the raid."

"They don't even know I was in the room."

"They don't even know *I* was in the room. Bogdan is the only name in the frame, remember? Everything I told them about myself might equally be true of him. See how similar we are, John? We both like to be free, to slip away, invisible, to be loyal only to ourselves."

"I don't treat people like that."

"Really?" A meaningful pause.

"Well, only if they deserve it."

"Me too, John! Me too. So what happens next? It's up to you. I'd like us to call a truce. Now we both know who we are. Let's spend some time together. See if we can work something out."

"That's easy for you to say when you're pointing a gun at me."

Grom looked thoughtful. "Fair enough." Without warning he tossed the gun down. It skittered off out of sight beyond the beam of the torch. Fairchild did his best to work out exactly where it was. Grom was closer to it. But Fairchild could be faster.

"See?" said Grom. "If I wanted to kill you I'd have done it by now. That's not what I want. I want a chance to show you who I really am."

"You've already done that. You've done nothing but lie to me."

"Oh, nonsense! I'm the one who gave you the truth! In the only way that would have let you believe it. It's the Service cabal that's been leading you a merry dance your whole life. Forget about them, John. Spend more time with me and you'll realise that what you've discovered so far is the least of it. They've drummed it into you for so long that I'm the enemy, you can't see how alike we are. Your network, your modus operandi, your roving statelessness, where do you think you got all that from?"

"I've lived that way for one reason only, and that was to find out what happened to my parents."

"Your parents?"

"To the people who raised me."

"Then why are you still doing it? Don't tell me you don't enjoy this life. This constant shifting, getting to know people, understanding their motivations, using them for your own ends. You don't fit anywhere else now. In the UK, in Hungary, you're a stranger everywhere. You were a cuckoo's egg, always in the wrong nest. I'm your only family now. In the whole wide world, John, I am the person most like you. Don't dismiss it. Don't dismiss me. Give me a chance. We can be cuckoos together."

"I've given you plenty of chances. I've told you before. I'm not you. I don't want to be and I never will be."

Grom gave a mock sigh. "That's a shame. I was hoping to see some strength in you but you seem to prefer weakness. I suppose what you think you want is for me to have no further role in your life."

"You could put it like that." Fairchild managed to avoid looking in the direction of the gun, though his thoughts went there.

"Very well, then. I have another proposal for you. I said I was the person in the whole world most like you. But that may not be true. There's another, isn't there?"

He waited to see if Fairchild caught on. He did. Grom was talking about Fairchild's mother. "You must be curious about her." His own face in shadow, Grom was watching Fairchild's expression. "Find her for me. Find her, and I'll leave you alone. You can do it. Your global reach, I don't say this often, John, but it's better than I ever managed. You could track her down. You want to, don't tell me otherwise. You could satisfy your own curiosity and get me off your back forever. And that means I'll walk away from everyone else you know as well."

He meant Rose, and by association, MI6. A world without Grom was certainly an attractive idea, but he couldn't be trusted. "How do you know she's still alive?"

"I don't. That's what I want to know. And if she is, where she is."

"What for?"

"Reconciliation. At my time in life, John, you reflect on your own mortality and what it all means. She and I had a child together. That child grew up into a remarkable man. The three of us, we share something special, whether you want to admit it or not. It's time to put the past behind us now."

"Bullshit. You want to find her so you can punish her. She hid from you for a reason. I won't lead you to her."

Grom sniffed. "That's your final answer, is it?"

"Absolutely."

Grom raised his hands. "I guess there's nothing else to talk about."

"That's right."

Neither man moved.

"You can leave, you know," said Grom. "Walk away."

Fairchild didn't. He was thinking about the gun again.

"Well, go on, then, if you're going!" Grom was practically shooing him off. "Good luck getting out, by the way. You know there are ten miles of cave down here? I know the layout, studied it, memorised it. I bet you don't."

Grom was right but it didn't matter. This wasn't about walking away. It was about finishing the job. In one sudden movement, he dived for the gun. But Grom had anticipated. He stepped in front and shoved Fairchild hard into the wall. Grom was on his knees in front of him scrabbling in the dark. The torch was on the ground pointing away.

A glint of metal. They both saw it at the same time. Grom got there first. He turned the gun as Fairchild lunged to grab him – and fired.

The noise amplified into an echoing roar. The pain was red-hot. Fairchild's knees gave way. Grom was on his feet. Fairchild rolled on the gritty floor. He put his hand on his stomach. It was wet. Grom was within reach but Fairchild had no strength.

Grom sniffed again. "Disappointing." He picked up the torch, casting the beam over Fairchild's hunched body. "Looks like you'll have a little while to ponder your life choices. Not too long, though."

Grom turned to walk away. The pain, the pain flowed through Fairchild's whole body. But it was only pain. It would be over. Grom wasn't walking away, not this time.

Fairchild pulled himself up and launched himself at the man, leading with his shoulder. Grom stumbled forward. Fairchild pressed his face into the cave wall, grabbed his right arm and twisted it. Grom yelped with pain and dropped the gun. But his other elbow caught Fairchild in the face. Pulling back, Grom rammed the torch into the side of Fairchild's head. Dazed, he thrashed out, going for Grom's own face. He found it and punched again. Grom backed up against the wall and dropped the torch – or did he throw it? The bulb smashed and they were in darkness.

Fairchild grabbed to pin him to the wall but somehow Grom dodged beneath his grip, going for the gun again. Fairchild threw himself down. Grom was on the ground beneath him. A wave of pain engulfed him. Grom was reaching out. A grind of metal on stone told him Grom had found the gun. Ignoring the dizziness, Fairchild launched himself forward on top of Grom's prone body, and felt for the man's outstretched arm. He jammed his knee into the man's shoulder and neck. Grom couldn't lift his arm. Fairchild's fingers met Grom's, gripping the gun. He couldn't prise the old man's fingers off the thing. He rammed down hard with his fist, again and again, on his hand and wrist. The man was gasping and spluttering underneath him. Eventually his grip weakened. Fairchild pulled the gun from between his fingers. But his strength was ebbing.

A force pushed up into his abdomen. The pain was intense, paralysing. Grom pushed again, rolling him back into the wall. Fairchild could hear his rasping breaths inches away but he couldn't move. The man was climbing to his feet. Fairchild set his teeth. If this were the last thing he was going to do, so be it. He tightened his grip on the gun.

A foot smacked into his chest. Grom was aiming for his wound again, but missed. In the pitch black Grom was just a mass above him, preparing for the next assault. Fairchild lifted himself up, though it felt like he was being ripped apart, aimed the gun, and fired.

Grom gave a long guttural sound, like some animal, and fell, hard, onto Fairchild. Pain exploded. That was enough, now. That was all he could manage.

The gun slipped from his grasp and he passed out.

Chapter 54

Sounds were distorted. All around and echoing, but somehow far off. Rumbling engines, sirens, shouting. Rose opened her eyes.

She was sitting up against a vaulted brick wall in a space lit with fluorescent tubes. Zsuzsanna was sitting watching her, looking deeply calm, the ghost of a smile on her face.

"The tunnel," Rose said.

"Yes. This is how I got in. How they were planning to leave. We can get out here." She pointed to a metal gate. Behind it was the bottom of a flight of spiral steps.

"What happened?"

"You got a knock on the head. I pulled you down here. We only just got clear."

Rose felt her forehead. It was painful and sticky. She couldn't see the end of the tunnel. "You dragged me here?"

"I managed. You should go to a hospital."

"Again?"

Zsuzsanna looked ashamed. "Sorry about before. I was angry with you for a long time. But now you have set me free. In a way I didn't expect."

Set her free? It made no sense. Rose looked down. A gun was lying by her hand. "What's this?"

"It's Marko's gun. The one you shot him with."

"I didn't shoot him."

"But you did. I wasn't there."

Zsuzsanna searched Rose's face for comprehension. The penny dropped. "Okay. I killed Marko to try and prevent him detonating the bomb. You weren't involved in any way. I haven't seen you for weeks, in fact. It was just me in there."

Zsuzsanna's face lit up with a broad smile. "Thank you."

After everything that had happened to the woman, it was the least Rose could do. "I came looking for you. Your office was empty."

"We were shut down. I said they were trying to close us. It doesn't matter. It's time to move on, anyway."

"How did you manage to overpower two men and take their weapons?"

"I was waiting for them. They weren't expecting me. I've spent some time with some bad people these past few years. Learning what I needed to know. I realised I'd never be free while Marko was alive. Now the job is done I can forget all that." She got up. "Time to disappear."

"Thank you for saving me."

"Thank you for saving *me*." Her voice was relaxed and melodious, echoing in the tunnel, the voice that Rose remembered from years ago.

"Where will you go?"

"Anywhere I like. Take care, Anna." She turned to go.

"Rose." Zsuzsanna turned back, frowning. "My name is Rose Clarke. My real name. Goodbye, Tihana."

She nodded and walked away, squeezing through the gate and stepping lightly up to the street.

Chapter 55

When they finally found each other, Danny's delight that Rose had survived gave way to concern, and a very fast journey to the emergency department. Explaining that not all the blood was hers didn't change the imperative that she had to stay there overnight. She protested, but when she finally awoke was told she'd been asleep for the best part of two days. Danny came by shortly afterwards, carrying Hungarian pastries. Better than grapes, he said, though they tasted like sawdust to Rose.

They updated each other. Danny told her the explosion killed two people in the ruin bar. The shattering glass caused a lot of injuries, mostly minor. Setting off the fire alarm had drastically reduced the number of casualties. The resultant five-minute blackout had caused a few more incidents, but it wasn't long enough for major issues such as looting to really get going. Danny passed on what Rapp had told him about events at Buda Castle.

"The five-minute timescale was planned. Merely an example of the kind of service this Grom character wanted to provide Fire Sappers in exchange for enormous sums of money. Thanks to Fairchild's alert, Bogdan was caught red-handed."

"Where is Bogdan?"

"Stateside somewhere. Rapp had him flown out of the country within the hour. I expect he'll give up the whole lot in exchange for leniency. Sounds like that will include the entire upper echelon. Fire Sappers is completely compromised. Bogdan is the one Rapp was interested in. Grom had the ideas but it was Bogdan who handled the mechanics and would know how to find these people."

"What about Fairchild?"

"Luckily, Zack was fine despite being shot. They were all in bulletproof vests. He led a massive hunt of the entire Buda Castle labyrinth. You know how many miles of cave there are down there? Rapp would have given up after a couple of hours but Zack insisted on carrying on. We pulled everyone in and combed the place. Fairchild was close to bleeding out. Zack saved him twice in one night."

"Where is Fairchild now?"

"Receiving treatment somewhere. Zack isn't saying."

"And Grom?"

"Never found him. There were people posted at every exit. He didn't walk out, that's for sure."

"You mean he's still down there?"

"When someone enlightens us with Fairchild's account of what happened, we'll have a better idea. But he wasn't near where Fairchild was found. The labyrinth is vast. People have been lost wandering around down there before."

"And Penny?"

"Who? Oh, the woman who called me from your phone? No idea. Sorry we were too late to stop it. You saved a lot of lives, Rose."

"So what happened to Kornai?"

"Died of his injuries."

"My God."

"Someone in the crowd brought a gun in. No ticketing, no screening, no bag searches. Kornai just seemed to think everyone loved him."

"We've no idea who?"

"A man dressed as a woman, apparently. In the blackout confusion he managed to get away. But the gun is the same type as Marko's."

"So they were connected?"

"Maybe. The two you shot were the only leads, so they're all underground now."

"Is the election still on?"

"Oh yes. Kornai's deputy has stepped up. Their party is massively ahead in the polls. Kornai's being painted as a victim of porous borders and liberal attitudes to crime. Whoever shot him isn't much of a political analyst. There's a huge investigation, of course. That's a much bigger affair locally than the explosion and blackout. They may never get to the bottom of it. A lot of people didn't have much time for Kornai. It's the kind of thing that will spin conspiracy theories for decades."

"So it hasn't changed anything? It will all carry on here?"

"There's a lot of talk about the death in custody of that teacher, the one who painted the statues. Sounds like it was made to look like a suicide but doesn't really stack up. Raises all kinds of issues about the unhealthy relationship between government, police and judiciary. That might do some damage, in time."

"So that's it, then?"

"What else is there? Fire Sappers will fold when Bogdan starts to talk. Grom is almost certainly dead. All a bit messy, but could have been worse. What about you? Back to London?"

"I guess." The thought didn't fill her with joy. Things seemed unfinished.

She got a taxi back to her hotel a few hours later. She'd been in her room ten minutes when the knock came. She opened the door to Penny and Walter, standing side by side.

"How did you know I was here?"

"My dear, it's our business to know." It was Walter's usual spy mystique, but it irritated her. "May we?" They swept in and sat.

Penny leaned over to Rose. "I'm glad you were okay, dear. I was a little worried. It sounds like you were the hero of the hour. You'll be wanting this back." She passed Rose her phone.

"I'd never have got there without you." Rose scrolled through the multitude of messages. She'd catch up with them all later. None from Fairchild, she noted.

"Is Grom really dead?" she said to Walter.

Walter raised his hands. "Everyone is assuming so, given his disappearance. Salisbury included. It seems reasonable unless we hear otherwise."

"But we've been here before, Walter."

"Indeed." He seemed to have nothing further to say.

"What do you know about Fairchild?"

Walter gave that regretful look that often appeared on mention of the name. "I can't get anything out of Zack. His injuries were serious. He seems to have voluntarily gone into hiding somewhere."

"He's definitely not dead?" Rose's throat was suddenly dry.

"I'd like to think that Zack would share that much with us at least."

Walter was making her angry again. Not long ago he was suggesting that Fairchild should be killed, if he was with Grom. So it was a bit rich now to be expressing relief at his survival.

"I've put you up for a commendation," he said. "You're the toast of the Service. Even Salisbury found something positive to say. You will do well from all this. Quite a few people will be keen to have you on their team."

"That's great." She sounded flat, she knew. In years gone by this would have been exactly what she wanted to hear. But it didn't seem all that important any more.

Something else was niggling at her. "What was the promise?" The question was aimed more at Penny than Walter. "You said Fairchild's parents – so-called – didn't tell him the truth because they made a promise not to. And so did Walter."

She was looking at two pairs of troubled eyes. It was Penny who spoke first. "I'm sure I said. I told you about her, didn't I?"

Rose thought back. "Fairchild's mother? She didn't want Fairchild knowing about her? Why?"

"To protect herself and to protect him, my dear," said Walter. "She knew his best bet for survival was if Grom didn't even know of his existence. Which meant not knowing about her, either. If Fairchild tried to find her, you see, it would put both of them at risk. She went to enormous lengths to hide from Sutherland."

"So all the secrecy, this whole time, was to protect this woman?"

"Indeed. To make sure Sutherland would never find her. Which meant cutting her off entirely."

"Do you even know if she's still alive?"

Penny came in. "We have no contact with her at all. She's gone. That's all we know."

"And that's the way it needs to stay," said Walter. "We must stay true to that promise. You too, Rose, since you're now privy to it. If and when Fairchild discovers the truth, he must be persuaded not to go looking for her. He has to respect her wishes. She sacrificed a lot so that he could live a free and unencumbered life. That's what he should do now. You'll say that to him, won't you?"

"What makes you think I'll see him? Nobody seems to know where he is, at least nobody who's telling."

Walter gave the smallest of shrugs. "Yet, somehow, I think you will."

Chapter 56

Tas sat on a train heading east. It was early. The sky was raw and blank. Power lines crisscrossed against thin white cloud. Budapest rolled by, faster and faster. From here to the border. Across, somehow. After that he didn't know.

Warm air from under the seat made his legs hot. His clothes stank. He still tasted the coffee from a mouthful of thick espresso in a tiny paper cup bought at a kiosk. He stared out of the window. Wide roads busy with traffic, tramlines and train stations, blocks of flats and building sites, gradually it all disappeared and gave way to fields. He'd said his goodbyes already. The cold muddy Danube had swallowed him up but he'd pulled himself free and hidden, shivering, until it was safe to retrieve Bálint's money. Now it was time to go.

He was learning. He was learning how not to think about the things that hurt and made you cry. He was learning how people talk when looking up the barrel of a gun. He was learning how it felt to kill, what it was to take a life. He was learning how to pass unseen, his make-up now to disguise and camouflage the scratches on his skin: no more *gorgeous boy*. He was learning how to find people who would help, how you needed to talk to such people.

The guy opposite was reading a newspaper. Kornai's face on the front was huge, like it was on all those billboards. Was it the right thing, what Tas did? Had it made any difference? He didn't know. Who cared about any of them? What was done was done.

Got to move now, got to keep moving to survive. He'd grown up, knew he had to look after himself. Bálint taught him that. You've got to make up your own mind where you stand. He couldn't follow others. He didn't belong. He didn't fit anywhere, but it didn't matter. There was always somewhere else you could go.

Hungary flew past, woods and roads and villages and churches. No one knew his face. No one was coming after him. No one would miss him. With a bag full of cash and nothing else in the world, he was leaving for good. This place was no more to him.

He'd never come back here again.

Spies Without Borders

Two Months Later

London

Spies Without Borders

Chapter 57

Want to meet? said Zack's text. Rose didn't hesitate. She suggested the rose garden in Regent's Park. It was in full bloom and would have looked lovely if it weren't for the rain. Zack zipped up his jacket, unimpressed. Rose produced an umbrella and they walked.

"Nice to hear from you at last," she said. "What's the occasion? Something must have changed."

"As far as I'm concerned, nothing's changed. Our mutual friend, on the other hand, insisted on it. I don't like the idea. He isn't listening to me, though. Nothing new there."

"I get that you don't like me, Zack. But thanks for the reminder. What does Fairchild want?"

"He wants to know if you want to know where he is."

"Zack, I've asked you that a dozen times. Yes, I want to know. He wants you to tell me, does he?" Zack pursed his lips. "Why is he hiding, anyway? Darcy Tang got what she wanted, didn't she?"

"Sure! Bogdan gave everything up – the high command, their security protocols. Fire Sappers is no more. Plenty of their hackers still out there, though."

"So what's Fairchild's problem?"

The American pulled a face, though its full impact was lost behind the mirrored shades. "He's been through a lot. Physically, of course. He's still weak but over the worst. Mentally, though…"

"He knows, doesn't he?"

"Who his real daddy is? Yeah, he knows."

"You're a good friend to him, Zack."

"Right. Which is why I think it's a bad idea you going anywhere near him."

"But he's not listening to you. He wants me to know where he is. So you're going to tell me, aren't you?"

A deep sigh, and more gurning. "He's in a secret location on the Mediterranean coast."

"Any chance you could narrow that down at all?" Rose stopped. "Seriously, Zack. There have been times in the past when Fairchild and I haven't seen eye to eye. But things have moved on since then. I can see now that he's solid. Probably more solid than anything else."

Zack looked curious. "Are you off the job? Is that why you weren't at Vauxhall Cross when I went there?"

"Leave of absence. A bit of a time-out."

"Really? What for?"

"Counselling."

His eyebrows lifted. "You?"

Her natural defensiveness sprang awake, but she checked herself. "I guess you're right. I've been going around thinking you can live through these things and brush it all off. Foolish, really. Of course they affect you. You can deny it but it's all in there."

She felt a lot more at ease with herself having unlocked and replayed a number of distressing episodes: Paris, Tokyo, Monaco, Moscow. Georgia. And Beijing. She'd discovered a lot more about herself. A few things she didn't want to admit. But having done so she felt better. Human and fallible, but better.

"You don't go in for all that yourself?" she asked.

"Hell, yes. Get it all the time. What? You think I'm too macho or something? That's what you think of me, is it? A gun-toting beefcake with shit for brains?"

"And you think I'm a scheming manipulative bitch who climbs all over people to further her own career."

"No," he said, after some hesitation.

"Well, me neither."

Was this the start of a thaw in their relationship? Not much of one. Rose saw two reflections of herself in his shades as he studied her. "You'll treat him right, won't you?" he said. "Don't mess him up any more."

Rose looked herself straight in the eye. "I'll do my best."

A Secret Location on the Mediterranean Coast

Spies Without Borders

Chapter 58

Walking down the path, it didn't look like much of a place. The rough ground was dotted with clumps of weeds, with the occasional palm tree and a falling-down stone shed. Beyond that, the low front of a house with doors that didn't look used. What did Walter once say? *If he wants to be found, he'll stay in the best hotel in town. If he doesn't want to be found....*

Rose could see no fences, no cameras, no cars, no people. She took a route round the side, her skirt getting caught up in the overgrown vegetation. She smelled pine, something like rosemary, some heady flower. Her heart thumped. He was expecting her, she knew that, but even so.

Things were different around the back. She stopped some distance away, and saw a patio that ran the length of the villa, cushioned wooden loungers, a swinging seat big enough for two, a path directly through to the beach and a fabulous view of the sea. On one of the loungers lay a figure in a white shirt. She came closer. Fairchild sat up and turned. He watched her approach, then stood and came towards her.

"Nice place," she said.

"Belongs to a friend of mine."

"A little out of the way."

"But you found it. Drink?"

"Gin and tonic?"

He went inside. Rose stepped onto the patio. Everything was tidy, no dirty glasses, no books lying about. Fairchild's shirt was clean on – she could see crease marks from the ironing. He knew she was coming. The men in the village, maybe. She had to ask at the bar for directions. She took a seat on the swing. "How long were you in hospital?"

"Too long." He appeared in the doorway. "A month."

His movements were still slow and deliberate. His face seemed thinner, gaunt. She recalled, looking at him standing there, that he was closer to fifty now than forty. But there was more to it than that. He went back inside.

She called after him. "A month is a long time. You were lucky to survive."

No answer to this. She sat back and took in the view. She could hear insects buzzing and the dash of waves on the beach. It was warm. The drinks took a long time to make. She was tired – lack of sleep, an early flight, as ever. She closed her eyes. Tired of being tired. He emerged, put the drinks on the table and sat next to her.

"It's all wrapped up with Tang now, is it?" she asked.

"Darcy Tang has made it known that she's happy with the outcome."

"I'm glad to hear it. You paid a high price for that."

"And Grom?" he asked.

"Grom is presumed dead."

"But no one found a body."

She hesitated. "No."

"I shot him. He fell. But when they found me, he wasn't there."

"Crawled off somehow?"

"He wasn't anywhere nearby."

"They were watching all the exits. He never came out."

"He could have found another way out."

"Or he could have died down there."

His eyes were on the deep straight blue of the horizon. They registered pain. "Maybe."

"He was injured. And he's old, Fairchild." This didn't seem to help. Rose sipped some gin. He'd mixed it very strong. She sipped some more. "You're no longer persona non grata. You disrupted a potentially powerful terrorist group. You could come to the UK. Put it all behind you." Up close she could make out the lines on his face, the ones that weren't there before. "I know it's been – difficult." Such an inadequate word. She ploughed on. "You found a kind of home, then lost it again. But the UK could be a home for you. You could make it that way."

"I don't have a home. I'm a cuckoo's egg. You know that term?" Said with bitterness. "I have an exiled murdering father and a missing mother. Both in all likelihood dead, but I'll probably never know for sure. I don't belong anywhere."

"If you don't belong then neither do I."

He looked straight at her for the first time. "You do. You know where you're from. You're grounded. It's something I've always liked about you."

A warm feeling spread through her. The cynical mercenary she'd met all those years ago wouldn't have talked like that. He'd let life change him. But she'd done the same; that was why she was here. "My family thinks I'm amoral. The Service I work for is led by someone who's under the influence of a long-time traitor. My boss was prepared to sacrifice everything, including you, to keep his hands on the reins. You're saying I belong there?"

"You don't have to agree with everything that goes on to be a part of it. You know who you are. You believe in something."

"I'm not sure I do any more."

"Power plays and blowing people up aren't the same thing. No country is perfect. No organisation."

"You're defending them? Salisbury? Walter?"

"No. But that doesn't mean the thing they are a part of is worthless. There are good people everywhere. Zack. You. Plenty more."

"You're sounding like you have more loyalty than me, now."

"I'm loyal to people, not establishments."

"Maybe I am too." This was what she'd come here to say. Over these last two months Penny's words had returned to her again and again, along with her sadness, standing on that balcony, her regret at the years of inflicted loneliness. *Trust your instincts. Let them guide you. They know better than rationalising functionaries who dream up self-serving motives. Not everyone is like that.*

"Do you know why I was so keen to find you?" she asked.

He turned back to the horizon. He really didn't know. Of course he didn't; she'd gone out of her way to hide it from him. Words came into her head but they sounded lame; after years of dissembling, speaking honestly seemed beyond her. His look was intense, his eyes the colour of storm clouds. His jaw was rigid, his face set in a pattern of disillusion and defeat, maybe even fear. She could change that. She wanted to.

She reached out and stroked his cheekbone with her thumb. She turned his head towards her and kissed him on the lips, softly and lightly.

A pause, she couldn't have said how long. She felt his breath on her cheek. He pulled back. Her arm fell. But the disappointment must have shown in her face, because his eyes widened seeing it, and then he reached for her.

Chapter 59

He knew she'd come and find him, but still, it shocked him when she arrived. At least the phone call from the bar in the village gave him a few minutes to compose himself. Even so, he couldn't believe she was here. The last two months had been nightmares and cracked realities, the pain, the drugs they gave him, waking and sleeping. What was real and what wasn't? But she was always in his head if only just a shape, a presence. She responded to things, told him things, helped it make sense.

Now he was recovering, he was finding reality again but it was a bleak place, the beauty of the coast here only underlining that. No one except his local friends and Zack knew he was here. This was a haven, a place to recover; he'd used it as such before. But his life was a dead end now. He had no ideas for the future.

Give it time, Zack had said to him. Something will turn up. But neither of them thought it would be Rose.

When she walked in he wondered if it was real. He was seeing her in a flowing skirt. Rose didn't wear flowing skirts. But she did today, and this one was light enough that he could make out the shape of her legs. Her hair was up, revealing her bare neck, her shoulders and arms. She was so calm. Collected. As he'd said to her, grounded. How long ago had they first met? Not long, a few years. But he felt like he'd always known her.

When she reached for him, it was panic that paralysed him. He'd spoil everything. Taint her. He was the son of a murderer. But when he pulled back he saw the hurt in her eyes. He'd seen it before, in Georgia, when for a time she'd lost everything. He'd wanted to hold her then. He'd always wanted to. But she didn't, and now she did.

They were for her, his mouth, his hands, wherever she wanted them. It was fast, to begin with, the sudden intimacy of skin on skin admitting a need of extraordinary depth, that seemed to surprise them both. One step and she was falling, pulling him with her. He followed, with more than willingness. But as she wanted more of him, an urgency took hold. He fought it, but in the end it enveloped him and he was powerless, as desperate and grasping as she. They landed in a new world, a place neither had been before.

The sun set, night fell, the sun rose more than once before the ground felt solid. Their talk during this time was inconsequential; he could remember little of it. He had meals brought to them, local seafood and chilled wine, which they took outside at strange hours of the day. At times, relaxing in the cool night air, it felt like things were dissipating. But no more than a passing touch would summon the fever again, impossible to say who had started it.

The days passed and they began to talk. It was easy, the most natural thing in the world. They could share every secret they'd ever had. Everything was different; the world had been destroyed but it could be rebuilt. It would take time, though. He didn't want to think about what next. They could stay here forever, couldn't they? This was all he needed. But nothing was forever.

Rose came out of the shower one time wearing one of his shirts, endowing it with a shape and mystique it never had before. She sat, saying nothing, her mind elsewhere, eyes out to sea.

"So," he said.

"So?" When she looked at him, his thoughts fell all over each other like toy soldiers in some battle formation scattered by a running toddler or an energetic dog. A defence strategy downed in an instant.

"You're thinking about London?" he managed.

"I'm thinking about how not to think about London."

"You want to quit?"

She inclined her head. "Maybe."

"I don't think you should." Odd, that coming out. It didn't even sound like him.

She looked as surprised as he was. "Why?"

"It matters to you. It's the only thing that matters to you."

She looked at him quizzically. "Not the only thing."

He could feel himself flushing. "This isn't enough. This isn't a life. You know it."

"The Service is no good. I gave everything to it, and it's rotten to the core."

"Not as long as you're there. Not while you're a part of it." She waited, interested in what he was saying, fool that he was. "Nobody's perfect. But if you can make it better, you should. Salisbury's not forever. Walter certainly isn't. Who's next? Hang in there. You could make it all the way with your skills."

"What, to the top?"

"Someone's got to. Why not you?"

She frowned, looking out to sea again. "You can't do that without treading on a lot of ants."

"So tread. Better you than someone else."

She smiled, her eyes on him now, a shade of blue he'd never seen before. "You're speaking very out of character, John Fairchild."

"Am I? What does that mean? Not cynical enough?"

"So what about you? You've achieved your purpose."

"Have I?"

"Haven't you? You have all the answers now. And Grom's dead."

Is he? But that question remained unspoken. She was right. It was over – if he wanted it to be.

"I need to make a living. Like I have been doing. I suppose."

"But where?" She seemed insistent. Something inside him pulled taut.

"Anywhere. Wherever you want me to be."

She looked pleased and came over. His shirt looked even better on her close up. There was no more conversation for a while.

"I want to ask you something," she said one time. "Let's walk. On the beach."

They went barefoot, hand in hand on the soft sand like every clichéd honeymoon holiday ad he'd ever seen. It was a cliché for a reason, he was starting to realise. She got a piece of paper out of her pocket. "If Walter knew I was doing this I'd be fired. I'm still not sure about it. But you've been lied to often enough. If you want it, take it."

He read it. It was a woman's name and an address in London. Neither was familiar.

"Her name and last known contact details," she said. "I had to call in a few favours to get that. It goes back a good few years, obviously. No idea how useful it would be."

"You think I want to find my mother."

"Knowing you, it wouldn't surprise me. I wouldn't blame you, either." But there was trepidation in her voice. She didn't want him off on another quest. He was supposed to have finished all of that.

He kissed her. A casual everyday intimacy was growing between them, becoming more normal by the day. "I'm touched you did this for me."

"You're not going to use it?"

He folded the paper and tore it into small pieces. He waded into the water and threw the pieces across the waves, like someone scattering ashes. They danced in the wind, settled on the crest of an incoming wave, and sank into the water.

They walked on, but Rose was thoughtful. Eventually she asked him. "Did you do that because you don't want to find her? Or because you can't look for her because you think Grom is still alive?"

"She didn't want me to know about her. She doesn't want me coming after her. She may even be dead by now. I've spent enough time chasing wild geese. I've got something better."

She liked this answer as well. He could get used to pleasing her.

Much later, while Rose slept soundly, he lay awake. He removed himself without disturbing her and found a pen and paper. He wrote down the name and address, which he'd memorised on the beach, folded it small, and tucked it away in a pocket of his wallet.

He wouldn't need it. He wouldn't use it. But just in case.

Chapter 60

He seemed to know before she did. She was just sitting, she thought, on the patio, looking at the sea. He came out and stood watching her.

"You're going back to London, aren't you?" he said.

She was missing it despite everything. She'd told him about the counselling. With him there was no subject she couldn't broach. She'd talked about Beijing and how that had stayed with her. He'd held her and rocked her, and said sorry at least a hundred times. That wasn't the point, though. The point was that she knew why he did it and she might have done the same. Still might, if circumstances demanded it. Would he do it again, she asked? To someone else, obviously. Never, he said. I don't want to be that person any more. Just another reason, she reminded him, why he was nothing like Grom.

"Come with me," she said, on the spur of the moment. It made no sense; she knew he wouldn't. But now that she'd discovered this intimacy, the freedom of sharing, the rock solid trust, knowing that he was the only person anywhere who'd make her feel this way, panic rose at the idea of losing it.

His smile held regret. "London's not for me."

"Where, then?"

"You'll get posted, won't you?"

"Maybe. I'll go where they want me to go."

"If it's interesting enough I'll come and join you."

She saw the mischievous look in his eye, and mirrored it. "Honoured, I'm sure."

They walked to the village. One of the guys offered to drive her from there. It all seemed so matter-of-fact but Rose wanted to scream. She could change her mind and stay. But after a month, what would be different from after a week? She'd still end up going. They'd both made their choices. There was a lot to be said for knowing yourself better, even if you didn't like it much.

It was a swift goodbye in the end. A kiss, a few seconds of an embrace, her cheek on his chest, fingers entwined, suddenly, desperately, not wanting to let go. Some murmured reassurances, his breath warm in her ear. Pulling away felt like something being ripped up, but the car was here, and this was what they'd decided.

She got in and looked back as they drove off. The men were gathering round a table. Someone was already handing Fairchild a drink. He'd do his thing. She couldn't stop that and didn't want to. As for her – airport, plane, London, somewhere else. Whatever.

She sat back, wondering what it would be.

The Clarke and Fairchild series

Thank you for reading *Spies Without Borders*! If you want to stay in touch and hear about new releases in the series before anyone else, please join my mailing list on my website, www.tmparris.com. Members of the Clarke and Fairchild Readers' Club receive exclusive offers and updates. Claim a free copy of *Trade Winds*, a short story featuring John Fairchild and set in Manila. It takes place before the series starts, and before Fairchild and Clarke meet.

Another short story, *Crusaders*, is set in Croatia and features Rose Clarke's fall from grace from the British intelligence service. *Crusaders* also features Zsuzsanna and Marko, two characters from *Spies Without Borders*. Told in part from Zsuzsanna's point of view (she's named Tihana) it's about how the two of them met, in Zadar, on the Dalmatian coast during the Balkan war of 1992-3, how Tihana tried to get away from him and how she fell into working with Rose and the catastrophic consequences of that. This prequel is free to anyone joining the Reader Club!

Reviews are very important to independent authors, and I'd really appreciate it if you could leave a review of this book on Amazon. It doesn't have to be very long – just a sentence or two would be fine – but if you could, it would provide valuable feedback to me to and to potential readers.

Other books in the series are *Reborn* (Book 1, set in China, Tibet and Nepal), *Moscow Honey* (Book 2, set in Russia and Georgia), *The Colours* (Book 3, set in Monaco and the French Riviera) and *The Secret Meaning of Blossom* (Book 4, set in Japan).

While each book in this series stands on its own, *Spies Without Borders* completes a series story arc that started in

Book 1 (*Reborn*), with Fairchild now aware of his past and the relationship between the two of them moving to a different level. Future books will continue to be set in different locations with distinct themes, and will of course feature Rose and Fairchild as well as Zack, Walter and other characters from the series.

I hope you stay with us for the journey.

Sources and Acknowledgements

I knew nothing about Hungary when I was first offered a job there teaching English back in 1992. This was soon after the fall of communism and I spent a fascinating ten months of my early twenties in Budapest, over which time my study of the language got me as far as the subjunctive. My boss at that time was indulgent enough to take me on some of his nights out, which included one of the few gay night clubs in Budapest. In October 2021, a mere 29 years later, I was lucky enough to manage a few days back in the country. As Penny Galloway said, I was struck at the same time by how completely and utterly some things had changed, and how in other ways it hadn't changed at all.

Most of the locations featured in this book I visited myself during that trip, but as ever I have altered details in order to fit with the story. These include the club *Tilos az A*, nowadays known as *Tilos a Tilos*, the Cafe MŰvész, the Széchenyi Baths, the Gellért Hotel, the British Embassy and nearby park, Rose and Danny's unfortunate route downhill from the Fisherman's Bastion, and Fairchild's wanderings culminating on the tip of Margaret Island. The *Electrotechnikai something-or-other* is in fact a museum. The building used to house a direct current substation which served much of the downtown, and there was a pop-up bar in the courtyard when I was there. There are tunnels – a substantial number underneath downtown Buda, and a few in Pest in the location explored by Penny and Rose, with rumours of a nuclear bunker and a supposed access point in a courtyard which was being renovated when I was there. There is a sizeable prison at the end of a tram line opposite a cemetery. The entrance and lift to Penny Galloway's flat is like the one to my own flat when I lived there in 1992-3, though in a different location. The ruin bar where Fairchild and Rose meet is a combination of the fascinating Szimpla Kert and another venue nearby.

I'm especially grateful to Sándor from the hostel where I stayed in Budapest, for taking the time to inform me of the wonderful sights of Budapest and the political events of the time. He helped in the discovery or rediscovery of many of the elements listed above. It was following our conversations that I included the struggling industrial city of Ózd in the book, as well as the term *cuckoo's egg* and probably one or two other things besides.

As with all the books in the series, I did a lot of reading in order to research the political and cultural context, and this is where my story ideas come from. Below are my main sources.

I made much use of the writing of Paul Lendvai in his books *The Hungarians* and his biography of Viktor Orbán.

For the accounts of the background to the fall of the Berlin Wall, I read *1989: The Year that Changed the World* by Michael Meyer, a journalist and first hand witness of many of those world-changing events.

Homeland by Nick Ryan is a fascinating glance into the mindset of Europe's right wing extremists in the late 1990s and early 2000s.

Orbanland by Danish journalist Lasse Skyt is an interesting and sympathetic liberal view on the conservative outlook of many of Hungary's Orbán supporters.

The film *Children of Glory* (2006) brought alive the Hungarian Revolution of 1956, and features the famous "blood in the water" match and victory of the Hungarian water polo team competing in the Melbourne Olympic Games of that same year.

The sections based in the village owe a lot to *Getting Hungary* by Jennifer Self, an uplifting and descriptive true account of a British couple who decide to move to Hungary and live a self-sufficient rural life.

As well as these, I read numerous online articles from a variety of sources on subjects including the politics of Hungary, its neighbours and the EU, the development of right wing extremism, hacking groups and how they operate, Roma communities in Hungary's north east and elsewhere, hidden beach resorts around the world, and many others. While I have taken a lot from all of these, this is a work of fiction and the world I have created in this book differs from reality in many significant ways.

About the author

T.M. Parris is the fiction pen name of Tracey Hill. After graduating from Oxford with a history degree, Parris taught English as a foreign language, first in Budapest then in Tokyo. Her first career was in market research, during which she travelled extensively to numerous countries and had a longer stay in Hong Kong which involved visiting many of the surrounding countries. She has also taken sabbaticals for a long road trip in the USA and to travel by train from the UK through Russia and Mongolia to Beijing and around China to Tibet and Nepal.

More recently she has played a role in politics, serving as a city councillor in Brighton and Hove on the south coast of the UK. She currently lives in Belper, a lively market town near the Peak District National Park in the centre of England.

She started writing seriously in 2011. She published her first novel, *Reborn*, in 2020, the first in a series of international spy thrillers. Her first non fiction book, *We're Not All the Same*, was published in 2022. The common themes of her writing are people, place and politics, and her work explores how these elements interact.

Crime and action thrillers are her favourite book, film and TV choices. She occasionally plays the trumpet or the Irish flute. She enjoys walking, running, cycling and generally being outdoors in beautiful countryside, as well as cooking and baking and, of course, travelling.

Email: hello@tmparris.com
Facebook: @tmparrisauthor
Twitter: @parris_tm

Printed in Great Britain
by Amazon

21857829R00182